Courage of a Highlander

Katy Baker

Published by Katy Baker, 2018.

COURAGE OF A HIGHLANDER

First edition. June 2, 2018.

Written by Katy Baker.

Chapter 1

KARA BUCHANAN SHIFTED uncomfortably in her chair. It was one of those big brown leather ones that seemed far too big for any mere mortal and squeaked every time she moved. The huge reception area in this swanky high rise office was all but empty—just herself and the receptionist and a spectacular view of the skyscrapers of the city through the windows. Ostentatious wasn't the word. Downright gaudy was more like it. She glanced at her watch and stifled a growl of annoyance.

He was over half an hour late already. Was this deliberate?

The receptionist, a pretty brunette showing way too much cleavage, let out a high-pitched giggle that made Kara jump.

"No way! He did *not!* So what did she do next?"

The young woman, maybe a few years younger than Kara herself, had been on the phone for the last ten minutes, giggling loudly at whatever her friend was saying. It was starting to drive Kara crazy.

"Um, excuse me?"

"Well, honey, if it were me *I* wouldn't take him back. You tell her that from me. She deserves better."

Kara cleared her throat. "Excuse me!"

The receptionist glanced up from behind her desk, seeming slightly surprised to see Kara sitting there. "Yes?"

"Will Mr. Devereux be long?"

The woman shrugged. "He's a busy man. I can reschedule if you'd like."

"No, no, that's fine," Kara said quickly. "I'll wait." It had taken weeks to pin the man down and Kara wasn't about to squander this chance. If he wanted to play games, she'd play along. For now.

She picked up a magazine and began idly flipping through it, not really seeing the pages. Mentally, she went through all the questions she would ask Michael Devereux, all carefully designed to discover what she needed. She'd get the truth, she was determined about that.

Finally the intercom on the receptionist's desk beeped. The woman put down her phone, placed her hands on the desk, and looked at Kara with a condescending little smile on her face.

"Mr. Devereux will see you now."

Nodding her thanks, Kara grabbed her leather briefcase, making sure she had her voice recorder, notepad and pen ready, brushed down her business suit, and pushed through the big polished doors.

Inside she found a large office with a sofa by one wall, a large desk under the window, and almost every available space along the walls taken up with tall glass cases. Kara goggled despite herself. The cases contained treasures. In one sat a large golden goblet with rubies around the edge. In another she spotted a leather-bound book mottled with age. A third held a large sword, its blade neatly broken in half.

Kara snapped her mouth shut, determined not to gawk like an idiot. She knew Devereux was an avid collector but this was ridiculous! There was enough stuff in this office to kit out a museum!

"Ah, Miss Buchanan!" Michael Devereux rose from his seat behind the desk and held out a hand.

Kara crossed the room and shook it firmly, meeting his eyes and trying to project an air of confidence. She'd learned from experience that with predators like Devereux you couldn't afford to show the slightest weakness. "Mr. Devereux, thank you for agreeing to see me." She didn't add, *at last*.

He waved a hand. "Call me Michael. Please, take a seat."

Kara folded onto another over-stuffed leather chair, studying Michael Devereux. Somewhere in his 40s, he had dark hair with a sprinkling of gray running through it, ice-blue eyes and the kind of features Kara guessed many women would swoon over. But he didn't fool Kara. That smile was a little too easy, a little too charming. What did it hide underneath?

Kara placed her voice recorder on the desk then settled herself on the edge of the seat, pad and pencil in hand. Just as her parents had taught her, Kara never relied solely on technology when conducting an interview. Sure, the device would record her interviewee's words but what about the other nuances? The body language? The fleeting expressions that might cross their face? The look in their eyes? It was often these things that told a journalist far more than the words that came out of their mouth and Kara suspected this would be doubly important with a man like Devereux, so used to smooth-talking his way out of things.

A faint look of amusement crossed his face at her meticulous preparations. He steepled his fingers. "So, Miss Buchanan. You've hounded me into submission. I have to admire your persistence. What is it now? Around thirty emails and just as many phone calls?"

Kara smiled. Yes, she'd been persistent in her attempts to get an interview with this man. He was as slippery as an eel and had rebuffed all her attempts to pin him down. But Kara had refused to be brushed off and her stubborn streak had won out in the end.

"This is quite a collection you have here," Kara said, glancing around the office. "I bet the local museum would give their back teeth to get a look at some of these pieces."

He gave a small smile. "No doubt. But these pieces are far too important to allow some grubby museum curator to touch."

"Oh?" Kara said lightly. "And why is that?"

Devereux laughed although there was no mirth in it. "Now that's the question isn't it? I'm afraid I can't answer that. If I told you that I'd have to kill you." He spoke jokingly but his eyes were cold.

Involuntarily, a shiver walked down Kara's spine. She could easily understand how this man was able to intimidate so many people into getting what he wanted. He had the bearing and air of someone who expected to be obeyed, as though to do otherwise was preposterous. But Kara was used to dealing with such men.

She gave a small smile of her own. "A different question then. What do you want with the estate of the late Margaret McQueen?"

Devereux's jaw tightened. Good. She'd hit a nerve. "That is none of your concern."

"Really? Mr. Devereux, you must know that there are all sorts of rumors flying around about how you acquired the McQueen estate. Those rumors mention extortion, racketeering and intimidation. The McQueen estate was promised to the National Museum of Scotland in Edinburgh but out of nowhere, you acquire everything she owned. I know the police didn't find anything incriminating after her family accused you of fraud and intimidation but that doesn't stop the rumors. Now you have the chance to tell your side of the story."

And incriminate yourself, you smooth bastard, she thought. *Come on. Men like you can't help but show off. Tell me what I need to know.*

"Margaret McQueen was the last of a noble Scottish line," Devereux said. "Her collection of rare artifacts was far too precious to allow into a museum. She had no idea what she had in her possession. But I do." His eyes glittered.

"And what is that?"

He regarded her for a long moment. Kara lifted her chin, forced herself to meet his gaze, and waited.

Devereux climbed to his feet, moved around the desk and perched on it, gazing down on Kara. "You should be sure you're ready for the answers when you ask such questions. They might take you down paths you aren't ready to tread."

Devereux leaned forward and whispered. "You really want to know?"

Kara swallowed. "Yes."

His face was only inches away from hers now. He smelled of sandalwood and spices. "Power," he whispered. "Power beyond your imagining."

Kara blinked. "I...I.... How can a bunch of old Scottish artifacts bring you power? You already have more money than any sane person would ever need."

He barked a laugh and sprang to his feet. Spreading his arms wide, he turned in a circle, indicating the cases around the room. "Money? You think that's what power is? Oh, my dear, it is far more than that. These things might look like bits of broken treasure, heirlooms from a bygone age, but they are something else entirely." He fixed her with a piercing gaze. "They were all made by the Fae and when I discover what I'm searching for, I will hold the greatest power of them all. The power of time."

Kara stared at him. What the hell was he talking about? Was he totally crazy? Or was he just messing with her?

"Are you serious? Fairies? Magic? That's insane! There's no such thing as magic in the world."

He cocked an eyebrow. "Oh? Are you sure about that?"

"Of course I'm sure," Kara growled, annoyed now. "How about you stop playing games and tell me what is really going on?"

"I warned you," he said in a low, dangerous voice. "I warned you about asking such questions. You think yourself a tenacious reporter, Miss Buchanan. You see yourself as a champion of the downtrodden, bringing to light the evils of those who would exploit others. You think yourself wise in the ways of the world. You are none of those things. You are a child meddling in things of which you understand nothing." He stalked across the room towards her and leaned down. His eyes flashed. "Go back to your stories of church fetes and school plays, Miss Buchanan. Do not step into my world. If you do, you will regret it."

Alarmed now, Kara scrambled to her feet and backed away. "If you had no intention of giving me a proper interview, why did you agree to meet me?"

"To give you a warning," he growled. "Go back to your life whilst you still can and do not meddle in mine. Your father never learned that lesson, and he paid the price."

"My father?" she cried, caught off guard by this sudden change of topic. "What do you know about my father?"

"That he was a good journalist, as you are. But he didn't know where the line was drawn. He didn't understand that some stories are never to be told. Don't make the same mistake."

Kara's heart began to thump in her chest. Grabbing her briefcase and equipment, she turned on her heel and headed to the door. Devereux's derisive laughter followed her out.

ALL THE WAY HOME THROUGH the city rush hour, Kara's mind whirled. She replayed the conversation with Devereux over and over. She'd gone in there with such high hopes and instead he'd toyed with her, spinning all that crap about magic and Fae, rather than giving her any honest answers.

She should have expected as much. Men like Devereux didn't give up their secrets easily and any journalist worth their salt would have realized that and found some other angle to come at him from. Instead, she'd floundered like a rookie, thrown off guard by that comment about her father. This is what he'd planned, of course. She was naive to think he wouldn't have done his research on her. Naive and stupid.

Idiot! she chided herself, slapping the steering wheel as she sat at the lights. *You should have realized he'd investigate your background and been prepared!*

Now what was she going to do? There was no way she could approach any of her regular papers with the story of Michael Devereux collecting magical artifacts—they would laugh in her face. No, what her editors were after was a story about how a corrupt multi-millionaire was running some kind of criminal network collecting precious artefacts and national treasures. That was the story she was after. But she had no evidence. Yet.

She finally pulled into the parking lot of her little apartment block and turned off the engine. She was so lost in her own thoughts as she strode towards the door that she didn't see the small elderly woman making her way along the path towards her. Kara smacked right into her, almost knocking the poor woman flying. Kara grabbed the woman's wrist to stop her falling flat on her face.

"Oh! Sorry!" Kara cried, aghast. "I didn't see you there. Are you okay?"

The old woman straightened herself and gave Kara a crooked smile. "Aye, I'm fine, lass," she said in a broad Scottish accent.

"Good. Well, sorry again," Kara replied and began walking away.

"Wait!" the old woman called.

Kara glanced over her shoulder.

The old woman was holding out Kara's notebook. "Ye dropped this, dearie."

"Oh," Kara said, taking it from her. How had that happened? She'd been sure she'd put her notebook in her briefcase. "Thanks."

"Nay bother, dearie. Tis nay wonder ye dropped it, lost in thought as ye were."

The old woman had small black eyes that sparkled with good humor. A grey bun was pinned to the back of her head and a burgundy coat was draped over her shoulders that appeared at least two sizes two big. She looked every inch like someone's eccentric grandma.

"Yeah. Sorry, I was miles away. It's been one of those mornings." Kara smiled ruefully.

The old woman cocked her head. "Aye, ye look like a warrior readying herself for battle, lass."

Kara snorted. "Then it's a battle I lost."

"Nonsense. Ye may have lost a battle but the war still rages. Ye only truly lose when ye stop fighting." She stuck out a wrinkled hand. "I'm Irene by the way, dearie. Irene MacAskill."

Kara took the old woman's hand and shook it. Her skin felt as dry as old parchment. "Kara Buchanan. Pleased to meet you."

"Not half as pleased as I am to meet ye, my dear." Her expression turned thoughtful and she tapped her lip as though thinking. "Aye," she said. "Ye will do just fine. There is a strength in ye, girl. A strength ye will need if ye are to find yer destiny."

"My destiny?" Kara replied, puzzled by the strange talk. "What's that supposed to mean?"

Irene stared at Kara, unblinking. A shiver of unease walked down Kara's spine. Those eyes...they seemed to look right into her soul.

Then Irene blinked, the warm smile returning, and the moment passed. "Surely ye know what destiny means, lass?"

"Of course I know what it means," Kara replied. "But I don't believe there's any such thing any more than I believe in fairy stories. You make your own fate."

"Well said, lass," Irene smiled. "And mayhap ye are right—to a degree. But there are other forces at work in this world, forces ye canna escape or deny. Destiny is one of them, whether ye like it or no. Blood will out. Yer path will soon fork, lass, and ye will have a choice to make. Do ye continue on yer lonely quest to save the world? Do ye continue to close out all others, to harden yer heart and walk alone? Or do ye take the second fork and open yer heart to yer true path, one that will take ye away from all ye know?"

"What...what are you talking about?" Kara stammered, alarmed at how the old woman's words stirred something inside her. "Lonely? Quest? I'm dedicated to my job. What's wrong with that?"

"Naught, lass, if it's done for the right reasons. If it's not done to fill a hole in yer heart or to fulfill yer parent's legacy—something that canna be fulfilled."

Kara's eyes widened. "You knew my parents?"

"Nay, lass. Not personally but I'm sure they wouldnae want this life for ye. Not everything in this world should be done alone."

Right. Now she was officially freaked out. Who the hell was this woman to turn up out of nowhere and start lecturing her? Kara held up her hands. "Okay, I'm gonna go now. It was nice meeting you."

She took two steps but Irene's hand shot out and caught her wrist. The old woman's grip was like iron. "Yer choice is coming, lass. Someone will come into yer life and lead ye to a crossroads. There ye must choose: continue on yer lonely path with only yer cause to fill yer heart or step aside, follow a different path, and in so doing, maybe find what it was ye were looking for all along. Destiny is reaching out for ye, lass. Will ye let it guide ye? Or will ye keep running?"

Kara snatched her wrist from Irene's grip. "What the hell are you talking about? You don't know anything about me!"

Irene smiled. "Oh, I ken more than ye think, dearie. And we are much more alike than ye might believe. Choices. It's always about choices. Ye might want to start with what ye are holding."

Kara glanced down and realized that Irene had placed a scrap of paper in her hand. What the hell? Kara glanced up, a hundred questions on her lips, and gasped. Irene MacAskill had disappeared.

Startled, Kara spun around, searching the parking lot for the diminutive old woman. There was no sign of her. It was as if Irene MacAskill had disappeared in a puff of smoke.

Kara rubbed her temple where a headache was starting to form. What a day. What a crazy-ass day. First her disastrous interview with Devereux and then being accosted by a strange old woman who was clearly a little unhinged. She curled her fingers around the bit of paper, crumpling it into a tight ball, and dropped it in her pocket.

Once inside her apartment, she kicked the door shut, slipped off her shoes, and made her way into the kitchen where she slung her purse and coat onto the table before crossing to the fridge and pouring herself a large glass of wine.

Hell, she thought. *With the day I've had, I've earned it.*

With a groan she settled onto the sofa in the living room. It was just about the only piece of furniture she owned besides a table in the kitchen and a bed and tiny wardrobe in the bedroom. Kara had never really given much thought to her apartment. It was small but suited her needs. There was Wi-Fi so she could work on her laptop. What more did she need? She was always too busy to spend much time here: chasing down her next lead, researching her stories, writing her reports.

She sighed and took a sip of wine. *Do ye continue on yer lonely quest to save the world?* Irene MacAskill's words echoed in her head. That's not what she was doing. Was it? And she wasn't lonely! What a ridiculous thing to suggest!

Her eyes strayed to her empty living room. There was nothing here to suggest this was a home. Nothing to suggest it belonged to Kara or who she was. It was just a place to sleep, somewhere she could leave quickly when she got a new lead, a temporary resting place before she moved on to the next city, the next town, the next story.

But when she got that story it never really brought her peace. There was always the next bad guy to bring to justice. There was always the next corrupt corporation to expose.

She glanced up at the only decoration in the room. Above her mantelpiece were clippings of old newspapers. They were faded and yellow with age but still readable. The biggest one showed a photograph of a smiling man in his early thirties. Above read the headline, "Journalist murdered in gangland style execution."

Kara closed her eyes. She had only been ten when it had happened but the memories still felt as clear and jagged as broken glass. Her mom had moved them across country after that and she remembered little of her early childhood but for that one sharp, cold January morning when the police had come knocking.

Her mom, also a reporter, had succumbed to cancer when Kara was fifteen, leaving her to carry on their fight to bring people to justice. To carry on their legacy.

Kara paused suddenly. That's what Irene MacAskill had said. Was that what Kara's crusade was? Was she trying to live up to her parent's legacy? Had Irene MacAskill somehow known?

"Don't be idiotic!" Kara said, annoyed with herself for thinking such stupid thoughts. Her meeting with Devereux had unsettled her. That was the only reason she was thinking such things. She took another sip of wine and gazed up at her father's picture.

"What would you have done, Dad? How would you have pinned that bastard down?"

She suddenly remembered the scrap of paper Irene had given her. Retrieving it from her coat pocket, she unrolled the scrap, smoothed it out, and then read the spidery writing scrawled on it.

You might want to investigate why Michael Devereux is so interested in this.

There was an address written hastily below the message.

Kara stared at the bit of paper then reread the message several times to ensure she'd got it down right. She had no idea why Irene MacAskill had given her this or how she was connected to Devereux. Anyone with any sense would leave this well alone.

But Kara knew she wouldn't. That spark was burning in her belly again. That spark that wouldn't let her rest until she had her story.

Chapter 2

AIDEN HARRIS LED HIS horse up a switch-back trail to the top of the cliff and looked out over the wild, rolling landscape of the Isle of Skye. It spread out before him like a map, a wind-blown panorama of heather-clad hills, rocky ravines and storm-lashed cliffs. One by one his brothers-in-arms reached the top and came to a halt, each one staring in silence, just as Aiden did. It had been three years since any of them had set eyes on home.

It felt like a lifetime.

"My, my," breathed Fraser by Aiden's side. "That's a sight for sore eyes and nay mistake. Ah, there were times when I wondered if we would ever see it again."

Aiden nodded. "Aye, but here we are, with purses full of gold, a few months' rest ahead and the king's thanks to take home with us."

His men nodded their agreement. It had been a long, hard road from Edinburgh but they had been in good spirits for the journey. After all, they were returning home victorious, having beaten back a Danish fleet set on raiding all along the eastern coast. For that, King James had rewarded them handsomely and given them leave to return home.

Angus, the youngest of them, pale with fiery red hair, gave a wide smile. "I've nay intention of ever leaving again. Besides, my Maisie will skin me if I even think of it."

Fraser bellowed a laugh. "Aye, that lass of yers is a fearsome one. When do ye plan on making an honest woman of her?"

"As soon as I can find a priest, if she'll have me. I plan on raising a few crops and some bairns besides. I've had enough adventure for a lifetime."

There were rumbles of agreement. Aiden knew the men had sorely missed their families and many of them would never leave Skye again. He envied them.

"How about ye, lad?" Fraser asked him. "Will ye break the hearts of every lass on Skye and take a wife?"

Fraser meant the words lightly but they cut through Aiden like glass. Aye, he'd like nothing more than to be content with a simple life. To settle down into his role as his father's heir, to fall in love and raise a family. But it wasn't for him. He'd always known a different path was laid out for him. A restless energy burned within him, one that would not let him settle. It was this restlessness that had driven him from his ancestral home and sent him traveling all over Europe, fighting for his king. And besides, what did he have to offer any woman? He was a warrior. He was rough, uncouth. All he knew was fighting. What woman would want that for a husband?

"I dinna think so," Aiden replied quietly.

"What?" Fraser boomed. "Ye will have the pick of the ladies! The laird's only son and a hero to boot? Captain Aiden Harris, hero of the Battle of Dun Crenin!"

Aiden forced a smile. "Hero? Surely that title belongs to ye? What did they name ye? The Bear of Skye?"

"Aye, because he stinks like one!" Malcolm piped up.

"And has a temper like one too!" David added.

Fraser scowled at them and Aiden smiled at their teasing. Nudging his horse into a walk he led his men onto the coastal road, winding their way steadily north. As they traveled Aiden's band dwindled as each of the men peeled off to make their way to their homes on different parts of the island until finally Aiden found himself on the road alone. It was just as well. He was in no mood for company.

It was a glorious late autumn day. The sun sparkled on the waves and the cry of seagulls echoed on the wind. The breath of winter was in the air but for the moment, held itself at bay. Aiden breathed deeply, savoring it. Aye, he'd missed this place. Perhaps he'd not realized how much until now.

He topped a rise and found himself looking out over a headland that jutted out into the sea. Here the road split and he would turn inland and travel north towards Dun Arnwick, his childhood home and seat of the Harris clan. Aiden pulled his horse up and just sat for a moment, staring at the road that would lead him home.

Memories assailed him. Weapons training with his father and adopted uncle, Jamie. Sitting in the Great Hall on a winter's night listening to his mother play the fiddle and tell stories of America, her distant homeland. Picking through the rock pools at low tide with his sister and the other castle children, pouncing on crabs and crayfish.

It seemed another life. Aiden was a different man to the one who had ridden out of Dun Arnwick all those years ago to join the king's warriors. Could he ever settle into this life again? Did he want to?

A great weight settled onto his shoulders. As the only son of Laird Andrew Harris, he was the heir to the lairdship. His clan looked for him to take his place among them, to lead them. But King James had offered Aiden another choice, one that, should he accept it, would take him away from this place forever.

Aiden shook his head. Curse it all, he should be glad to be home but Aiden felt more conflicted than ever. If he chose to leave how would he tell his family, his people? If he chose to stay, how would he tell his king?

Lord, what a mess.

He pulled his horse off the road, dismounted, and led him down a rocky trail to the beach. Walking by the sea always helped Aiden to think. It was low tide and a wide strip of golden sand lay between the base of the cliffs and the whispering waves.

Leading the horse, he strolled along the edge of the wet sand, feeling the cold water seep through his leather boots and sting his skin.

Up ahead, he noticed that part of the cliff had fallen away, leaving a great gouge in the cliff face. The only part of the section still standing was a spur that arched out of the cliff and down onto the beach, forming a natural archway through which Aiden could see the endless miles of ocean stretching away.

Intrigued, Aiden walked closer. Erosion was an ever present danger when living on the islands and was one of the reasons why his father had put a stop to the building of settlements right on the cliff edge. He dropped the horse's reins, leaving him to wander, and approached the arch. He craned his head back, examining the structure. Lines of minerals sparkled in the sunlight and water dripped slowly from its apex, gathering in a puddle below.

A voice suddenly spoke behind him.

"I wouldnae move any further unless ye are sure where it will take ye."

Aiden spun, yanking his sword from its scabbard and holding it in a two-handed grip.

But when he saw it was an old woman standing behind him, looking calmly at the great silver blade resting against her throat, a wave of shame washed through him. He quickly sheathed his broadsword and gave her a bow.

"My apologies, my lady," he said formally. "Ye startled me. How may I be of service?"

The old woman raised an eyebrow and merriment twinkled in her dark, dark eyes. She seemed old beyond measure with skin so wrinkled it was difficult to see where one ended and another began. But for all that, she radiated a kind of solidity, as though she was as strong as the roots of an old oak tree.

"Now that, my lad, is the second dangerous thing ye have done in the last few moments. Has nobody ever told ye ye shouldnae offer yer service until ye ken what ye will be asked to do?"

Aiden frowned. There was something about this woman. She stirred memories that were buried deep. "Have we met?"

She smiled broadly. "Aye, lad, though I doubt ye'd remember. Ye must have only been around three when last I laid eyes on ye. I came to Dun Arnwick to help yer mother birth yer sister, just as I helped her birth ye. My name is Irene. Irene MacAskill."

Aiden's eyes widened. Despite himself he took a pace backwards. Irene watched him, an unreadable look on her weathered face.

"I can see by yer reaction that ye recognize my name."

"Aye," he breathed. "That I do."

He had been brought up on stories of Irene MacAskill. She was a guardian of Clan Harris and it was because of her that his mother, Lucy, had been able to travel from her home in the twenty-first century to the Highlands of the sixteenth where she met his father. Without Irene, Aiden would never have been born.

But she was also the woman spoken of with caution by his father and by Dougie, the steward of Dun Arnwick, and Mona, the old housekeeper before she died. The tales claimed this woman was of the Fae, and the Fae always had an agenda of their own, one that went far beyond the understanding of mortal men.

He cleared his throat and pushed his unease aside. "It has been many a year since ye have been seen on Skye, my lady. What brings ye here this day?"

Irene's smile deepened. Her eyes roved over him, taking in his Harris clan plaid with the sash over the top bearing the king's colors. "Ye have come far, young Aiden. Ye are a loyal warrior, like yer father before ye. But loyal to who and to what? I know of that ache inside ye, lad. The one that willnae let ye rest. The one that drove ye to leave yer family."

"I left to do my duty. To my country. My king."

"And yer duty to yer family?"

"I know my duty," he grated. "I dinna need to be reminded of it."

If she noticed the edge in his voice, she didn't show it. Instead, she cocked her head to one side and regarded him with her dark eyes. Aiden forced himself to meet her gaze squarely. He'd faced down terrible enemies on the battlefield, men who would have killed him without a second's thought. He'd be damned if he'd be intimidated by an old woman.

"Ye are marked for a different path, Aiden Harris. It is time ye walked it."

Aiden sighed. "And how do I do that? I dinna even know what it is I want."

Irene smiled. "Ye will in time."

"Ye speak in riddles, woman."

"Do I? Then mayhap I'll speak plainly." She stepped forward. She was so tiny she barely reached Aiden's chest but even so, it was Aiden who suddenly felt small. "I have come to ask yer help, lad. If ye accept, maybe we'll both get what we want. I will stop something terrible from happening and ye may finally find the path ye were meant to walk." She looked up at him. "Will ye help me?"

"Aye," Aiden replied without thinking. "I took a vow to help all those in need."

Irene patted his arm. "Ah, ye are a good one, Aiden Harris."

"What do ye need me to do?"

She clasped her hands in front of her. "The secret of time-travel is known only to a few—yer family being one of them—and there is good reason why it is kept so. In the wrong hands the power of time could wreak great evil. There is a man who meddles with that which ought not to be meddled with. He searches for the Iuchair, the Key of Ages. If it falls into his hands, then all could be lost. Ye must protect the key at all costs."

"Very well," Aiden nodded. "Where do I find this man? I'll ride there anon and arrest him."

"It isnae that easy, lad," Irene replied. "He doesnae reside on the Isle of Skye, nor even in this time. Ye will have to travel to the future to find him."

Aiden went very still. His mother was a time-traveler and so the concept was not alien to him but the idea of traveling through time himself was both terrifying and exhilarating at the same time.

Irene pointed and Aiden turned to see that the space beneath the archway was shimmering like heat-haze over a bonfire. He could no longer see the sky or the sea, only a blur of colors that shifted and melded and then became a view of a vast city, far bigger than anything Aiden had ever seen. Great crowds of people walked along the streets and metal boxes—cars his mother had called them—whizzed along at terrifying speeds.

"What is this?" he murmured in awe.

"The future, lad. None other can take this step. None other can do what must be done. Do ye accept this task?"

He turned to look at her. "How will I know what I'm looking for?"

Irene smiled. "Oh, ye will know, lad. Just remember: protect the Iuchair at all costs. It is yer destiny."

Aiden nodded. Then he pulled in a deep breath and walked through the arch.

There was a strange sensation of falling, as though his stomach was rising into his chest and Aiden gritted his teeth. It lasted for only a heartbeat before his boots smacked into something solid, his knees buckled, and he staggered onto hard, smooth ground. His vision swam, nausea twisting his guts, and Aiden sucked in deep, heaving breaths. After a moment it passed and Aiden scrambled to his feet, hand going to the hilt of his sword.

Irene MacAskill was gone. The beach, the sea, the stone archway were gone. Even the Isle of Skye itself had disappeared.

Instead, he found himself standing beneath a broad, smooth archway that was made of orange stones precisely cut into rectangles—bricks he'd heard his mother call them. The archway formed a short tunnel and across the top, stretching out in either direction two sets of metal railings were set into the ground. Aiden racked his brain for any mention his mother might have made of such things. A railway?

Stepping away from the archway into the shadows by its wall, Aiden took a moment to survey his surroundings. Ahead of him stretched a wasteland of old buildings and burned-out vehicles. A cracked road wound its way through the buildings. Weeds had grown up in those cracks, giving the area an abandoned, desolate look. The crowds of people he'd spotted through the archway were gone. It had spat him out in another part of the city and there was not another soul in sight and Aiden heard nothing but the low moan of the wind.

Cautiously, hand still on his sword hilt, he stepped out from his hiding place. Irene had said he would know what he was looking for when he saw it but there was nothing in this lonely place that gave him any clues. Then his eyes settled on a building to his left. It was bigger than the others and though still dilapidated, it showed signs of recent activity. Car tracks and footprints led up to the door.

"Well, let's get this started," he muttered to himself.

He stepped out from his hiding place and began a careful perimeter of the building. He moved silently, years of scouting enemy camps aiding him now. If there were enemies around he'd expect to find pickets posted around the outside but he found nothing. Whoever or whatever was inside the building, they didn't expect company.

He'd completed a full circuit and was approaching the doors again when the hairs rose on the back of his neck. Someone was coming. He pressed himself against the wall, relying on the shadows to hide him, and waited. Seconds passed. Stealthy footsteps approached and Aiden tensed. A figure appeared out of the darkness, moving hesitantly towards him.

Aiden startled. It wasn't a vagabond or ruffian—the kind of person he'd expected to find wandering this place at night.

It was a woman.

She looked to be around Aiden's age and was wearing trews like a man, with long hair spilling down her back. She was moving cautiously, as though unsure of where she was going, but nevertheless, the set of her shoulders spoke of a steely determination. The woman walked past Aiden's hiding place and moved further into the complex.

Intrigued, he followed her.

Chapter 3

WHAT ARE YOU DOING? Kara asked herself as she made her way along the street. *This is crazy. Go home before you get yourself into trouble!*

It was good advice. Anybody with half a brain would realize that this was a fool's errand. Anybody with half an ounce of common sense would give this up as a bad job and go write that gossip column about the local vegetable competition instead.

Not Kara. She'd come to realize that common sense didn't really enter her vocabulary much these days.

She checked the address scrawled on the bit of paper for the hundredth time. Yes, this was definitely the place. Pausing in the shadow of one of the buildings, she looked around. She'd arrived in a part of town she'd never visited. Around her lay an abandoned industrial unit that looked as though it hadn't seen activity in decades. The roads were pitted and cracked, the windows smashed, the buildings seeming empty and forlorn.

She gulped. Yes, this was definitely a bad idea. For all she knew Irene MacAskill might be a plant sent by Devereux and this was a set-up designed to make Kara look like an idiot. If that was so, it was working.

But she couldn't leave now, no matter how much her common sense was telling her to. That fire in her belly wouldn't let her rest. Her instincts were screaming at her that there was something here, something important, and she could no more have ignored them than she could have stopped breathing.

Kara stuck her head out and looked around. It was getting dark now and she saw no sign of anyone. From across the street a stray cat arched its back and hissed before scampering away.

Kara steeled her resolve and moved. Above her reared a huge warehouse. On first glance it appeared as abandoned as the others but there were fresh tire tracks indicating somebody had been here recently. A tall fence surrounded it.

Carefully, Kara crept round the back. She hoped to find a gap in the fence or an open gate or anything that would let her get closer to the building for a good look. She didn't find a hole but around the back of the building she found an old garbage can leaning against the fence. She paused, glanced around, then climbed up onto the garbage can and used the extra height to boost herself onto the fence and over the other side.

She paused as she hit the ground, heart hammering. She had no idea who owned this building and although it seemed abandoned, the fence around it suggested otherwise. She was probably trespassing and had probably committed several felonies just by vaulting that fence. *Nothing for it now,* she thought. She had to go on.

Moving quickly, she crept across a wide tarmacked area and soon found herself in a jumble of yards separated by crumbling walls. Kara guessed that these must once have been storage areas. She kept moving, searching for a door into the warehouse, heart thumping so loud she felt sure anyone in the vicinity would hear it. Finally, she spotted a door. It was small and battered, probably used for taking deliveries. She hurried over to it and set her ear against the rotting wood. Nothing. All was eerily quiet.

Then, just as she was about to put her hand on the door handle, an explosion of barking sounded behind her. She whirled in terror. A huge black and tan dog came hurtling towards her, its claws making a skittering noise on the tarmac.

Panic surged through Kara. She ran, pelting deeper into the warren of storage yards. She didn't need to look behind her to know the dog was hot on her tail—she could hear it panting as it bore down on her, could almost feel its hot breath on the back of her legs.

With a surge of panic she saw that the yard she'd entered had no exit. It was surrounded by tall walls. Kara didn't slow: she leapt, arms outstretched at the wall. For a heartbeat her fingers brushed the top but then she was falling, to land on her back on the hard ground with enough force to knock the breath from her lungs. Gasping, she flipped onto her belly and then backed up, pressing her back against the wall.

The dog skittered to a halt not three feet away, head hanging low, lips pulled back in a snarl. It bunched its muscles to spring and Kara threw a hand across her face, a scream forming in her throat.

Then everything seemed to happen at once.

The dog leapt at her, jaws snapping for her throat. But suddenly a man appeared, putting himself between her and the slavering beast. The dog slammed into him but he crouched down on one knee, drove his shoulder into its chest and the dog went tumbling away. It landed on its side and scrabbled to its feet, shaking its head as if dazed.

"Hurry!" the man snapped. He held out his hand and hauled Kara unceremoniously to her feet.

He grabbed her around the waist and suddenly she was being lifted onto the wall. She clutched at the stone to steady herself and then dropped down the other side. The man boosted himself after her, clearing the wall just as the dog made a leap at his feet. Kara collapsed onto her knees, panting in terror, and the man dropped down beside her.

"It's all right, lass," he said in a deep voice. "He canna get in here."

Kara squeezed her eyes shut, concentrating on calming her racing heart. For a moment her head swam and she feared she might faint so she curled her hands into fists, digging her fingernails into her palms to steady her. Finally her heart rate began to calm and she opened her eyes, fixing her bleary gaze on her savior.

He knelt next to her, regarding her with a concerned expression on his face. He was tall and broad-shouldered. Jet-black hair fell in lazy tangles onto his shoulders, framing a face of high cheekbones and a strong chin laced with stubble. Stormy blue eyes watched her steadily.

"Thanks," she gasped. "I owe you one."

"Ye are welcome, my lady."

He spoke with a lilting Scottish accent and now that she noticed it, he seemed to be wearing traditional Scottish dress. He wore a long plaid over a simple linen shirt. The plaid came to his knees below which he wore knee-high leather boots. A sash crossed his chest which bore an insignia she didn't recognize. And was Kara imagining it or was that a sword strapped to his side? *Well I shouldn't be surprised,* she thought. *It's no crazier than anything else that's happened today.*

"Who are you?" he asked.

She eyed him. Giving her name seemed like a dumb thing to do. What if he was a security guard? But lying wouldn't get her anywhere either. "Kara," she muttered. "My name's Kara. And you are?"

"My name is Aiden. Aiden Harris."

"Right. Do you work here?" *And are you going to call the police?* she wondered silently.

"Nay, lass. I'm...looking for something. Something I hope might be found here." He regarded her with an inquisitive expression, his deep blue eyes full of questions. "Tell me, what would a lass like ye be doing in an abandoned place like this?"

Kara lifted her chin. "Same as you. Looking for something."

"Really? And what would that be?"

Kara bit back an angry retort. What did it have to do with him? But he had saved her from that dog and deserved a bit of common courtesy. "Answers. Answers to questions I don't know how to ask."

She glanced at their surroundings. They were in another small yard. To the left rose the wall of the warehouse with two large windows looking out that were mostly broken. A high fence circled the yard, with a locked gate sealing them in. There was no sign of Devereux. Why had Irene sent her here? More and more she was beginning to think this was some elaborate trick of Devereux's. An attempt to teach her a lesson for sticking her nose into his business.

"If I ever see Irene MacAskill again, I'm going to give her the rough side of my tongue," she muttered.

Aiden's head came up at that. He fixed her with a stare. "What did ye say?"

"Nothing. It doesn't matter."

"Did ye say Irene MacAskill?"

Kara watched him warily. "Yes. What of it?"

Aiden looked equally wary. "It was Irene MacAskill who sent me here."

Kara barked a sardonic laugh. "You too? Seems we've both been had. I think we've been sent on some wild goose chase."

"Ye dinna understand," Aiden replied, shaking his head. "She sent me to protect the Iuchair—the Key of Ages. Why would she send ye as well? Ye are no warrior. It doesnae make any sense."

"You've got it right there," Kara replied. "None of this makes any damned sense." She climbed to her feet. Iuchair? Key of Ages? What the hell was he talking about? She suddenly felt uneasy, as though she'd lost control of this situation. There was something going on here, something she was missing. Aiden knew Irene MacAskill. Did he know Michael Devereux as well? How was he caught up in all of this?

"Listen, I—" she began but Aiden suddenly put his hand up for silence.

He rose to his feet in one fluid motion and stood still, head cocked as if listening. Kara froze as well and then she heard it—the unmistakable sound of a car engine. Aiden crept over to the locked gate, signaling for her to stay put. Kara ignored him and followed, crouching by the gate and peering through the tiny gap between gate and fence post.

A car pulled to a halt on the other side and four men got out. Kara gasped as she recognized Devereux. He held a small metal lock-box.

"Hurry!" he snapped to his men. "Open the door."

His men hurried over to a large set of double doors that were chained and padlocked. One of them took out a bunch of keys. The doors squealed as he pushed them open, the sound setting Kara's teeth on edge. With one last look around at the deserted landscape, Devereux went inside.

Aiden let out a string of curses under his breath, his eyes tracking every movement of Devereux and his men. Then he stood and looked at Kara.

"Ye should leave, lass. Those are dangerous men if ever I saw them. It isnae safe for ye here."

"What are you going to do?"

He glanced at her as if deciding how much he could tell her then drew in a breath. "I came to get the Iuchair. Those men must have it or else why would Irene MacAskill send me to this place? I'm going to get it from them. I willnae leave without it."

"But there are lots of them and only one of you!"

He shrugged as though this detail was unimportant. "I made a vow. I'll nay break it."

Kara stood and squared her shoulders. "Then I'm coming with you."

"Nay, lass," he said, shaking his head. "It's too dangerous."

Indignation welled up inside Kara. "I've been investigating that man for months! This is my chance to find out just what the hell he's up to!"

Anger flashed in his deep blue eyes. "If ye enter that building, I canna guarantee I can keep ye safe."

"I'm not asking you to!" She crossed her arms and tapped her foot, glaring at him. "Listen. I'm going into that warehouse whether you like it or not. Now I think we've got a better chance if we work together but if I have to go alone, I will. You'll not stop me short of tying me up."

"Dinna tempt me," Aiden growled. Then he sighed. "Fine. We'll need to sneak inside and get a look before we make a plan of action. This way."

He led the way over to the warehouse wall, pressing themselves flat against it. Aiden cautiously peered through one of the broken windows then ducked down next to Kara.

"I canna see them. They must be in another part of the building. It's clear within. Come on."

He moved silently to the doors and peered through the crack, hand resting on his sword-hilt.

After a few tense moments Aiden relaxed, taking his hand from his sword and nodding to indicate they should go inside. Kara swallowed, a strange mix of near-panic and excitement swirling in her stomach. The rational part of her screamed that this was crazy. She was breaking into a building with a stranger she'd only just met on the off chance she'd be able to find out what Devereux was up to. But the other part of her, that part that had always followed her instincts, churned with excitement. Without knowing how, she felt sure she was on the right path. Tonight she would discover the truth. One way or another.

She followed Aiden Harris as he led the way inside the warehouse.

Kara couldn't have said what this place used to be but there were bits of rusted machinery scattered about the floor. A thin layer of dust covered everything, disturbed only by the footprints of rodents.

She and Aiden moved carefully, quietly into the room. Aiden's eyes scanned everywhere, alert for danger, and everything about his posture suggested he was tense, ready to spring in any direction. He made not a sound as he slowly padded across the room to a door on the other side. Kara felt clumsy in comparison. Although she tried to move as quietly as he did, she failed miserably and her footsteps sounded as loud as gunshots to her ears.

Aiden paused by the door and pressed his ear against it. Kara hunkered down next to him.

"What is it?"

"There are voices on the other side."

Kara pressed her ear to the thick wood. Sure enough, she could hear muted voices although she couldn't make out the words.

"What do we do?" she asked.

Aiden looked around and his eyes alighted on a metal gantry that ran around the perimeter of the room. "This way."

They hurried over to a metal staircase that led up to the gantry. It was rickety, had clearly seen better days and rocked alarmingly when Kara set her foot on the first step.

"I will go first," Aiden said. "Come up only when I signal."

Kara nodded and Aiden set his foot on the first step. Although it creaked, the metal held as he climbed and stepped out onto the gantry. He nodded at Kara who gritted her teeth and began to climb. As the steps shook under her weight she cursed herself for a fool for the hundredth time tonight. What the hell was she doing? She could very well fall to her death in the pursuit of her stupid story!

But she reached the gantry without mishap. From up there she could see what had caught Aiden's attention. The top half of the wall was taken up by windows and there was a big metal box at the far end that seemed to straddle the wall between this room and the one beyond where the voices were coming from. The metal box had windows just like the wall as well as a door on this side. Kara guessed it had been a foreman's office, situated where he could keep one eye on the workers in both rooms below.

They hurried along the gantry and through the open door into the foreman's office. It smelled musty with disuse and a rodent had made a nest in one corner. Kara followed Aiden inside.

They crouched low then crawled over to the window. Kara got a great view of the room below. It was larger than the first and rows of workbenches had been pushed to the sides, leaving a clear space in the middle. This space was taken up by a structure that looked wholly out of place in this industrial setting.

A set of ancient standing stones.

Two large upright stones sat in the middle of a circle inscribed with chalk. They looked to be gray basalt and were taller than Kara, probably taller than Aiden. Across the top of these lay a third stone, forming a rudimentary gateway. This odd location with its lifting equipment dangling from the ceiling above suddenly made sense. Moving those stones would take a mammoth effort. But that still didn't explain why the hell Devereux had constructed this thing in the first place. She shook her head, trying to make sense of what she was seeing.

The chalk circle around the stones was inscribed with words but in a language that Kara couldn't read. Devereux's men stood at equidistant points on the circle and Devereux himself knelt on the edge closest to Kara and Aiden, fiddling with the strongbox he'd been carrying.

"What is that?" Kara whispered, nodding at the standing stones.

Aiden's eyes, fixed on the scene below, flickered with unease. "An arch through time," he muttered.

A what? She opened her mouth to ask Aiden what he was talking about when a sudden gasp from him drew her eyes back to Devereux. He'd opened the strong-box and held a strange object up to the light.

To Kara's un-expert eye it looked like some kind of Celtic decorative piece. Made of beaten and flattened gold, it was about the size of her two palms together and was three-pronged, each of its prongs fashioned into swirling knotwork. From the way Devereux held it up reverently, it clearly had some importance.

Beside her Aiden tensed, letting out a long, slow breath. He leaned forward, the expression on his face tense and wary. "That's it," he muttered.

Devereux suddenly laughed, a harsh sound that cut through the air like a whip crack. "Ha!" he barked. "Finally! I knew that old bitch McQueen would give me what I wanted! All these years she had this in her possession and she never even knew what she had!"

"So that's what he was after from the McQueen estate," Kara breathed. "What is it?"

Aiden didn't look at her. His attention was still fixed on Devereux. "The Iuchair," he breathed. "The Key of Ages. The reason Irene MacAskill sent me here."

Key of Ages? Arch through time? What on Earth was he talking about?

"I don't understand," she began. "None of this is making any sense. I—"

She cut off suddenly as Devereux stepped up to the stone archway. Now that she looked closer she realized that one of the uprights had a depression carved into it, a depression that was exactly the same shape as the artifact in his hand.

"Aiden, I think he's going to—" Kara began then stopped as she realized that Aiden was no longer crouching by her side.

"Stop," his voice suddenly rang out from below. He stepped out from the bottom of the stairs. Kara cursed under her breath. Damn the man! He moved so quietly that she hadn't even heard him leave.

Devereux spun at the sound of Aiden's voice. His eyes fixed on Aiden for a second before he looked around, checking if Aiden was alone. Kara ducked low as Devereux's gaze flicked over the foreman's office.

"Who the hell are you?" Devereux demanded.

Aiden stepped further into the room. "Who I am doesnae matter. What I'm here for is what's important."

Devereux raised an eyebrow. "Oh? And what is that?"

"To return the Iuchair to its rightful owner."

"I *am* its rightful owner!" Devereux growled. "Have the McQueen family sent you here? Stupid of them. And stupid of you thinking you could walk in here—and walk back out again in one piece."

Aiden met Devereux's gaze squarely. "I dinna ken who ye are speaking of but no matter yer claims, that key doesnae belong to ye. Ye will give it to me. Now."

Aiden's voice held the crack of command, as though he was used to giving orders and being obeyed. Devereux though, only smiled.

"Do you even know what this is?" he asked Aiden. "It is the ticket to limitless power and you really think I'm going to hand it over to some McQueen thug just because you ask me to? You've obviously not done your homework."

"I know exactly what that is," Aiden replied. "And the power it holds. It is a power not meant for ye. I willnae let ye claim it."

Kara shook her head. She had no idea what these two were talking about. All Kara knew was that she was caught up in something way over her head, that Aiden was facing down five men alone, and that she must do something about it. Two of Devereux's lackeys had begun edging towards him, hands in their pockets where they no doubt held hidden weapons. Aiden hadn't noticed with his attention fixed on Devereux.

Kara took a deep breath and then crossed over to the door. Easing it open, she tiptoed down the stairs and into the room below. Nobody noticed her as she reached the bottom and ducked behind the cover of a large stack of crates, hiding her from the view of the men.

Peeking around the side, she took in the scene. Aiden stood maybe twenty paces away with his back to her. Beyond him lay the chalk circle and Devereux. To Aiden's left Devereux's two lackeys were getting closer, moving slowly so as to avoid notice. Kara chewed her lip, fear coursing through her veins. What did she think she was doing? She ought to run from here as fast as she could and call the police. She was no God-damned hero. But she didn't. Her instincts were screaming again, screaming that she had to help Aiden.

"As I'm in a good mood," Devereux said to Aiden. "I'll have my men beat you only a little senseless."

A wry smile twisted Aiden's lips. "Hand over the Key of Ages and nobody need get hurt."

"There are five of us, you damned fool!" Devereux replied. "Are you completely out of your mind?"

Aiden shrugged.

Then, without warning, Devereux's two lackeys exploded into motion. They sprang at Aiden, pulling guns. Kara's heart leapt into her throat and she opened her mouth to scream a warning but it wasn't needed. Aiden, it seemed, had been aware of them all along, for the instant they moved, he moved too. He pivoted away from them so they grappled with the empty air where he'd just been standing, kicked one of them in the wrist, forcing him to drop the gun and then kicked the weapon out of reach. He landed an upper-cut into the man's jaw that laid him out flat before spinning and grabbing the arm of the second man who was coming up behind him, twisting his wrist so savagely he also dropped his weapon, then landed a knee into his guts that doubled him over. A swift elbow to the temple, laid the second man out flat.

It all happened in a heartbeat, in the time it took Kara to draw breath.

Aiden glanced over his shoulder and for a second met Kara's gaze. A look of annoyance flashed across his face at seeing her there, quickly replaced by worry.

"I dinna wish any more trouble," he said, turning back to Devereux and the rest of his men, who'd all pulled guns and trained them on Aiden. "Please give me the Key."

Kara looked around, searching for a means of escape. Behind her was another delivery door, all but obscured from view by a pile of half-broken crates. Doubled over so as to remain behind the crates, she crabbed over to it. It was held shut by a rusty iron bolt. Kara grabbed it and began gently easing out the pin. It scraped loudly enough to make her wince and she hoped the men behind her didn't hear.

"Who the hell are you?" Devereux demanded of Aiden. "Who the hell are you to walk in here and demand the Key?" His eyes narrowed and suspicion flared in them. "And why are you dressed like that and carrying a sword? Anyone knows not to bring a knife to a gun fight."

Aiden lifted his chin and faced the man squarely. "My name is Aiden Harris of Clan Harris of the Isle of Skye. Irene MacAskill sent me here to retrieve the Key of Ages. She is its rightful owner, not ye."

"Oh? And what gives this 'Irene MacAskill' the right to claim that?"

Aiden shrugged. "She is of the Fae."

He said it casually but the effect on Devereux was instantaneous. For the first time since Kara met him, he looked taken aback. "The Fae? But..." His surprise lasted only a moment. Understanding dawned in his eyes. "You're one of them aren't you? A time-traveler?" He made a sweeping gesture at his men. "Take him! Don't let him get away!"

They sprang at Aiden. They were skilled fighters and they worked with more coordination than the ones Aiden had already disabled. Whilst one aimed a roundhouse kick to Aiden's mid-riff, forcing him to jump back, the other came up from behind and grabbed Aiden around the chest in a bear-hug. The man, taller and broader than Aiden with a neck like a bull, lifted him off the ground, squeezing tight enough to crush ribs. Aiden growled then threw his head back, smashing the back of his skull into the man's nose. There was a loud crunch and the man's grip slackened a little. Aiden took the opportunity to ram his elbow into the man's gut. With an 'oomph', the man released Aiden who landed lightly on his feet, spun, and took the man out with a swinging haymaker to his cheek.

The second man closed in on Aiden and they grappled back and forth, neither able to find purchase on the other. Then suddenly Aiden ducked low, drove his shoulder into the man's stomach, and tackled him to the ground. The man's head smacked into the floor and he went limp, unconscious. Without pausing, Aiden sprang to his feet and hurled himself at a shocked Devereux. Before the man could react, Aiden ripped the key from Devereux's grasp and then sprinted towards Kara's hiding place.

"Now!" he bellowed.

Kara pushed the door open just as Aiden reached her. He grabbed her hand and the two of them were suddenly pelting into the yard. Heart thudding, she ran by Aiden's side, not daring to look back, expecting to hear gun shots ringing out behind them. They ran across the storage yard and towards a pair of gates on the far side that stood open.

Then two police cars suddenly screamed up to the gates, lights flashing. Kara's heart jumped into her mouth. Damn it! They must have tripped an alarm! They were going to get arrested! But before the cars had even skidded to a stop, Aiden yanked Kara behind a storage shed out of sight.

"Here!" he said, pushing the key into her hands.

"What are you doing?" she cried, her voice shrill with panic.

"They havenae seen ye, neither the men inside nor those in the cars. Nobody knows ye are here. I canna let the key fall into their hands. Will ye keep it safe for me?"

"I...what....?" Kara struggled for words. Everything was happening too fast.

"I need yer help. Will ye do this for me, lass?"

Kara met his gaze and felt something shift inside her. She curled her hands around the key and before she realized it, she was speaking. "Of course, I promise I'll keep it safe. But what are you—?"

Before she could finish the question, Aiden stepped out from behind the shed, holding his hands up. Two police officers got out of the car and approached.

"The alarm was tripped. What's going on here?"

"I dinna want any trouble," Aiden called.

Devereux suddenly appeared at the doorway of the warehouse and came running towards them. "Officers! Arrest that man!" he shouted. "He's broken into my property, stolen a precious artifact and assaulted my men!"

Kara gritted her teeth. It took all her willpower to stay still and hidden. She felt like a coward but her promise to Aiden echoed in her ears. For whatever reason, this Key of Ages was important enough that he'd risk arrest. And, she suspected, it held the key to discovering the truth she'd been searching for.

The police officer looked at Devereux. "You own this property?"

When Devereux nodded the officer turned his gaze on Aiden. "You care to explain yourself, son?"

Aiden's eyes strayed to Kara's hiding place and then back to the police officer. He straightened his shoulders. "I'll come quietly. There's nay need for trouble."

Kara kept still and quiet as the officers approached Aiden, pinned his hands behind his back, cuffed him and marched him to the car. He never made a murmur nor so much as glanced in her direction. The doors slammed shut, the wheels skidded and one of the police cars sped away. Devereux watched them go for a moment, utter fury on his face, before he turned to the second officer who had a pad in his hand and began asking questions. They walked back to the warehouse and disappeared inside.

Kara watched them go with her heart hammering in her chest. She counted to a hundred then crept carefully from her hiding place and out through the gates. Only when she was clear of the warehouse and any prying eyes did she allow herself to break into a panicked run for home.

Once there she stood leaning on the closed door whilst her heart fluttered in her chest like a caged bird. What the hell had just happened? She glanced down at the Key clutched in a white-knuckled grip and swallowed. Things had got out of hand very quickly. This should have been a straightforward story. Now she was embroiled in something way over her head.

She set the Key down on the kitchen counter, slumped onto the sofa in the living room, and picked up her cell phone ready to call the police and tell them all about her part in tonight's activities. She'd probably get arrested for tres-passing at the very least but there was nothing to be done for that. If she spoke to the police, gave them the Key of Ages, and let them deal with Aiden Harris, then maybe, just maybe, she could forget all this had happened and go back to her normal life.

Her fingers hovered over the keypad but she didn't dial. Aiden's face flashed in her mind and his words. *I canna let the key fall into their hands. Will ye keep it safe for me?* She'd made a promise, dammit. How could she break it now?

And besides, her instincts were screaming at her again. Screaming that this was something she couldn't drop. That this was something she had to follow through. She'd wanted a story hadn't she? Now she was living right in the middle of one!

With a cry of exasperation she jumped up, grabbed her purse and headed out the door.

She only hoped she wouldn't regret it.

Chapter 4

AIDEN SAT CROSS-LEGGED, hands resting on his knees with his back against the cold stone wall. They'd taken his sword and his hunting knife, of course. Weaponless, he waited.

He pulled in long, steady breaths, the way he did before a battle, keeping his body calm and his mind focused. He'd often dreamed of traveling in time the way his mother had but he'd never dreamed that his first foray into the future would end up like this: sitting in a jail cell. Still, he was used to it. He'd been captured and ransomed several times whilst on campaign. He'd learned to be patient.

His thoughts strayed to the events of the day. The arch had spat him out right where he needed to be: close to where Michael Devereux had been attempting to use the Key of Ages. That bit of the mission had gone smoothly. What hadn't gone so smoothly had been bumping into Kara Buchanan and getting her mixed up in this mess.

Her face appeared in his memory. She was beautiful enough to quicken his breath, and fierce enough to rival any warrior under his command. What part did she play in this? Why had Irene MacAskill sent her to that warehouse?

He'd given her the Key of Ages because he'd had no other choice. It was that or have the law keepers take it. But, he realized suddenly, it wasn't *only* that. There was something about Kara Buchanan that made him want to trust her. For an unaccountable reason he knew the key would be safe in her hands.

Aiden examined his surroundings. The cell was large, built to hold up to ten people. Including Aiden there were six in it now. One fellow stood up at the bars, shouting obscenities and waving his hands around, trying unsuccessfully to get the attention of the law keepers outside. Two other prisoners were slumped unconscious in the corner, stinking of spirits. Another sat at the back, hunched over with his arms wrapped around himself, whimpering slightly.

It seemed to Aiden that no matter what time you lived in, jail cells were always filled with the same: drunks, petty criminals or those who'd just been in the wrong place at the wrong time.

The man shouting obscenities starting banging on the bars, howling for all his worth. It set Aiden's hair on end.

"Give over, man," he growled. "They'll willnae respond. All ye are doing is giving the rest of us a headache."

The man spun, glaring at Aiden. "What the hell has it got to do with you?"

"Everything," Aiden replied. "When ye are ruining my peace."

"Yeah? You want to make something of it?" The man's eyes were red-rimmed and his features twisted with anger.

Aiden sighed. "I dinna want any trouble. I merely wish for ye to be quiet."

"And are you gonna make me?"

Aiden stood. Did this man think himself intimidating? He was just a petty thug who had doubtless never seen a true battle in his life. Aiden stepped forward, towering over the man and fixing him with a hard stare. "I would be grateful," he said, his voice low and soft. "If ye'd cease yer wailing. That way maybe we can all get some sleep. What do ye reckon?"

The man swallowed, his confidence wavering. "Yeah, well, perhaps I could do with a nap after all."

He found a spot over by the far wall and wrapped himself in his coat, falling blessedly silent. Aiden sighed, watching the man. He knew the type. The man was a bully who would look to throw his weight around if Aiden showed any signs of weakness. He sat, laid his head back against the wall, and closed his eyes.

What was happening at home right now? Were his family gathering in the Great Hall for dinner? Was his mother playing for them whilst his sister sang? Was Uncle Jamie soundly beating his father at cards the way he always did? And what about his men? Had they all made it back to their families without mishap? Had the king reached Edinburgh safely after his campaign in the north?

Impatience burned inside Aiden. He couldn't tarry here. He was needed in his own time. Somehow he had to get out of this cell.

He was startled out of his thoughts by the sound of the door sliding open. One of the law keepers stood there. The pot-bellied man crooked a finger at Aiden. "Time to go, pretty boy."

Aiden scrambled to his feet and followed the man from the cell and down a corridor. "I'm being released?"

The man glanced at him. "You've been charged with trespassing and affray. You'll need to produce your identity documents at this station tomorrow or you'll be rearrested. After that you'll be given a court date. Until then, don't break the terms of your bail."

"My bail?" Aiden asked. "What's that?"

The law maker raised an eyebrow. "Don't try to be funny. Seems you have a guardian angel, friend."

Aiden said not a word as he followed the law maker into a small room where his belongings were returned—minus his sword—and made to sign some paperwork. After this he was led into a small waiting room and came face to face with his benefactor.

It was Kara Buchanan.

KARA WAITED WITH ILL grace. She chewed on her bottom lip and paced in the tiny waiting room.

Come on, she thought. *Hurry!*

The longer she waited, the worse her nerves became and she'd almost spun on her heel and marched out twice already. She still couldn't believe she was doing this. The door opened with a click and Kara spun. Aiden Harris strode in behind a pot-bellied police officer. His eyes scanned the room, noting every detail before fixing on her.

Kara found herself staring at him. He stood straight-backed and alert, his eyes raking over her with an intensity that made her stomach do a little flip. Who was this guy? He stood there like he owned the place rather than like someone who'd just been released from jail.

The police officer was speaking to her so she forced her attention away from Aiden Harris and focused on the man's words. He had her sign some documents and then he walked out, leaving Kara alone with Aiden.

Aiden Harris didn't say anything. He just watched her steadily. Kara cleared her throat.

"Are you okay?"

"Okay?" he echoed. A small smile lifted the corners of his mouth. "Aye, lass, I'm okay. Thanks to ye." To Kara's surprise he gave her a formal bow, putting his arm across his chest and bending at the waist. "I am in yer debt."

"Actually, I'd say we're about even. You saved me from getting savaged by that dog, remember?" She looked around the room, taking in the security cameras that would be recording everything they said. This was not the place to discuss things. "Let's get out of here."

She turned to the door and took two steps before she realized Aiden wasn't following. She glanced over her shoulder. "What are you waiting for?"

"Where are we going?"

"My apartment. Or would you rather stay here?"

Aiden glanced around. He opened his mouth as if to speak then seemed to think better of it. "Nay. I wouldnae."

"Come on then," Kara pushed through the door and led Aiden out into the parking lot where she'd parked her beaten-up sedan.

Aiden halted in front of the vehicle, staring. "A car," he breathed, almost under his breath. "My mother has told me of such things."

Kara raised an eyebrow. "What, they don't have cars in Scotland?"

He looked at her and the intensity of his gaze made her mirth drain away. "Nay, lass. We dinna have anything like this in my homeland."

You're a time-traveler aren't you? Devereux had said. She pushed that thought away. It would lead her down dangerous paths.

"Right. Whatever. Well, don't just stand there. Get in."

She slid into the driver's seat and after a moment Aiden climbed in beside her. He was so tall that his head brushed the ceiling and his bare knees were pressed up against the dashboard.

Kara started the car and they pulled smoothly out of the lot. It was late and the roads were quiet, for which Kara was grateful.

"Where is the Key of Ages?" Aiden asked softly.

"Safe," Kara replied. "I left it at my apartment." She glanced at him. "You mind telling me what they hell is going on?"

He shook his head. "I should never had got ye tangled up in this in the first place, lass. The less ye know about me, the better."

"Oh no you don't!" Kara replied, pulling up at a red light and turning to look at him. "Tonight I've trespassed on private property, accepted stolen goods and hid from the police, so don't tell me I shouldn't get involved. It's a little late for that! Who are you? Where are you from? What's going on between you and Michael Devereux?"

The light changed and they pulled away. Aiden didn't answer for a long time. He watched the buildings speeding by.

Finally, he spoke. "As a boy I was fascinated by tales of my mother's homeland. It sounded so grand and exciting. I would have given anything to come here." He smiled ruefully. "These were not the circumstances I had in mind. Mayhap ye should be careful what ye wish for."

Kara nodded. "Isn't that the truth? This morning all I wanted was a decent lead on Michael Devereux. This afternoon I got that lead. This evening I'm mixed up with a guy who carries a sword and beats up four men as easy as breathing."

Now that she said it aloud she realized how crazy it all sounded. What was she doing? She ought to pull the car over, drop Aiden Harris off, then drive home and forget she'd ever met him.

But she knew she wouldn't.

She was relieved when they finally pulled into her parking lot. Aiden looked around, eyes roving everywhere, seemingly alert for danger.

"What is this place?"

"My apartment block. I didn't have an address for you and they wouldn't have given you bail without one. Besides, you want your Key back don't you? This way."

She walked off and after a moment he caught up with her. They made their way up to her apartment in silence.

"Where is the Key, lass?" he asked the second the door closed behind them.

Kara crossed to where her purse lay on the kitchen counter. Taking out a cloth-wrapped bundle, she handed it to Aiden.

"Here."

He took it reverently and then unwrapped it. The gold scrollwork glinted in the light. It didn't look anything particularly special to Kara. She'd inspected it closely, and whilst finely made, it looked like nothing more than a piece of decorative work."

"What is it?" she asked leaning forward. "Why was Devereux so interested in it?"

Aiden ran his hands over the spiraling metal. "Something important. Something very dangerous in the wrong hands."

Annoyance flared in Kara's stomach. "You don't like answering questions, do you? You've still not even told me who you are or what the hell your connection to Devereux is."

Aiden sighed. "That, I'm afraid, is a long story."

"That's fine. I like long stories and we've got all night." She jabbed a finger in his direction. "So start talking."

AIDEN WATCHED KARA steadily. Her eyes glinted and her chin was tilted defiantly as she glared at him from across the room. She was a fierce one all right. Fierce and brave and beautiful.

He blew out a breath and ran a hand through his hair. Lord above, how had he ended up in this situation? He was supposed to come here, stop whoever was meddling with time—this Devereux character—rescue the Key and then go home. A quick mission, in and out.

He gripped the edge of the table so hard his knuckles went white. What, by all that's holy, was Irene MacAskill up to? Curse the woman. Why had he ever listened to her?

Kara stared at him, arms crossed, unblinking. Waiting.

He blew out a breath. "Very well, lass. I'll tell ye what ye want to know."

She relaxed slightly, inclining her head, although her gaze remained fierce. "Why don't you start with who you really are and where you're from?"

"I've already told ye that bit. I come from the Isle of Skye in the Highlands of Scotland. My father, Andrew, is laird of the Harris clan." He shook his head. "Nay, lass, it isnae such much *where* I come from that ye should ask but *when.*"

She frowned. "What's that supposed to mean?"

Aiden placed his palms flat against the table top and leaned forward, meeting her gaze squarely. "I was born in the year of our Lord 1518, during the reign of King James the fifth of Scotland. The arch that Devereux had in that warehouse was an arch through time. They are constructs made by the Fae—portals through the fabric of time. I came through one such not a mile from that warehouse. I'm a time-traveler, lass."

She stared at him in silence. Then her eyes roved over him, taking in his plaid, his boots, the empty scabbard strapped to his waist. He could see her working things out, putting the pieces together. Then she shook her head.

"That's ridiculous. I'm sure you could come up with a better story than that."

"It's the truth, lass."

Silence settled between them. Then she shook her head again angrily.

"No, I don't believe you. Time-travel, fairies, magic? You really expect me to swallow that? No way. There's no such thing."

"Really, lass? Are ye so sure of that?"

She pointed a finger at him. "Now you're making fun of me. You think I'm some kind of gullible idiot who'll fall for this crap? Well, think again, mister."

Aiden spread his hands wide. "Do ye have an alternative explanation?"

Kara opened her mouth and then shut it again. She cast around as though trying to think of what to say. Then she threw up her hands. "I don't know! But there could be a hundred other explanations for all of this!"

"Such as?" He kept his voice patient. He wasn't surprised by her distrust. After all, who would believe such a tale? It sounded like the kind of thing one would tell a child at bedtime.

She walked into the next room and started pacing. Aiden followed. The room was so small that it only took five steps before she had to turn around and come back the other way. The room, like the whole abode, was shockingly bare. No ornamentation, no trinkets, no paintings hanging on the wall. It reminded Aiden of an army camp. Transitory, containing only the bare essentials needed to survive.

"So let me get this straight. You're really from sixteenth century Scotland and you were sent here by Irene MacAskill who is actually a fairy. She sent you to retrieve that key thingy to stop Devereux from using it?"

"Aye, lass, that's about the right of it."

She paused, looking at him. "So Devereux knows about these arches too, right?"

Aiden nodded. "It would seem that way. How he learned of them I dinna ken but it seems clear he wants the power of time for himself. Like I said, lass, in the wrong hands such power can wreak terrible destruction."

"This is crazy," Kara whispered under her breath as she began pacing again. "I can't even believe I'm asking these questions." She paused again and looked at him.

"Hang on a second. If Irene MacAskill sent you to get the Key, where do I fit into all this? Why did she send *me* to that warehouse?"

"I dinna have the faintest idea. The Fae are known to be meddlesome and have their own reasons for what they do—reasons that dinna always make sense to us."

"You can say that again," she muttered before slumping onto the sofa and pressing the heels of her hands against her eyes. "This has got to be the craziest day of my life."

"Now ye know the truth. What will ye do, lass?" Aiden asked gently, folding onto a chair opposite hers.

"I have absolutely no idea. Journalism school didn't prepare me for this."

She glanced at the faded picture of a man pinned above the mantelpiece and a look of sadness crossed her face.

"Who is he?" Aiden asked gently.

"My father," she muttered. "He'd know what to do. He always did."

Aiden said nothing. From the sorrow in her eyes he guessed thoughts of her father caused her pain and he had no wish to intrude on it.

"I need to record all this," she muttered suddenly. She crossed to a bag and pulled out what looked to be a pad for writing and some sort of small metal device. She placed these on her knee and faced him. "I'm gonna need some quotes."

"Quotes?"

"For my story. You didn't think I'd not report all this did you? I can at least report how he threatened to kill you and had his heavies try to kick the crap out of you. That might at least expose him for the rat he is. It's a start until I figure out what the hell is really going on."

A shot of alarm went through Aiden. The last thing he needed was his visit to be publicized to all and sundry. He made a big show of letting out a yawn. "In the morning, lass. I'll tell ye all ye wish to know in the morning."

She sighed and put down the pad. "Yes, I guess you're right. I'm pretty beat." She stood. "You can have the sofa. I'll get you a blanket."

She disappeared into the bed chamber and returned a moment later carrying a folded woolen blanket. "It's all I have."

"It will be fine, lass. Ye have my thanks for all ye have done for me this night." He reached out to take the bundle and his finger brushed hers for a moment.

A thrill shivered across his skin. He glanced up to find her watching him, eyes huge. She was so close he could smell her: a faint hint of lavender.

"Goodnight, lass," he said hoarsely.

Kara blinked. "Um...yes...goodnight."

She gave a weak smile and then made her way into her bed chamber and shut the door behind her. Aiden stared at the closed door then blew out a breath. Lord, what a mess. The sooner he returned home, the better.

Clasping the Key in his hands, he sat on the sofa and rested his hands on his knees. Going very still and counting his breaths the way he did to calm himself before a battle, he waited, watching as the hands on the clock slowly counted out the time. When he judged enough time had passed he stood, crept slowly over to the door of Kara's bedchamber and pressed his ear against the wood. No sound came from within. Good. The lass was asleep.

Silently he padded over to the door in the hallway, turned the key, and eased the door open. With one last regretful look back at the apartment, he left, stealing silently out into the night.

SLEEP WOULDN'T COME. Kara had lain awake for the last hour, staring at the ceiling. She was too wired to sleep. The day's events kept running through her head. Meeting Aiden at the abandoned warehouse. His confrontation with Michael Devereux. Getting him out of jail. But most of all the sight of him standing in front her, only inches away, blue eyes so deep she could drown in them.

The morning, she told herself. *It will all be better in the morning. You're just strung-out after everything that's happened. Come the morning it will all make sense, you can get your story on Devereux and life can go back to normal.*

Life, she thought suddenly. *What life? Moving onto the next story? Is that all there is?*

She paused. Where the hell had that thought come from?

Suddenly a sound intruded on her senses and she bolted upright. She'd lived alone for so long that her senses were finely tuned to any sound that didn't belong. Was that the front door opening?

Hurling back the covers, she jumped out of bed and ran over to the window. Below her, a figure hurried across the parking lot, quickly disappearing into the night. A shot of alarm went through Kara. There was no mistaking the tall, broad figure of Aiden Harris.

What the hell was he doing? He was running out on her! Damn the man!

Throwing a coat over her pajamas, she pulled on a pair of boots. If he thought he was going to just disappear without so much as a by-your-leave he had another think coming! She bolted out the door and took the stairs two at a time. By the time she reached the parking lot Aiden was just a dark speck in the distance.

Kara jogged after him, careful to keep far enough back that he didn't notice her following. He seemed to know exactly where he was going. He walked at a brisk pace through the streets and it soon became clear that he was heading back towards the warehouse. Kara slowed, suspicion flaring inside. Why would he be going back there?

Perhaps he's a plant, Kara thought. *Perhaps everything he told me was a pack of lies and he was working with Devereux all along.*

The thought sent a pang of hopelessness through her.

She pushed it aside. *You're a reporter, damn you,* she told herself. *So report. Follow him. Find out what the hell he's up to and how he's connected to Irene MacAskill and Michael Devereux.*

The industrial unit soon came into view. All was dark and forbidding. Up ahead, the abandoned warehouse loomed out of the night—a darker shadow against the blackness. But instead of heading towards it, Aiden suddenly turned left and picked his way across wasteland to an old railway bridge. Kara followed, diving behind a burned-out car to watch him.

Aiden marched up to the bridge and paused below it. Crumbling brickwork formed an archway above him. What the hell was he doing?

"Ye can come out, lass," he said suddenly into the darkness. He turned and his gaze fell on Kara's hiding place.

With a curse, she stepped out. "How did you know I was following you?"

Was that an amused smile? "It wasnae difficult, lass. Ye make enough racket to wake the dead."

She frowned. And here she was thinking she was being stealthy.

She jabbed an angry finger at him. "You ran out on me."

He grimaced. "Aye. I'm sorry. I thought it was for the best."

"For the best? Leaving me to face the music when you disappear while on bail? Leaving me with more questions than I can name? Telling me a crazy story then leaving me to figure out which bits are true and which bits are a roaring pack of lies?"

Aiden said nothing. He just watched her. Then he shook his head. "What would ye have me do, woman?" There was anger in his own voice now. "I've told ye the truth but ye dinna believe a word I say."

"And you're surprised by that? You seriously expect me to believe in magic? That there are fairies and time-travel? Why would I believe such a crazy tale?"

"Because I gave ye my word! Isnae that enough?"

"No!" she yelled. "Don't you get it? People are liars! I've been a reporter long enough to know people will say whatever they need to save their own skin. People cannot be trusted!"

"*I* can, lass," Aiden said quietly. "I wouldnae lie to ye."

His eyes glinted in the darkness. She opened her mouth to speak but found no words would come out. Her anger leaked away like water from a broken bottle. Instead she let out a deep sigh.

"Could you at least tell me what you're doing out here in the middle of the night?"

"I'm going home, lass. I've tarried here too long already."

"To Scotland? Then you're going the wrong way. The airport is five miles in the other direction."

"I dinna need this 'airport', lass, whatever that may be. I have all I need right here." He nodded at the railway bridge.

Kara glanced up at it. In the darkness the space below looked like some bottomless pit that would swallow her up. No, wait. As she looked closer she thought she could see something within. There were swirling shapes like mist and beyond that, so faint she could barely make it out, something moved. Something that looked like waves crashing against a shore.

She shook her head. Yes, she was finally losing it. She could add hallucinations to the other crazy things she'd experienced today.

Aiden took a step towards her, hand held out pleadingly. "Kara, lass. Listen. I—"

A sudden sound made him pause. Kara heard it too. It came from the shadows behind them. Aiden whirled, hand going automatically to where his sword had hung. But it wasn't there any longer, of course. The police had confiscated it.

The sound came again, echoed at three other points all around them. Kara's neck prickled as she realized what it was.

Laughter.

Four shadows detached themselves from the darkness. Aiden grabbed her, pushing her behind him.

His eyes tracked the shadows as they stalked closer. "Who are ye?" he demanded. "Show yerselves!"

The shadows revealed themselves into four men, each carrying a handgun that was trained on Aiden. Kara's heart leaped into her mouth.

"Look," she said. "We don't want any trouble. I haven't got much money but you can take what I have—"

"You think it's money I want?" said a familiar voice. "I thought you knew me better than that, Miss Buchanan."

A fifth figure materialized from the darkness and Kara's breath caught as she recognized Michael Devereux.

He halted a few paces from them. He was wearing the same sharp business suit he'd been wearing earlier and looked neatly styled, despite the hour. He smiled at Aiden.

"I have to hand it to you," he said in a conversational tone. "You did quite a number on me earlier. Not many things surprise me these days but you showing up like that? Well, that was a real eye-opener. Give me the Key of Ages."

Aiden glared at Devereux, fists clenched, body tense.

"Like that, is it?" Devereux continued. "You know I have ways to make you cooperate. If you don't do as I say, you'll force me to hurt the girl."

"If ye touch her, I will kill ye," Aiden growled.

"How did you know we were here," Kara demanded.

"It wasn't hard to have one of my men follow Aiden when he was bailed," Devereux replied. "I suspected he had an accomplice here earlier and I suppose I should have suspected you. After all, you seem a little too preoccupied with poking your nose into my business, Miss Buchanan. Still, all's well that ends well, eh?" He stepped closer, eyes fixed on Aiden. "It all makes sense now. I think I even know who you are. Tell me if I'm right. You're Aiden Harris, of Clan Harris, son of Andrew and Lucy Harris. According to the records you were born in 1518 on the Isle of Skye. Am I right?"

Aiden's scowl deepened. His shoulders had gone tense and his fingers worked, as if he wanted to leap forward and throttle the man.

"I'm right, aren't I? Did the Fae send you here?" Devereux's eyes strayed to the archway beneath the railway bridge. "And this must be your arch! How perfect! Shall we go through now? No time like the present is there? Although the term 'present' probably has very little meaning for somebody like you."

"Hang on," Kara said, holding out a hand and trying to make sense of all this. "Are you telling me you *knew* about this? That you really believe that crazy story you told me about Fae and magic powers? That's why you bought all those artifacts? To get hold of some trinket you thought had magic powers? Do you know how insane that sounds?"

"Ah, Miss Buchanan, ever the realist. Always fighting for the truth. I'm afraid the truth this time, my dear, is a little beyond you. Yes, I bought those artifacts because I was searching. Searching for a power more ancient than the bones of the Earth. The power of time." He nodded to his heavies and they raised their guns, aiming straight at Aiden. "And you, Aiden Harris, will give me what I need. Now."

"Stay behind me, lass," Aiden said. He didn't look afraid. He was staring at Devereux, unblinking.

Kara took a step back and found herself standing almost directly below the arch.

"It doesnae work like that," Aiden said to Devereux. "The power canna be taken. It must be granted—and ye havenae been granted it. Nor will ye ever be. As long as there is breath in my body ye will never hold the power of time. This I vow."

His hand suddenly snapped out and gripped Kara's. He turned to look at her. "Do ye trust me?" he whispered urgently.

"What?"

"Do ye trust me?"

"I...I..." she struggled to answer. Then she met his eyes and the answer became obvious. "Yes, I trust you."

"Good."

Then, before Devereux or his men could react, Aiden spun and yanked them both into the darkness under the railway bridge.

"Stop them!" Devereux yelled.

There was the sharp retort of gun fire then they both went tumbling. Kara curled her fingers around Aiden's just as everything went black.

Chapter 5

A SOUND SLOWLY INTRUDED on the blackness. A soft, sighing sound. Next came smells: saltwater and wet earth. Kara opened her eyes.

A gray sky arched above her, the sun a pale ball behind the clouds. Birds crisscrossed the sky, crying raucously to one another. Kara blinked, expecting the vision to disappear as dreams always did. It didn't.

A second later a face appeared above her. A chiseled, handsome face with a strong mouth and eyes like polished sapphires. Hair as dark as a raven's wing fell around his face and brushed her forehead.

"Kara. Are ye well, lass?"

Aiden. That was his name. Aiden Harris. A Scotsman. The guy who claimed to be a time traveler. It all came rushing back and she bolted upright, looking around wildly.

The industrial unit was gone. The railway tunnel was gone. Devereux and his men were gone. There was only Aiden and herself on a stretch of wintry beach. With a trembling hand she reached out and laid her palm against the damp sand. It felt cold and grainy under her touch.

Wide-eyed, she looked around. Gentle waves lapped at the beach not five paces from where she sat. A rock archway reared above and on the other side miles of endless ocean stretched to the horizon.

Kara pressed the heel of her hand to her forehead. "Oh God. I've gone and done it. I've lost my mind."

Aiden's hand settled on her shoulder. "Nay, lass, ye havenae. We passed through the archway. We've traveled to my home. To the Isle of Skye."

She forced herself to take a long, slow breath and then let it out, pushing back the panic that threatened to overwhelm her. Then she looked at Aiden.

"Your home? In the sixteenth century, you mean?"

He nodded gently. "Aye, lass. There was nay choice. If we hadnae, those men would have shot ye. I couldnae let ye get hurt."

Kara reached up and ran a shaky hand through her hair then forced herself to stand. Aiden held out a hand to steady her and she clung onto his arm as she looked around. Sudden dizziness took her and she staggered forward. Aiden caught her. She sagged against him, feeling faint and disoriented. She rested her head against his hard chest and his arms came around and held her.

"I'm sorry, lass," he murmured in her ear. "I didnae want this for ye."

"Sorry?" she muttered, fighting the dizziness with an effort of will. "Sorry?" she lifted her head and pushed away from him.

"This is your damned fault! Why did you bring me here? I didn't ask for it!" A part of her knew she was being unfair. Like he said, if he hadn't pushed her through the archway Devereux's men would have shot them. But fear-fueled anger coursed through her, sending rationality out the window. "If you hadn't ran out on me none of this would have happened!"

"If ye remember," Aiden replied, sounding a little exasperated. "It was *ye* who followed *me*, just as it was ye who was sneaking around that warehouse—and getting yerself cornered by a guard dog."

"I was doing just fine. I didn't need your help."

"Oh? If I hadn't turned up ye would have ended up as that guard dog's dinner!"

"And if *I* hadn't turned up Devereux would have got the Key of Ages and you'd still be in a jail cell!"

They glared at each other. Aiden's chest heaved, his eyes alight with anger. He was so close that Kara could have reached out and kissed him. Or slapped him.

Right now she didn't know which she'd rather do. Oh God. What the hell was going on?

AIDEN GLARED AT KARA. Lord, she must be the most stubborn, pig-headed woman he'd ever come across! Her dark eyes glinted with fury and the set of her shoulders told Aiden she was considering slapping him.

He held up his hands in surrender. "Ye have every right to be angry, lass," he breathed. "I dinna know how I would react if I was ripped from my time against my will but I doubt I'd be any less annoyed."

She stared at him for a moment, defiance in her eyes, then she seemed to crumple. She blew out a long breath and her shoulders sagged. She sat down heavily on the wet sand.

"Oh God," she murmured. "What am I going to do?"

There it was, that vulnerability that hid underneath the hard exterior. The sight of it twisted Aiden's heart. He crouched in front of her, put a finger under her chin and lifted it so she looked at him. He gave her an encouraging smile.

"Dinna worry, lass. Irene will fix this, ye'll see."

He climbed to his feet and turned in a slow circle, taking in the arch, the cliffs, the sea, the beach, searching for Irene MacAskill. Surely, she'd be here waiting for him to return with the Key? But he found nothing. In all directions the beach was empty, with not even footprints in the wet sand to show Irene had ever been here.

He cupped his hands around his mouth. "Ho! Irene!" he bellowed. "Where are ye?"

His shout echoed off the cliffs and sent a flock of seagulls flapping into the air. The noise quickly faded into silence and Irene MacAskill did not appear. The cry of the wind sounded oddly like mocking laughter to Aiden's ears.

This couldn't be right. Irene had sent him on this mission, so why was she not here to greet him?

"Irene!" he yelled. "Come out, curse ye!"

Nothing.

Aiden let forth a string of curses that any sailor would have been proud of. Why had he trusted the old woman? He should have heeded his father's warning and not got caught up in that woman's schemes. Where had it led him? Into a whole heap of trouble, that's where. He pulled in a deep breath then turned to Kara who was watching him with wide eyes.

"What's wrong?" she asked.

"I expected Irene to be here but she isnae."

"We hold the Key don't we? If it activates the arches surely we can use it to send me back?"

"It isnae that simple. Devereux will be waiting on the other side. Without Irene to send ye to an alternative location, I canna risk it. I willnae put ye in danger."

Her eyes flashed. "Put me in danger? Don't you think it's a little late for that? Take me back right now!"

Despite her ire, he shook his head. "I canna do that, lass."

"Fine!" she exploded. "Then I'll go myself!"

She whirled and stomped towards the archway.

Aiden grabbed her wrist just as she was about to step under it. Did the lass have no common sense at all? "What are ye doing?" he growled. "Have ye lost yer senses? Ye would walk right back into their clutches?"

"What would you have me do?" she shot back. "Stay here with you?"

Aye, a traitorous little voice said in the back of his head. *That's exactly what I'd have ye do.*

Aiden closed his eyes for a second. Then he sucked a breath through his nose, took out the Key of Ages and held it in his left hand, while holding his other hand out to Kara. "Very well. Ready?"

She looked at him, puzzled. "What are you doing?"

"I'm coming with ye. I willnae let harm come to ye, lass. This I vow. I'll find a way to keep Devereux from harming ye."

She seemed a little taken aback. "You'd do that for me?"

"Did I not give ye my word? I said I'd protect ye, lass. Are ye ready?"

Kara reached out and grasped his hand. Her hand seemed tiny in his meaty fist, as fragile as a bird's wing. He looked up and their gazes locked. His breath left him in a whoosh.

She nodded. "Ready."

Together they stepped through the arch—

—and straight onto the beach on the other side.

Aiden stumbled, nearly taking them both crashing to the ground. He spun, looking back at the archway. What, by all that's holy—?

"What happened?" Kara asked. "Why didn't it work?"

"I...I dinna understand," Aiden muttered.

He let go of Kara's hand and glanced down at the golden prongs of the Key of Ages. What had happened? This thing was supposed to bestow the gift of time-travel for pity's sake! He strode back through the archway. Sure enough, he emerged onto the beach on the other side. No shimmering veil of time, no gut-wrenching tug into the distant future, just a cold seascape on an early winter's day.

"Irene," he growled. "This is more of her meddling! I swear when I find her I will wring her neck!"

He stomped off down the beach, determined to find the old woman's trail. She couldn't have vanished into thin air. She must have left footprints or something. And when he found her, he would make sure she regretted meddling in his life!

KARA FOUGHT THE PANIC that swatted at the edges of her consciousness. She was in the sixteenth century, and, from the expression on Aiden's face, wouldn't be going home any time soon.

Aiden had stomped off down the beach and kept kneeling every so often to examine the sand. He did not look happy. After a moment he returned and shook his head.

"Nay sign of her."

Pulling in a deep breath, Kara said, "So what now?"

Aiden turned to look at her and the fury in his eyes softened into compassion. "We must discover where Irene MacAskill has gone, lass," he said. "She's the only one who can send ye home."

Kara nodded. "Okay, so we have a plan. How do we find her?"

"That's the problem," he replied. "I dinna have the first idea—but my family will. They've had dealings with Irene MacAskill before, especially my mother, and if anyone knows how to find Irene, she will."

Kara brightened a little. "Great! So we go find your mom, right?"

Aiden smiled in return. "Right. There's only one snag."

"And that is?"

"My family live at Dun Arnwick on the very northern tip of the island which is thirty miles away." He turned, scanning the terrain. "And it looks as though my horse has run off." He fixed her with his blue eyes. "Looks like we must walk and I reckon the journey will take at least two days."

Kara digested this in silence. She could deal with two measly days in this time, couldn't she?

"Right," she said, squaring her shoulders. "We'd better get started then hadn't we?"

Aiden nodded. His eyes were still fixed on her and Kara felt a little thrill walk down her spine. Then Aiden cleared his throat and looked quickly away. "This way. There's a trail that leads up to the clifftop."

They walked a little way along the beach to where a switchback trail made its way up the cliff. Kara couldn't help looking over her shoulder at the archway. It looked forlorn and abandoned, nothing more than a broken piece of rock.

Kara was puffing by the time they reached the top of the cliff although Aiden was barely out of breath. He eyed her but wisely made no comment. Kara leaned over, resting her hands on her knees as she caught her breath. She was doubly glad she thought to put on her coat as the wind up here was biting, plucking at her clothes with icy fingers and sending her hair streaming out behind her.

When she'd recovered, she straightened and took her first look at the Isle of Skye. The coastline to her right was rugged, composed of tall, jagged cliffs that tumbled down into the churning sea below. To her left the land spread out in a brown and purple carpet, stands of heather covering the undulating ground. In the far distance, their tops wreathed in cloud, Kara saw a line of dark mountains with a loch glimmering at their feet.

It was wild, untamed, utterly unlike anything Kara had ever experienced. She stared and felt something stir within her. Yes, it was wild, untamed. But it was also something else. Unfettered. Free. It felt like home.

"Beautiful," she whispered. "It's beautiful."

"Aye," Aiden agreed, standing beside her. "It is. Sometimes I forget how much." This last was said under his breath, as if to himself.

They started walking. The exercise warmed her a little, for which Kara was profoundly grateful, and she found herself beginning to relax a little. There was something...reassuring about Aiden's presence by her side.

For his part, he remained silent and she couldn't figure out what was going on behind those storm-blue eyes of his. His mood seemed somber, apprehensive even.

"So we'll follow the coastline to your home, right?" she asked.

"Only for a short time," Aiden replied. "The coastline is full of inlets and bays that means we'll have to walk three times the distance if we follow the contours of the coast. Nay, in a few miles time we'll hit the inland road and take that. It leads into the heart of Skye and crosses the uplands and the base of the mountains. It will be our quickest way home."

Kara nodded but said nothing. It looked to be somewhere around mid morning but back home she guessed the sun would just be coming up. Her stomach growled, reminding her she'd not had anything to eat since yesterday afternoon.

As if sensing her thoughts Aiden said, "If we're lucky we'll pass a croft soon where we can get something to eat."

"And if we're not lucky?"

Aiden shrugged. "Then we'll discover how good a hunter I am."

"You should have warned me we were going to travel back in time. I would have packed us breakfast."

Aiden snorted. "Oh? And what would that involve?"

Kara pursed her lips in thought. "Well, croissants for starters. You can't possibly have breakfast without croissants. And yoghurt. And then pizza for lunch. Pepperoni, ham and pineapple, take your pick."

"I've nay heard of these things, lass. What is a 'pizza'?"

Kara looked at him incredulously. "You don't know what a pizza is?" She pointed at him. "You, my friend, are an uncivilized barbarian."

He laughed again and the sound of it did something funny to Kara's insides. She found herself grinning in return.

"Ye'll find nay argument from me on that score, lass."

It turned out they were unlucky. They reached the fork in the path without encountering another soul, let alone a cottage where they might beg some breakfast. At the crossroads Aiden hesitated. From here the path they'd been following carried straight on, disappearing into the cliffs in the distance. To the left it snaked inland and rose up onto high moorland that looked cold, windswept, and uninviting.

Aiden glanced down the trail then at the cliff that dropped down onto a beach on their right. He seemed to make a decision.

"I canna offer ye croissants or pizza, lass, but mayhap I can rustle up a bit of breakfast before we move on. What do ye say?"

Kara nodded. "That is the most sensible thing you've said since I met you."

Aiden led the way to the cliff edge. It wasn't as steep as the one where the arch had been and Kara was able to scramble down it after Aiden. At the bottom wasn't a sandy beach as Kara had been expecting but a wide tumble of rocks worn smooth by the relentless passage of the waves. The tide was out so the area was filled with a myriad of rock pools, all sparkling in the sunlight.

"Here," Aiden held out his hand to help Kara down onto a large, flat rock.

Kara took his hand and stepped down, his fingers feeling warm and rough where they touched hers. "Thanks," she mumbled. "What's this place?"

"Skye's kitchen," Aiden replied with a smile. "If ye would take a seat, my lady, I will bring yer breakfast anon."

She raised an eyebrow at him and then folded into a cross-legged position on the flat rock. With a sigh, she leaned back on her hands and gazed out at the sea. Somewhere out there was her homeland. Thousands of miles and hundreds of years away.

Aiden jumped down from the rock and began scouting around on the beach, crouching every now and then to pick up bits of driftwood. When he had enough he returned to the rock, set the wood down in a depression, then took flint and tinder from his sporran and struck a spark. In only a few moments, much to Kara's delight, a merry fire was crackling, sheltered from the sea breeze by the rocks.

Closing her eyes in delight, Kara held her hands out to the flames, enjoying the sensation of warmth on her cold fingers.

"I'll be back soon," Aiden said, jumping down onto the beach once more.

"Where are you going?" Kara asked.

Aiden gave a wicked smile. "Didnae I say I'd bring ye breakfast? Stay here and try to keep out of trouble."

Kara inclined her head. "I'll do my best."

Aiden nodded and then disappeared round a large boulder. Kara shuffled closer to the fire and soon found herself drowsing. Fractured images spun through her head: Michael Devereux. Irene MacAskill. The Key of Ages. But most of the images were of a tall, dark-haired man with eyes she could drown in. Those images sent a warmth right into her core.

She came awake with a start. The fire was getting low so Kara added another branch. She had no idea how much time had passed. There was no sign of Aiden. Kara scrambled to her feet and hurried to the edge of the boulder, looking left and right down the beach. There was nobody in sight. Kara could have been the only person in the whole world. She felt panic begin to bubble in her belly and fought it down.

No, she thought. *He'll be back soon. He gave his word.* Then another, panicky voice replied, *that didn't stop him running out on you in the apartment, did it? What makes you think he can be trusted any more than anyone else? He's only looking out for himself, just like everyone.*

She pressed her hand against her chest to try to still her suddenly thumping heart. Then she heard a scrabbling sound and Aiden climbed up onto the rock. His boots and plaid were wet and he was cradling something in the crook of his arm.

At the sight of him Kara's legs went wobbly with relief. Aiden saw her standing there and a look of concern flashed across his face.

"Are ye well, lass?" he asked. "Ye look as if ye've seen a ghost."

Kara wiped a hand across her brow. "I'm fine. What have you got there?"

"Breakfast. Highland style. Can ye find me a flattish stone I can lay these on?"

Kara cast around and found what he was looking for, a flat stone about the size of a dinner plate. She put it down near the fire. Aiden crouched next to it then carefully placed the items he'd been cradling on the rock. Shrimps. Lots of them. He sprinkled bits of seaweed on top and then placed the stone in the fire, allowing the shrimps to fry in their own juices. In no time at all a delicious smell wafted out, making Kara's stomach rumble all over again.

"I trust ye like seafood?" Aiden asked.

"You trust right," Kara replied. "Especially seafood as fresh as this."

"None better," Aiden said with pride. "When I was a boy I used to spend whole days exploring the coast, living on whatever I caught. Skye will show ye her bounty if ye know where to look."

He took the shrimps from the fire and laid several out on another, smaller rock for Kara to use as a plate. "Welcome to yer first Highland meal, lass."

There were no knives or forks, salt and pepper, or fancy sauces to go with the shrimps but even so it was possibly one of the best meals Kara had ever eaten. She'd never tasted seafood as fresh or as well-cooked. In no time at all she'd polished off her share and sat licking her fingers.

"Wow," she said. "That was delicious. Have you ever thought of moving to my time? You'd make an excellent chef. I know a dozen swanky hotels who'd snap you up."

Aiden licked his own fingers and then smiled. "I'm nay sure they'd ever get used to my ways, lass. What was it ye called me? An uncivilized barbarian?"

"Well, maybe after that meal I need to reassess that statement."

She looked up and found him watching her. Their gazes locked and Kara felt a tremble inside. She cleared her throat and jumped to her feet. "Right. Hadn't we better be going?"

Kara poured some sand onto the fire to quench it, then they climbed the trail back to the clifftop. Now that she'd eaten she felt refreshed and a little more normal—whatever normal was these days. They took the path that led inland, towards the mountains. There was soft, springy turf underfoot and the trail was flat. The going was relatively easy and they made good time.

The road was wide enough that they were able to walk side by side although Kara was pretty sure Aiden slowed his pace to account for her. Kara watched the landscape change as they walked. The coast was soon left behind and they entered an upland area of purple heather and peat bogs. Aiden picked their way with care, warning her about straying too far from the path as the peat bogs could be treacherous.

The clouds rolled back and the sun shone although there was a bite in the air that suggested winter wasn't far away. The scent of heather and peat filled her nostrils and she breathed the clean, fresh air deeply, savoring its feel in her lungs.

To Kara's surprise, she found herself beginning to relax. The near-panic that had filled her retreated and was replaced by something else, something she couldn't quite put a name to. She felt calm. Almost peaceful. There was something about trekking through this landscape with Aiden that chased away all her thoughts, her worries, leaving only the crystal clear moment of right now.

Aiden pointed things out as they walked: the names of flowers and plants, types of birds and their nesting habits, the names of abandoned settlements they passed through. Kara listened attentively, tucking it all away, and found herself watching Aiden as they traveled. He seemed utterly at home here. He moved with an economy of movement, a sort of languid grace that suggested he was used to long days of walking in this sort of terrain. His stormy blue eyes scanned the landscape, taking in everything, spotting things that Kara wouldn't have noticed had she tripped over them: the red deer crouching in the heather, the tracks of a fox crossing the trail, a golden eagle riding the thermals high above them, a clutch of blue eggs that he collected for their supper.

Dusk was falling when Aiden called a halt for the night. They were walking by the banks of a stream that gurgled along the base of a wooded valley and the temperature was rapidly dropping. For the last half an hour Aiden had been studying their trail intently, looking for something. Kara had watched him, bemused, as he stopped to check a piece of scuffed turf or the grazed bark of a tree. When she'd asked him about it he'd merely smiled and told her to wait.

Now he went stock still, staring at the trail ahead. Then he gave a quick shout and dashed forward. Kara hurried after and found him around a bend in the stream, standing under an overhang leading to a cave in the hillside.

Kara looked up and something on the far side of the valley caught her eye. A ring of standing stones stood high on the hillside, their silhouettes black against the sky.

"What's that?" she asked, pointing.

Aiden followed her gaze and a look of unease passed across his face. "It's called Cullmaggin. An ancient place that's best avoided. Dinna worry, lass. Our path tomorrow willnae take us near it."

Kara squinted up at Cullmaggin. The stones looked like clawed fingers erupting from the ground, beckoning her closer...

She shook her head at the foolish notion and turned her attention to the cave that Aiden had found. The floor inside was made of fine gravel that looked like it had been swept in by the stream and at the back was a neatly stacked pile of firewood and two pottery jugs.

"What is this place?" Kara asked as she entered the small, dry space.

"This is a waypoint," Aiden replied. "A place for travelers to rest. With so few settlements in the uplands, these spots are a lifeline for travelers. There's always some firewood, a water jug and, if we're very lucky, a bit more than that. Whoever creates the waypoint leaves markers for other people to follow."

"So that's what you were looking at?" Kara asked.

"Aye. We'll sleep warm and dry tonight, lass."

Kara looked around the rudimentary shelter. It looked downright uncomfortable to her but she didn't say this to Aiden. "Great. I'm so exhausted I think I could sleep standing up."

"I'm going to take a look around. I willnae be long."

Before she could reply he disappeared into the gathering dusk. Kara put her hands on her hips and looked around. She crossed to the back of the cave and inspected the jugs. One was full and sealed with wax but the other was empty. She took this down to the stream and filled it with the icy water, drinking her fill before returning to the cave.

Next she inspected the woodpile and found flint and tinder wrapped in a pouch. Kara had been a girl scout in her youth and was no stranger to making a fire. She arranged the sticks neatly in a depression in the center of the cave, added kindling and then struck a spark. It was a long time since she'd done anything like this and she wasn't as practiced as Aiden was so she was swearing and cursing under her breath by the time she managed to get a spark into the kindling. As a tiny plume of smoke rose up, she went onto her belly and blew gently on it, carefully coaxing it to life. She fed in smaller twigs, whilst simultaneously blowing on it and eventually the spark took, eating into the wood and soon becoming a bright blaze.

"Ha!" she cried, punching the air. "Take that, Aiden Harris!"

She was surprised by how such a simple act of making a fire gave her so much pleasure. Back home she'd never thought twice about it, just taken it for granted as she lit a match or pressed the ignition button on her gas cooker.

There was a rustle and Kara spun just as Aiden stepped inside. He paused as he took in the merrily burning fire.

"How did ye do that?"

Kara placed her hands on her hips. "I'm not completely useless you know."

Aiden held up his hands. "I wouldnae dream of suggesting ye were. I'm just a little...surprised is all, ye being a city lass and all."

"Well this city lass won 'best girl scout' two years in a row I'll have you know."

"Aye? Well, I'm glad of it."

He moved to the back of the cave and took out the wrapped bundle he'd placed there, carefully uncovering a clutch of eggs he'd collected earlier as they moved through the heather. Kara folded into a cross-legged position as Aiden found a flat stone and placed it into the fire. When it was hot enough he cracked the eggs onto it and began to cook them gently.

Kara propped her chin on her hand and watched him. "Where did you learn all this?"

He glanced up at her. "From my father and Uncle Jamie mostly. Uncle Jamie used to take me on long expeditions when I was a lad. We'd spend days out in the wilds, living on what we could catch. The king's guard taught me more. When ye are constantly moving ye soon learn that a hot meal might not be as forthcoming as ye might wish. Ye learn to take what ye can, when ye can."

Kara cocked her head. "King's guard? You mean you're a soldier?"

Aiden shifted uncomfortably and Kara got the impression he didn't really want to talk about it. "Aye, something like that."

She changed the subject. "Did you find anything when you were scouting?"

"Nay, lass. There is not a soul for miles nor any sign of dangerous animals. We should be fine here tonight."

"And tomorrow we'll reach Dun Arnwick?"

"Aye, providing the weather holds."

Kara swallowed a sudden feeling of unease. She would meet Aiden's family. She'd never been good at meeting families. Somehow she always managed to say something stupid and make an idiot of herself. This time though, her whole future hung on the help Aiden's family might be able to give her.

"Tell me about them," Kara said. "Your family, I mean."

Aiden tipped the fried eggs onto two large leaves to use as plates and passed one to Kara. She took it gratefully and tucked in. The eggs were delicious, although she would give her back teeth for a dollop of ketchup and some salt. And a fork. A fork would be great. Eating fried eggs with her fingers was decidedly tricky.

"There's nay much to tell," Aiden replied, sitting back and tucking into his own meal. "There's my mother and father and my younger sister, Beth. I think ye will get on with her—she's as opinionated as ye are."

"Opinionated?" Kara said. "I'm not opinionated!"

Aiden just grinned. "Then there is my Uncle Jamie – my parents took him in when he was a boy so he's not a blood relative. Annis is the housekeeper who is more like a surrogate aunt and my ma's closest friend. Old Dougie is the steward. Then there is the extended clan. Everyone in Dun Arnwick is related to somebody else in some way. When I was a lad I couldnae get up to anything without my parents finding out about it. Ye could say I was brought up by the whole clan."

"That sounds nice," Kara whispered. How different it sounded to her own upbringing. There had only been her and her parents, then only her and her mom after her father had died. Although she and her mom had been very close, her mom had always been busy. Always chasing a story. Always on the hunt for the next lead. In a lot of ways it had been a lonely life.

Am I any different? Kara thought suddenly. *Am I lonely because I choose to be?*

"Yer turn, lass," Aiden said, screwing up his leaf-plate and tossing it into the fire. "Tell me something about yerself."

"What do you want to know?" Kara asked, a sudden wariness making her tone sharp. She wasn't used to people asking questions and even less used to answering them. But fair was fair.

"Why were ye at the warehouse? Ye say ye didnae know anything about the Key of Ages but ye still havenae explained why ye were looking into Devereux in the first place."

Kara set aside her plate and glanced out into the gathering gloom. How to explain? She gathered her thoughts for a moment and then looked back at Aiden. He was watching her steadily, the firelight dancing in his eyes.

"Michael Devereux is a bad man. There are rumors of things he's done—terrible things—including racketeering, extortion, beatings. Even murder. But nobody was ever able to nail him. The police would build a case for it to fall apart when a witness disappeared or an alibi was suddenly produced from nowhere. I'm an investigative reporter. It's my job to stop these people. To bring their crimes into the light of day."

"Why?" Aiden asked.

"Why what?"

"Why do ye do such things? Surely it's the province of yer law keepers to stop these men. Why put yer life in danger?"

"I..." Kara floundered for words. How could she explain? How could she make him understand that relentless tug she felt inside herself? That her instincts always drove her? How could she explain that she had no control over it? That it was a drive that would never let her rest because there was always the next story. Always the next bad guy to bring down? That it was the only way she knew to fill the hole inside herself?

"I...I..." she opened her mouth and then shut it again.

For the first time she realized she felt different. That tugging sensation was gone. That relentless yearning had fallen silent.

She ought to be burning with desperation to get home. She ought to be hungry to get back so she could take down Devereux. But she wasn't. Instead of that insatiable fire in her belly, she felt calm. No, wait. That wasn't it. She felt...she scrabbled around in her brain trying to find a word to describe the feeling. It had been so long since she'd experienced anything like it that it took her a while. Then she had it and her mouth formed a little O of surprise.

She felt at peace.

"I don't really know why I do it," she said at last. "It's just something I do. It's like something pushes me, whether I want to or not. Do you know what I mean?"

His blue eyes fixed on hers and she saw a shadow of sorrow in them. "Aye, lass," he breathed. "I know exactly what ye mean."

Then, before Kara could reply, he gathered up a stick and hunched over the fire, precluding further conversation.

Chapter 6

AIDEN REACHED HIS HANDS towards the fire, savoring the warmth that bled into his stiff fingers. It was going to be a cold night and they'd need the fire if they were going to pass it in even a modicum of comfort. Aiden would have dearly loved to have found an isolated croft where they could have slept in the barn—Kara deserved a finer introduction to his country than sleeping in a cave —but it seemed fate was not on his side and this was the best he could offer.

He glanced at her. Her cheeks were rosy from the fire and her hair was spilling over her shoulders and framing her face in a way that accentuated her beauty. It was a careless sort of beauty, as though she was either unaware of it or didn't care. Either way, the sight of her sent Aiden's pulse racing in a way that made him decidedly uneasy. He picked up a twig and began idly shredding it. Anything to keep his mind off the flame-haired beauty sitting not four paces away.

Suddenly Kara let out an enormous yawn.

"Sorry," she mumbled. "Don't know where that came from."

"It's been a long day," Aiden replied. "Why dinna ye get some sleep? Dinna worry, ye'll be perfectly safe. I'll sleep across the entrance."

Kara nodded then lay down, head cradled on her arms. In moments her eyes drifted closed and her breathing evened out, a little wisp of hair rising and falling with each breath.

Aiden glanced out of the entrance. Darkness had fallen and he was night-blinded by the firelight so could see nothing beyond its light. He didn't think any wild animals would venture near with the scent of two humans so strong in the area but he would take no chances. What he wouldn't give for his claymore but that had been taken by the police in the twenty-first century. He had to content himself with a stout branch as his only weapon.

He shuffled backwards to lean against the wall of the cave and stretch his legs out in front of him. He was exhausted. His limbs felt heavy and awkward and the bruises he'd suffered at the hands of Devereux's thugs sent a dull ache throbbing through his body. He glanced at Kara who looked peaceful in sleep.

Irene, he thought. *Where are ye? What are ye up to?*

The sooner they reached Dun Arnwick and he could speak to his family, the better. Maybe they could make sense of all this. The thought of his home sent a pang through him. It was a strange mixture of homesickness and wariness. Homesickness because he'd missed them all, wariness because when he got there he knew he'd have to tell them. Tell them he was leaving. Tell them he couldn't fulfill their expectations of him.

He sighed and scrubbed a hand through his hair. Ah, Lord. What a mess. He could well imagine their reaction when he told them. His mother would be heartbroken. His father would be furious. His sister would be disappointed.

But what else could he do? He had a duty to his king, his country. He knew of no other way to still that restlessness inside him.

He paused suddenly as he realized something. The restlessness was gone. For the first time since he could remember, that ache that kept him forever moving, forever searching for something was gone and he felt...content.

He glanced over at Kara. And wondered.

The fire was getting low so he dropped a few more logs into the flames and then sat back, leaning his head against the cave wall, staff clutched across his knees, staring out into the darkness.

But exhaustion soon took him and pulled him under.

KARA WOKE WITH A START. She sat up, looking around. Something had woken her but she wasn't sure what. The fire had burned low and cast eerie shadows on the walls of the cave. Aiden sat by the entrance, head back, snoring softly. Kara rubbed her eyes, trying to brush away the last vestiges of sleep. She'd been dreaming about something. Something that had been calling to her...

Something wasn't right. She sensed it in the air around her and in the ground beneath her feet. The air felt charged, like it did just before a thunderstorm. Slowly, she stood and, careful not to wake Aiden, made her way to the mouth of the cave. A fat round moon hung in the sky above, dusting the landscape with silver. In its light Kara saw the landscape spreading out from their hiding place: the valley, the trees, the stream sparkling silver in the moonlight.

Her eyes strayed to the top of the valley. There she saw the stones of Cullmaggin silhouetted against the stars. From here they looked like a set of jagged fangs sticking up into the night.

Just as when she'd first laid eyes on it, Kara felt drawn to it. The fire in her belly was back suddenly, pulling her, urging her on... She hadn't realized she'd left the cave until her feet settled onto the soft, muddy ground of the stream bank. She looked around, confused. How had she gotten down here? The cave was behind her and she could still make out the faint light from the fire burning within. She ought to return. It was crazy being out here alone in the dark. What did she think she was doing?

But she didn't turn around. Instead she began walking along the riverbank as it meandered closer to the valley's edge. Above her the broken stones of Cullmaggin grew closer, towering into the sky like eerie sentinels. Watching her. Calling her onward.

Before she knew it Kara had splashed through the stream and begun climbing up through the vegetation on the far side of the valley. Brambles snagged her clothing, branches pulled at her hair and scraped her face but Kara barely noticed them. The pull was getting stronger, more insistent. She must answer.

Come, the wind seemed to whisper. *Come to us.*

Finally she stepped out onto the windblown upland and found Cullmaggin rising before her. The stones were enormous. Easily twice Kara's height, they stood in a rough circle maybe fifty feet across. Weathered and pitted by time and the elements, they nevertheless radiated a kind of immovable strength, as though they had stood sentinel over this valley since ages long past and would continue to stand sentinel long after all memory of them had passed from the land.

Come to us.

Kara stepped forward, approaching one of the stones, but halted on the threshold without crossing into the ring. A faint voice inside was screaming at her, telling her this was stupid, warning her back. But that voice was drowned out by the overwhelming urge to step inside.

Kara reached out a trembling hand and laid her palm flat against the stone. It felt warm to her touch and her skin tingled where it brushed the rough granite.

Come to us.

Kara looked up and saw that the moonlight falling through the scattered clouds illuminated the center of the circle. Slowly, hesitantly, Kara crossed the threshold and entered the stones of Cullmaggin.

The temperature plummeted but she didn't slow as she walked to stand in the exact center, in the circle of moonlight. Around her a cacophony of whispering voices spoke up.

Ye have come!

Ye are ours! Ours!

Ye canna escape us now. Ye canna escape yer destiny. Ye are one of us!

Embrace it! Embrace who ye are!

An icy wind blew through the stones, running freezing fingers along Kara's skin. She wrapped her arms around herself, her teeth suddenly chattering.

"Who are you?" she shouted. "What do you want with me?"

There was laughter. Harsh, cruel, laughter.

Do ye not know?

The voices echoed all around her, blending until she could no longer make out words. The cold intensified, seeming to seep into her very soul.

"Leave me alone!" she yelled.

Cold. So cold. Can't stay awake. Kara crashed to her knees and then onto her side. Darkness rushed up to claim her.

AIDEN SNAPPED AWAKE, a sick sense of dread knotting his stomach. Reflexively he reached for his sword only to realize it was no longer there so grabbed the staff instead, looking around for the enemy. There was none. The cavern was empty.

A shot of pure panic went through him as he realized the spot where Kara had been sleeping was bare. He jumped to his feet and ran to the cave entrance.

"Kara!" he bellowed into the night. "Kara!"

There was no answer.

Returning to the cave, he grabbed a smoldering brand from the fire, blew it into life, and, holding it aloft, ran out of the cave and then crouched in the mud, eyes scanning the ground. There. A set of footprints led away from the cave. Holding the torch in one hand and his staff in the other, Aiden followed the trail down to the river bank where it turned left, following the contours of the watercourse.

Aiden moved as quickly as possible in the dark, stopping every now and then to check he hadn't lost the trail. Panic churned in his gut. What was she doing? Why, by all that's holy, had she gone out into the woods alone at night?

He cursed himself for a fool. He'd been meant to stand watch, to keep her safe, and instead he'd fallen asleep and let her slip past him. *Ye are a damned fool*, he growled at himself. Even the newest, greenest warrior knew never to fall asleep on guard duty.

Biting back his worry, he forced himself to concentrate on the trail. He followed it through the stream and then picked it up again on the other side. It seemed to be climbing the valley side. Heading towards...

He glanced up. Cullmaggin rose on the horizon, a darker shadow against the blackness of the night sky. The hairs on the back of Aiden's neck rose. Cullmaggin. What on God's clean earth would possess her to approach that haunted place? There were stories of Cullmaggin and its like. Stories told to Highland children since time immemorial. Stories of how such places belonged to the Fae and they did not suffer mortals to pass.

Aiden sucked in a deep breath and steeled his courage. If Kara was up there then that's where he must go. He began to climb.

It was hard going, the trail little more than an animal track, and in places it was so steep that he had to use his hands and feet together. He was scratched and battered by the time he reached the top.

He paused for a second, his heart quailing at the sight of the dark monoliths rising from the ground ahead of him, then gritted his teeth and ploughed into the circle.

The darkness inside the circle was almost absolute and for the briefest of moments he thought he saw shadowy figures moving around the edges but when he blinked they were gone. The clouds suddenly parted and moonlight broke through, illuminating the center of the circle. It revealed a figure lying on the ground, curled on its side.

"Kara!" Aiden's heart thudded in his chest.

He scrambled to Kara's side and scooped her into his arms. She didn't stir. She was still breathing but her eyes were closed and her skin as cold as ice.

"Kara!" he said. "Wake up, lass!"

She didn't respond. He lifted her and turned to the shadows at the edge of the clearing.

"If ye have done aught to harm her," he growled. "Ye will answer to me!"

He thought he heard soft laughter but it could easily have been the sound of the breeze. Clasping Kara to his chest, he carried her from the circle and back down into the valley.

By the time he reached their cave he was sick with worry. Kara hadn't stirred the whole time, even when Aiden slipped and stumbled on the difficult trail, jolting her unconscious form. He had to warm her up. She was freezing.

Once in the cave he laid her near the fire then quickly built it up. In moments it was burning merrily again, casting heat and light into the small space. Aiden was glad of it. The warm light chased away the night and the memory of cold shadows and dark laughter.

He knelt beside Kara, grabbed one of her arms, and began rubbing it vigorously. It was a method they used in the king's guard when men were suffering from hypothermia. He needed to get Kara's circulation going. When he'd done one arm he moved onto the other and then her legs.

Part of him realized it was hardly decent for him to be rubbing a woman's legs like this—even if she was wearing a strange pair of flannel trews—but right now her wellbeing was more important than her modesty.

Kara stirred and mumbled something that he couldn't quite make out. Her color was better, the blue tinge gone from her lips, but her skin was still far too cold for Aiden's liking. He hesitated, deciding what to do. Then he lay down behind Kara, fitting his body along hers and wrapped his arm around her, holding her close, hoping that his body heat would warm her.

Kara sighed and pushed herself into him so that her back sat snugly against his chest. It felt good to have her pressed against him. It felt right.

His thoughts were becoming sluggish. It had been a challenging day and an even more challenging night and the warmth from the fire was making him drowsy. In only moments his eyes started to droop and, with his body curled protectively around Kara's, he fell asleep.

KARA WOKE SLOWLY. SHE felt warm and comfortable and her limbs held that heaviness that comes after a good night's sleep. There was a pleasant, warm pressure against her back and for some unaccountable reason, it made her feel very safe.

She opened her eyes. Beyond the cave's entrance sunlight glimmered through the trees and she realized the weight pressing against her back was Aiden's body curled protectively around her. His arm lay under his head as a rudimentary pillow and he was sound asleep.

Kara swallowed thickly. How had they ended up like this? She remembered a vague recollection of walking into the night. Of climbing a steep slope. Of stone teeth rising from the ground and a voice. A voice saying, *ye are ours*. Had that been a dream? Even as she tried to make sense of it the images began to fade as dreams will until Kara was left with only the barest impression of unease, as though she was missing something important.

Aiden shifted and Kara twisted to look at him. His dark hair was spread out around his head like a shadowy halo and his expression was peaceful in sleep. His shirt was twisted, pulled taught across his body, revealing the contours of muscle that lay beneath. Stubble dusted his chin.

Kara's stomach lurched Holy crap, but he was gorgeous. She reached out, gently running her fingertip along his cheek. He shifted slightly but didn't wake. What would it be like to wake up like this everyday? she wondered. To have Aiden by her side? The thought sent a delicious warmth uncoiling inside her.

She pushed the thought away ruthlessly and withdrew her hand. She shouldn't think such things. She would soon be going home and leaving Aiden Harris and sixteenth century Skye behind forever.

Careful not to wake him, she wriggled out from his grasp and climbed to her feet. She ached all over and little scratches marked her arms. How had that happened? She couldn't remember falling yesterday. No matter. She was determined to let Aiden sleep whilst she made herself useful so she quickly padded to the cave entrance and made her way out into the early morning sunlight.

The morning was crisp and clear, cold enough that Kara could see her breath in the air before her. There had been rain sometime in the night and now the leaves dripped with diamond droplets..

Kara pulled her coat closer about herself and scanned the area, searching for what she was after. She glanced up and saw the jagged stones of Cullmaggin rearing up on the hillside above her. Even in the morning light they seemed dark and full of shadow, as though they resisted the sunlight that tried to illuminate them.

Ye are ours. Ye must embrace who ye are.

A voice suddenly whispered in her head. Kara staggered, almost falling, and steadied herself on a tree trunk.

Hearing things now, Kara? she asked herself. *You really are going crazy.*

She pushed all thoughts of Cullmaggin from her mind and concentrated on her task. A little way from the riverbank she found what she was looking for. Stooping, she filled her pockets and then made her way back to the cave where Aiden was still sleeping.

She deposited her finds next to the fire then built it up until it was burning nicely. Then, using the same flat stone that Aiden had used yesterday, she laid her finds out on it and popped them into the fire.

She crossed her legs and propped her chin on her hand, watching Aiden and wondering exactly what had passed between them last night for her to wake with him the way she did. She wished she could remember. Fractured images and faint impressions were all she recalled. Kara shook her head.

Aiden shifted, reached out, found Kara gone, and suddenly bolted upright, looking around. Then his eyes settled on her and he relaxed.

"Morning," Kara said with a smile.

Aiden blew out a breath. "There ye are. For a moment I thought—"

"Thought what?" Kara asked, raising an eyebrow. "That I'd run out on you?"

"Nay, lass. I thought...I thought. It doesnae matter." He eyed her cautiously. "Are ye well, lass?"

"Never better," Kara shrugged. "I slept like a baby. Now, how about some breakfast? Roasted chestnuts—every girl scouts favorite!"

AIDEN TUCKED INTO HIS breakfast. The roasted chestnuts were good, he had to admit. Where Kara had found them he had no idea as he'd not spotted any chestnut trees as they were traveling yesterday. He watched Kara from across the fire. He'd gently asked her questions about last night but she didn't seem to remember any of it and Aiden didn't push the matter.

Perhaps she was merely sleepwalking, he told himself. *She wouldnae be the first lass to do that.*

He didn't believe it. Something told him the Fae were involved and that thought made him profoundly uneasy. What did they want with Kara? The woman herself seemed none the worse for her late-night jaunt. In fact, she seemed in high spirits and the sight of her smile and the healthy flush to her cheeks warmed Aiden's insides.

When they'd eaten their fill Aiden made his way down to the riverbank where he gave himself a quick wash in the icy water. It was a cold morning with a hint of winter in the air and Aiden hoped they'd make it back to Dun Arnwick before the first snows of the season that looked like they might arrive today.

They quickly packed up and left the cave. As they made their way along the trail at the valley bottom, Aiden deliberately didn't look up at Cullmaggin rearing above them, watching malevolently as they left its demesne.

They walked for several hours and Aiden soon found his worries evaporating in Kara's company. She asked a thousand questions—about the flora and fauna they spotted, about the settlements on Skye and the history of the Harris Clan. She was interested in everything and Aiden answered as best he could, amused by her child-like delight in learning about the migratory patterns of puffins or the way crofts were constructed from local stone and thatch.

"And everything on Skye belongs to the Harris clan?" Kara asked.

"Not everything. There are also the MacConnells and the MacKays although they both owe allegiance to the Harris Clan. In times of strife my father can call on their warriors for aid and similarly, if they have difficulties, they would come to my father for help. On Skye my father's word is law, above all save that of the king."

"So you're all one big happy family?" she said with a smile.

Aiden snorted. "Hardly. Although Skye has been peaceful since before I was born, the same canna be said for the Highlands. Highland politics can be...delicate and there's been many a clan war fought, particularly on the mainland. With clan ties the way they are with all the inter-marriages and alliances, a feud between two lairds can soon escalate into something more. The Murrays and the MacFarlanes for example, both friends to our clan, were at each other's throats for many years although now they are close allies."

"Sounds complicated," Kara said, picking a piece of grass from the side of the path and idly shredding it. She spent a moment in thought. "So a laird is like a chief and you're the chief's son. Does that mean you'll inherit eventually?"

The question was asked innocently enough but Aiden almost missed his step. He glanced at her to see her watching him expectantly. He scrabbled to find an answer. "Not necessarily," he said after a long pause. "The eldest son usually takes over the lairdship after his father but it isnae always so." He glanced out at the landscape around them. At the rolling moorland and mountains in the distance. Almost under his breath he added, "Not if his path lies elsewhere."

Kara seemed to sense his disquiet and didn't pursue the matter. She shrugged. "Families, eh? Seems no matter what era you live in, as much as you love them they can drive you crazy."

Aiden raised an eyebrow. "Ye never spoke a truer word, lass." He stepped over a muddy puddle lying in their path and then cocked his head at her. "How about ye? Willnae yer family be worrying about ye by now?"

A strange look crossed Kara's face and she glanced away, staring out over the moorland, just as he had done. She said nothing for a long time and Aiden had begun to suspect that she wouldn't answer at all when she finally looked back at him. There was an old, dull pain shining in her eyes.

"No," she breathed. "There'll be nobody worrying about me at home. I don't have any family. My dad died when I was ten, my mom when I was fifteen. I don't have any brothers and sisters."

Aiden's heart twisted for her. "Ah, lass," he breathed. "I'm sorry."

Kara shrugged. "It's fine. I've gotten used to it. What's that? I thought you said there weren't any crofts out here?"

Aiden looked ahead and saw a crumbling stone wall crossing their path. It stretched to left and right for a good distance before he lost sight of it against the brown of the moorland.

"There isnae," Aiden replied. "And this isnae a croft but the ruins of an old keep that was abandoned long before my father's time, when the land became too sparse to support a community. Most of it is gone, disappeared beneath the heather or else the stones robbed out for use elsewhere. Some of the walls still stand though." He glanced up at them. Most were not much higher than Aiden's head. "It will be a climb. Unless ye would rather go around?"

Kara looked at him indignantly. "I can climb, thank you very much," she said with a defiant lift of her chin.

She strode off along the trail and soon reached the wall. It was rough, the stone broken in places, giving plenty of foot and handholds.

Aiden looked at Kara and grinned. "Are ye sure ye wouldnae like me to carry ye over? Or is wall climbing part of the 'City Girl Scouts training'"

"You'd best get over this wall right now, Aiden Harris, before I do something you'll regret!" Kara retorted, placing her hands on her hips.

Aiden laughed then vaulted the wall and dropped down to the ground on the other side. A moment later Kara appeared atop the wall, swung her legs over the top and jumped down. As her feet touched the ground she lost her footing and stumbled. Aiden darted forward to catch her, his hands grasping her waist.

"Easy, lass. We dinna want ye breaking an ankle now, do we?"

Kara grabbed his forearms to steady herself. "No," she said in a low voice. "That would certainly put a crimp on my day."

Their gazes locked and Kara made no move to pull away. Aiden was suddenly all too aware of how close she was, how easy it would be to pull her into his arms and kiss her.

KARA'S THOUGHTS SCATTERED like leaves blown on the wind. All she could think about was how strong and reassuring Aiden's hands felt on her waist and how he was so close she could smell his scent: pine leaves and tilled earth. It would only take the barest movement, hardly even a step, and she'd be inside the circle of his arms. All he had to do was lean down just a little and his lips would be on hers...

Aiden cleared his throat and stepped away. He glanced at the path, then the sky, then the landscape. Anywhere but at her.

"If we make good time we should reach Dun Arnwick by mid-afternoon," he muttered.

"This afternoon. Right. Great," Kara said in a rush. "Let's go then shall we?" She marched off, trying desperately not to let Aiden see how flustered she was. She hoped to God he didn't notice the heat that had crept into her cheeks.

After a moment Aiden caught up with her. Neither spoke and they marched in silence for a good half an hour. Then suddenly Aiden went very still and stared intently at the path ahead, head cocked as if listening.

"What is it?"

He held up a hand for silence. Kara listened and then heard it, a faint drumming getting steadily closer.

Aiden swore and pushed Kara behind him. Grabbing his rudimentary staff with both hands, he stepped in front of her, blocking the path.

"What is it?" Kara asked again.

"Company," Aiden replied, eyes fixed on the road. "Stay behind me."

The drumming became louder and louder and soon revealed itself to be a single horseman speeding along the road towards them. The figure was crouched low in the saddle and the chestnut horse had lather flying from its mouth. The rider made no attempt to swerve and for one horrified moment Kara thought he would ride right over Aiden but at the last minute the rider yanked his mount to the side and instead rode around her and Aiden, pulling his mount in a tight circle so it danced around them, chomping at the bit and flinging up bits of mud from its churning hooves.

Aiden grabbed Kara and held her close behind him, turning continually to keep the circling horseman in front of them.

"Who are ye?" Aiden demanded. "Pull up yer horse, man, or by God ye'll regret it!"

Finally the horseman pulled the dancing horse to a stop. The man seated in the saddle looked to be around the same age as Aiden and had similar jet black hair. But there the similarity ended. Where Aiden was broad and well-muscled, the man in the saddle was wiry and had a slightly mocking look to his handsome face.

"Is that any way to greet an old friend, Aiden Harris?"

Aiden's eyes widened slightly. "Bhradain Garrick! What, by all that's holy, were ye playing at? Ye could have trampled us!"

Bhradain Garrick jumped lightly from the saddle. His mouth twisted into a lop-sided smile. "Do ye really think so little of my horsemanship? I'm hurt. And after I've ridden out here to find ye and all."

"Find me? What do ye mean?"

Bhradain's gaze flicked to Kara and back to Aiden. "Yer horse turned up rider less at Dun Arnwick and we received word that the rest of yer squad returned home days ago. Yer father has sent out scouts to scour the island for ye, fearing ye had fallen from yer horse or been attacked by brigands." He grinned as his dark-eyed gaze roved over Kara. "Although I can now see the real reason why ye were delayed. I canna say I blame ye. Tumbling a beauty like her is mightily preferable to the tedium of clan business."

Aiden moved like lightning. Before Kara could even blink he'd grabbed Bhradain's dagger from his belt and had pressed it up against the man's windpipe.

"If ye say anything like that again," he growled in a low, menacing voice. "It will be the last thing ye say. This is Lady Kara Buchanan, a visitor to our lands, and ye will show her the respect she deserves."

Kara gasped, taken aback by this sudden show of aggression. It was clear Bhradain and Aiden knew each other and it was also clear there was no love lost between them.

Bhradain's grin only widened. "Lord above, but ye havenae grown a sense of humor while ye've been away! Canna ye take a joke? I was only teasing ye!"

Aiden didn't move. "Ye will apologize. Now."

Bhradain rolled his eyes. "Fine! I'm sorry."

Aiden released him, flipped the knife over, and held it out to him, hilt first. "To the lady, not me."

Bhradain sheathed his dagger and gave Kara a flourishing bow that had a slightly mocking edge to it. "My lady. Ye have my deepest apologies. I didnae mean any offence. I am Bhradain Garrick, ward of Laird Andrew Harris, and it is my honor to welcome ye to Dun Arnwick which lies just a few miles yonder." He took Kara's hand in a courtly fashion and kissed the back of it. "If I can be of service during yer stay with us ye need only speak it. I am yers to command."

Kara shifted uncomfortably. There was something unsettling about Bhradain. Although his voice sounded sincere there was a kind of mocking amusement dancing in his eyes as though he was privy to some joke nobody else was.

"Um. Thanks," she muttered.

The drum of hoof beats filled the air once more. Bhradain held up a finger. "Ah! It seems like the rest of yer welcoming party has arrived."

Four riders rode towards them. As they pulled up the leader cried, "Curse ye, Bhradain! What were ye doing riding off like that? We were supposed to be searching the coast road!"

Bhradain spread his hands wide. "And if we'd done so we wouldnae have found our lost sheep would we?"

The man's eyes snapped to Kara and Aiden and widened in recognition. "Aiden! Blind my eyes, lad! Is that really you?"

"Aye, Jamie, ye old bastard!" Aiden replied, stepping forward with a grin. "I see yer temper hasnae improved while I've been away!"

"Ha!" the man cried. He jumped down from his horse and crossed the space in three strides, sweeping Aiden up into a bear-hug. He was a big man, maybe ten years older than Aiden, and had an open, friendly face.

The two men pounded each other on the back then Aiden moved over to greet the other men as warmly. "Drake!

Martin! Sam, is that ye? Ye've grown into a man! Where's the wide-eyed boy I knew?"

The three men returned Aiden's greetings and Kara found herself smiling at the sight of Aiden with his old friends. It was obvious they held him in high regard as every one of them was grinning and slapping him on the back.

"I'm glad we found ye," Jamie rumbled. "I fear if we had returned home empty-handed yer mother would have had me skinned and hung out on the battlements for all to see. She's been going out of her mind since yer horse came home rider less. Why did ye not send us word, lad?"

Aiden shook his head. "There wasnae time." He glanced at Kara. "Much has happened since I returned to Skye. Much that I must tell my father. And there is someone I must introduce ye to."

In short order Kara had been introduced to the men who all gave her respectful bows as if she was some medieval lady. Jamie—who turned out to be Aiden's adoptive uncle he'd told her about—rubbed his chin and glanced from Kara to Aiden and back again. "I suspect ye both have quite a tale to tell. Come, let's gets back to Dun Arnwick so ye can tell it. Drake, ride double with Martin. Aiden, Kara, ye can have Drake's horse. We should be home within the hour."

In no time at all Kara found herself seated in front of Aiden on a huge black horse Drake had been riding. She'd not ridden a horse since she was eight years old.

"My God," she muttered. "I never realized horseback was so damned high."

Aiden's arms circled her, holding the reins in front of them. "Dinna worry, lass," he replied as he kicked the horse and they moved off at a walk. "I will keep ye safe."

I know you will, the thought came unbidden to her mind. *I know you will.*

Chapter 7

KARA KNEW SHE WAS STARING like some wide-eyed idiot but she couldn't stop herself. Little over an hour ago they had ridden over a rise and she had gotten her first look at Dun Arnwick. It perched on a headland, a towering keep of stone with high walls, many windows and pennants snapping in the breeze.

Now, she and Aiden rode through a set of enormous gates into a large courtyard. Directly ahead a set of wide stone steps led up to the main doors of the castle and the courtyard was alive with sights, sounds, smells. Nearby a group of children were playing with a scruffy-faced puppy that was yapping excitedly as they threw it a leather ball. Over the far side several horses were tied to a post while boys brushed out their coats. Up on the walls a handful of eagle-eyed men with tall halberds kept watch over it all. It was full of sound and color and smells. It was so...so....alive.

Aiden swung easily out of the saddle and dropped to the ground. His eyes raked over his childhood home and rather than any joy at coming home, his eyes seemed troubled. He helped Kara down and the other men dismounted around them.

Bhradain sauntered over, a small smile on his face. "Well?" he asked Aiden. "Still remember the old place, eh? Although I'm sure it must seem very small and colloquial to someone of yer...standing."

Aiden ignored him. He was busy staring up at the doors, a slight frown marring his face.

"Come, lad," Jamie said, "I dinna know about ye but I'm just about ready for a jug of ale or three!"

Jamie took the steps two at a time. Kara made to follow but a sudden wave of dizziness overcame her and she stumbled. She suddenly felt very cold. Aiden was at her side in an instant.

"Are ye well, lass?" he said, taking her arm.

Kara nodded. "I'm fine."

Aiden escorted her up the steps and through the doors of the keep into an enormous chamber. Kara had seen enough movies to know this must be the Great Hall. A vaulted ceiling soared high overhead and the flagstone floor was covered with thick, colorful rugs. Rows of wooden tables marched down the hall's length and a huge fire burned in a fireplace at one end.

"Ho!" Jamie bellowed. "Look what I found! Our lost sheep!"

At the sound of his voice, a man and a woman rose from a table by the fire, turning to face them. They were both somewhere around middle age. The woman was beautiful, slim and with glossy hair cascading over her shoulders. The man had raven-dark hair like Aiden's and the two of them were so alike that Kara knew this must be his father.

There was a moment of stunned silence and then his parents were striding down the hall. His father slammed into Aiden, throwing his arms around him and slapping him on the back just as Jamie had done. Aiden grinned, returning his father's affection, before turning to his mother. Kara shifted uncomfortably, feeling out of place in this show of familial affection.

"You will be the death of me, Aiden Harris!" his mother cried, throwing her arms around him. "You couldn't have sent a letter? I've been going out of my mind with worry!"

Aiden smiled apologetically. "I couldnae, Mother. Ye have my apologies for worrying ye but I was unavoidably detained." He stepped aside. "Mother, Father, this is Kara Buchanan. Kara, I'd like ye to meet my parents, Andrew and Lucy Harris."

"I...I'm very pleased to meet you," Kara said, stepping forward and giving them a nervous smile.

Their reaction wasn't what she'd expected. As Kara spoke, a sudden look of shock crossed both their faces. They shared a long glance then Lucy turned to her son.

"How?"

Aiden flicked a glance behind to check nobody was in earshot then said in a low voice. "Irene MacAskill has been meddling again."

Lucy's eyes went wide. "Irene? After all this time?" She stepped forward and took Kara's hands. "I'm sorry, my dear. Your accent shocked me for a moment. I haven't heard it in many years. You must tell us everything."

Kara's jaw dropped as she finally puzzled out something that had been bugging her since she'd first heard Lucy speak. "*Your* accent," she stammered. "You're from America!"

Lucy smiled and nodded. "Of course. Did Aiden not tell you? I'm from the twenty-first century too."

Kara stared. "But...but..." Her brain whirled with questions. "How did you get here? Did Irene MacAskill bring you? How long have you been here? Do you know a way home?"

"I'll answer all of your questions, I promise. But might I suggest you go change first? Those pajamas don't look very warm."

Kara glanced down. What must she look like standing here in her pajamas, coat and boots, dirty and disheveled? As if summoned by her thoughts another fit of shivering took her. Aiden held out a hand to steady her.

"I'm fine," she muttered. "Just a bit cold."

An icy wind blew through the stones, running freezing fingers along Kara's skin. Whispering voices. Ye are ours!

Kara blinked away the strange sensation. Aiden's face had gone blurry. The sounds in the hall shifted, becoming muted, as though heard from far away. Then suddenly she was falling, the floor rushing up. Aiden caught her before she could hit the ground. He lifted her easily, as if she weighed no more than a doll.

"Take her to one of the guest rooms," Lucy said.

Then Kara was being carried, Aiden's strong arms holding her close to his chest. She felt woozy, barely able to lift her head, so she rested it against Aiden's hard chest, fighting against a sudden weakness that washed through her body like freezing water. A door opened and closed then she was laid on something soft, a blanket pulled up around her.

Dimly she heard Aiden's voice. "Nay, I willnae leave her side."

"She'll be safe here, I'll call ye as soon as she wakes."

No, she thought groggily. *Don't go.*

She heard receding footsteps and a door closing. Kara tried to call him back but the lassitude was spreading, reaching through her body, and pulling her under into darkness.

KARA DREAMED. IN IT, she was running, running. Men chased her, men with no faces and guns pointed at her back. She zig-zagged, trying to dodge, but no matter how she ran they were always behind. A man beckoned to her. "This way, darling, you'll be safe." It was her father. Kara ran towards him but as she got closer a gunshot sounded and suddenly a bright red stain erupted on her father's shirt. The vision shifted and now she heard Irene MacAskill saying, "Yer destiny, my dear. Ye cannot escape it." Then dark stones, cold fingers and voices whispering, whispering, "Embrace who ye are. Ye are ours!"

"No!" Kara cried, bolting upright in bed.

She looked around wildly, heart thumping. She found herself in a large, lavish bed chamber. The bed was large enough for several people and piled high with brocaded covers and cushions. Directly opposite a large window gave a spectacular view of the churning, wind-lashed sea stretching to the horizon. A fire burned in the hearth, making the room deliciously warm.

"Ah, curse it!" a voice said. "I almost had it then and ye've gone and moved."

Kara blinked. A young woman, around Kara's age, was sitting in a chair by the bed holding a sketchpad and charcoal in one hand.

Kara stared, trying to clear her thoughts. "I'm sorry?"

"Oh, dinna be," the young woman said, waving her hand. "I got some others while ye were asleep. I find sleeping people make good subjects. Dinna ye reckon?"

Kara opened and closed her mouth. Her confusion must have shown on her face because the young woman suddenly put down her sketch pad.

"Sorry! I was doing it again, wasnae I? My Ma reckons my mouth is often one step ahead of my brain. Ye were having a bad dream but ye are awake now and safe. I'm Beth and I'm very pleased to meet ye, Kara Buchanan." She stuck out her hand.

Kara reached out and took Beth's hand, who shook it vigorously.

"There," Beth said, smiling. "Now we're friends. Would ye mind sitting back slightly so I can finish my sketch? I had the light falling across yer face just so."

Beth had the same dark hair as Aiden and pale skin with a scattering of freckles across the bridge of her nose. But it was the smile that gave it away.

"You're Aiden's sister?"

Beth nodded without looking up from her sketch. "Aye, for my sins. My Ma asked me to watch over ye whilst ye slept but my brother hasnae made it easy, coming here every half a bell and all but breaking the door down to see how ye are."

"Aiden's been here?" Kara asked, pushing herself upright.

"Aye. More times than is good for him. The last time I had to threaten him with a broom."

Kara smiled. Yes, she could well imagine the scene. In the little time she'd known him, she'd come to realize that Aiden Harris had a stubborn streak around a mile wide.

Beth was watching her with a speculative look in her dark eyes. Kara cleared her throat. "So, you're an artist?"

Beth waved a hand. "Some might say that. Others would tell the truth."

"May I see?"

Beth shifted uncomfortably. "It's nay very good. I didnae have the right materials—"

"Please?"

Beth sighed then passed over the sketchpad. It wasn't paper, Kara realized as she took it, but very thin parchment. A charcoal sketch of a sleeping Kara filled the page. It was so lifelike it looked like a black-and-white photograph.

"Wow," Kara breathed. "This is amazing!"

Beth beamed. "Ye like it?"

"Like it? It's fabulous! You're very talented, Beth."

Beth's grin widened. "Would ye like to keep it?"

Kara looked up and met Beth's eyes, suddenly moved by this simple kindness. "I'd love to. Thanks."

"Ye are most welcome. Are ye feeling up to getting out of bed? Ye gave everyone a fright when ye keeled over like that but I reckon it was just exhaustion and the cold."

A memory of Kara's dream rose up, sending a shiver of unease through her. With an effort, she shrugged it off. "I feel fine. How long was I asleep?"

"All last night and this morning. It's almost midday. If ye are up to it I'll have a bath drawn for ye—I know it always makes me feel better."

Before Kara could reply she crossed to the door, stuck her head into the corridor, and shouted a few commands.

"We'll have to see about getting ye properly attired. Ye canna go around Dun Arnwick in those 'pajamas' ye arrived in, that's for sure."

She opened the door of a big wardrobe that sat in the corner of the room and took out a few dresses. "Which would ye prefer? I reckon the purple. It will bring out the color of yer eyes."

The dresses were beautiful. Made from the best quality velvet, they were elegant, flowing things that looked like they had been made for a medieval princess, not a twenty-first century journalist.

"I...um....I'm not sure they're really me—"

"Purple it is then," Beth interrupted. She gave Kara a wicked smile. "Purple is my brother's favorite color."

Kara flushed in embarrassment. To cover it, she threw back the covers and swung her feet out of bed. Only now did she notice that her sodden pajamas had been removed and she was dressed instead in a long linen nightdress. Her cheeks grew hot. Aiden had carried her to this room. Oh, God, he hadn't undressed her as well, had he?

As if sensing her thoughts, Beth said. "I undressed ye and lent ye one of my nightgowns. Yer own stuff is in the laundry."

Kara nodded, not sure whether to be relieved or embarrassed at having to be undressed by a stranger. "Um. Thanks. I think."

There was a knock on the door and a blonde-haired woman walked in followed by several servants carrying a bath tub and buckets of hot water.

Much to Kara's astonishment, the woman gave her a curtsey.

"I'm mighty pleased to meet ye, my lady," the woman said. "I'm Annis, the housekeeper here at Dun Arnwick. Are ye feeling any better after yer sleep?"

"I...um....I...." Kara stammered. *My lady?* Where the hell had they got that idea? "Please, just call me Kara. And yes, I feel much better, thanks."

Annis smiled. She instructed the servants to put the bath down in front of the fire and then empty the buckets into it. "If ye need anything, anything at all, just ring the bell and someone will come. I'll leave ye in Beth's capable hands."

"Um. Thanks."

Annis left, closing the door behind her. Beth rolled up her sleeves and then tipped a white powder into the bathwater. The smell of roses wafted through the room and the water frothed a little. Beth inspected it.

"Nay as good as yer bubble bath, but it will have to do," she announced.

"You know about bubble bath?" Kara asked, surprised.

Beth gave her a flat look. "Aye, of course," she said, as if this should be obvious. "My ma is a time-traveler after all." She said this with a certain amount of pride.

"Time travel," Kara breathed. "This time a week ago if you'd told me that I'd soon be sitting in a Scottish castle in the sixteenth century I would have thought you were crazy. But now look." She gestured helplessly at the room. "Here I am."

Beth cocked her head and regarded Kara. "Ye say that as if ye didnae know about time-travel."

"I didn't. This is all one big accident."

Beth watched her for a long moment, tapping her lips in thought. "My brother said Irene MacAskill was involved. Is that right?"

"Yes."

"Then it was nay an accident. If ye are here it is because she wanted ye to be."

"Me? Why on Earth would she want me to come here?"

Beth shrugged. "I havenae the faintest idea. Now, are ye gonna have this bath or not?"

It soon became clear that Beth had no intention of leaving Kara alone to bathe. It seemed that it was perfectly normal in the sixteenth century to have someone present during such things. Beth laughed when Kara asked her to turn her back whilst she got undressed then hurried in and lay down until the soapy water covered her all the way to her chin but it was a good-natured laugh, and Kara found herself joining in.

The water felt wonderful. The warmth soothed Kara's aches and pains. Beth bade her sit forward whilst she scrubbed her back then washed her hair, tending to Kara as though she was a lady's maid rather than the daughter of the laird.

"I will have words with Irene MacAskill when I see her," Beth griped. "Why did she choose my brother to go through the arch and not me? He's always the one that gets to go off and have adventures! Nay content with riding by the king's side, fighting battles and driving off invaders is he? Oh no, he has to go gallivanting through time as well. If I wasnae so pleased to see him home, I'd give him the rough side of my tongue!"

"He's been away a while then?" Kara asked. She realized suddenly that she knew very little about Aiden other than the scraps he'd told her.

Beth puffed herself up with pride. "Aye. He's captain of the king's guard. King James himself decorated him for valor after he rode all night with an arrow in his belly to bring word of an invading army to the king's ears. Didnae he tell ye any of this?"

"No," Kara replied. "He didn't."

Beth waved a hand. "I'm nay surprised. He doesnae often talk about it. I suppose he'll miss it when he becomes the laird. It will nay doubt seem dull around here compared to that."

Kara nodded. She'd known Aiden was a warrior, the way he'd dealt with Devereux's men had demonstrated that, and he'd told her he was a soldier, but she'd had no idea of any of the things Beth had told her. Aiden Harris was a closed book.

And more and more, Kara found herself wanting to open it.

After her bath, Beth helped Kara into the purple dress. It had so many buttons and hooks on the back that there was no way Kara would have been able to do it up herself. Dressing, she realized, must be something of a chore for women of this century.

She sighed. This was going to take some getting used to.

AIDEN DUNKED HIS HEAD into the water. It was icy cold, almost enough to make him gasp. He welcomed it. It helped to clear his thoughts a little. He held his head under for as long as he was able and then threw his head back, sending droplets scattering all over the floor of his room.

Grabbing a cloth, he dried his face then pushed the washbowl aside and leaned with both hands on the window sill, looking out. He could see his reflection in the bubbled glass and beyond this, the sweeping vista of the Isle of Skye. The weather had broken and spears of sunlight stabbed down through the rapidly thinning clouds. Birds darted through the sky, calling out to each other.

Aiden drew in a deep breath. Home. He was home, after all these years. The bailey outside was a hubbub of activity. Guardsmen chatting by the gate, leaning on their halberds as they shared a crust of bread. Serving girls laughing as they hauled water from the well. A gaggle of children arguing over the rules to some game.

For a moment, his heart swelled. Aye, he'd missed this place, far more than he'd thought he would. But then he remembered the scroll sitting in a drawer in his room and his contentment evaporated. This couldn't be. He wasn't meant for this place, this life. It felt as constricting now as it ever had, no matter how much he'd missed it.

He turned to take in his chambers. They'd been his since he was a boy. When he was younger they'd seemed enormous, big enough to get lost in, but now they seemed smaller, like they weren't large enough to contain his restless energy.

He settled onto the floor cross-legged and rested his sword, which he'd acquired from the armory, across his knees. Grabbing a rag, he methodically began polishing it. The familiar, rhythmic work soothed him. How many times had he done this whilst on campaign for the king? More times than he could remember.

As he worked, he found his thoughts turning towards Kara Buchanan. No matter how hard he tried to concentrate on the task at hand, he found her face filling his mind. Those large, dark eyes, so full of intelligence. That mouth, that formed dimples in her cheeks when she smiled. That skin that felt so soft and warm when he touched her...

He shook his head, cursing himself inwardly. *Remember yer duty*, he told himself. *Kara is under yer protection. Ye mustnae think of her this way.*

But Lord! It was hard. She was willful and strong-headed, stubborn and reckless but she stirred something in him Aiden had never experienced. Just the thought of her sent heat rushing straight to his groin. He longed to see her and had tried at least a dozen times last night but each time his sister had chased him off.

He jumped when his chamber door suddenly burst open. In an instant he was on his feet, sword in hand. Even here, in the heart of his clan, his warrior's instincts wouldn't let him relax.

Jamie grinned at him from the doorway. "Ye can put yer letter-opener away, lad," he said, amusement in his voice. "Unless ye are planning on sticking me with it?"

"My...my apologies," Aiden muttered. He sheathed the sword. "But ye startled me. Hasnae anyone ever told ye to knock?" He grumbled at his uncle but the words were tinged with affection. Jamie had never shown much in the way of manners.

"Where would be the fun in that?" Jamie replied. "If ye have finished polishing yer letter-opener, Annis has sent word that Lady Kara is up and about. Yer father has summoned ye both to give yer report. He suggested ye might—"

Aiden didn't hear the rest of his uncle's words. He bolted through the door in the direction of Kara's chamber.

IT WAS AMAZING, KARA reflected as she stared at the undulating landscape beyond the window, how something as simple as a bath could make you feel better.

The scritch-scratch of charcoal filled the room. Beth was seated cross-legged on the floor whilst she sketched Kara who was sitting by the window. Her brow was furrowed in concentration, the tip of her tongue sticking out the side of her mouth.

There was a knock on the door and Kara all but jumped out of her seat.

"I'll answer it!"

She hurried over to the stout wooden door and pulled it open. Aiden stood on the other side, one hand resting on the doorframe above his head. He'd washed and changed and now his slightly damp hair rested lightly on his shoulders, the odd curl clinging to the skin of his neck. His eyes widened slightly as they settled on her and he shifted his feet awkwardly.

"Kara," he said. "I trust ye are settling in well? My sister tells me yer collapse was naught but exhaustion. Is this true?"

"Of course it's true!" Beth called from inside the room. "Didnae I say as much?" Beth appeared at Kara's side and fixed her brother with a stern look. "But she still needs rest."

A ghost of a smile flickered over Aiden's face and he held out his hands in a placating gesture. "Aye, and I'll make sure she isnae overtaxed. I've come to escort ye to my father's study. He wants to talk to the pair of us. I imagine he has a hundred questions. Are ye ready?"

Kara nodded. "As ready as I'll ever be."

Aidan gave her a reassuring smile. "Dinna worry, lass. My family are used to dealing with time travelers, remember? I'll be at yer side the whole time."

Aidan held out his arm and she took it. Together they made their way through the castle. Aidan didn't speak and Kara was happy to keep silent, nerves flittering in her belly at the prospect of this meeting. The outcome of it could very well decide her fate. If she was very lucky, they would find a way to send her home.

And if you're not lucky? Kara asked herself. *What then? What if you're stuck here?* Involuntarily she glanced at Aidan, and her heart skipped a little. *Would that be so bad?* A traitorous little voice whispered inside her head.

She pushed the voice aside. She would *not* go down that road.

Instead, she focused on where she was walking. The corridors and rooms they passed were not what she'd expected from a medieval Highland castle. No drafty, dank, places here, oh no. There were brazier's set at regular intervals and their bright coals chased away the worst of the chill. Herbs burned within them, filling the air with a delicious scent that reminded Kara of summer evenings. Thick rugs patterned in the colors of the Harris plaid covered the tile floors and tapestries and beautiful paintings adorned the walls.

No, nothing about her experience so far had been as Kara expected.

They reached a closed door and Aiden pushed it open without knocking. Kara followed him into a circular room done out as a study. A round table dominated the center, strewn with bits of parchment, tools and ink pots. Above the fireplace hung a large map of the Highlands and Kara found herself staring at it. The Isle of Skye was marked on the map to the far west and for the first time Kara was able to see a representation of the world she'd been thrown into. She didn't recognize many of the place names. Only a few stood out: Aberdeen in the north, Edinburgh to the east, the rest she'd never heard of.

Oh my God, she thought suddenly. *I'm really here. I'm in 16th century Scotland.*

She took a deep, shaky breath to calm her suddenly thumping heart. She forced her fractured thoughts together and focused on the people seated around the table.

Lucy gave her an encouraging smile and Andrew nodded a greeting. To Andrew's left sat Bhradain and Jamie. Bhradain was busy writing in a book, the scratch of the pen sounding loud in the still room but Jamie was lounging in his chair, grinning at them. Two seats had been left for her and Aidan.

"Be seated, both of you," Andrew said. "Would you like refreshment? I can have some wine brought if ye would like."

Kara folded onto the chair and shook her head. "No, I'm fine, thanks." The last thing she needed was a muddled head during this meeting.

Andrew nodded and leaned forward, clasping his hands on the table in front of him. He fixed Kara with a gaze that was every bit as powerful as Aidan's. She saw strength in that gaze, and fairness, but also a ruthlessness. It was the gaze of a man born to leadership, a man who knew how to take tough decisions. It was the gaze of a man who would do whatever he must to protect his family, his clan.

Kara understood where Aidan got it from.

Andrew cleared his throat. "I've asked for us to meet in this room so that we have some privacy. The truth of my wife's origins are known to only the closest kin and it must be kept that way. Gossip travels like wildfire in Dun Arnwick and I'd wager there are already a hundred stories in circulation of Lady Kara and where she might have come from." He smiled wryly. "Although I doubt any of them would have guessed the truth." He glanced from Aidan to Kara and back again. "It seems ye have had quite the adventure, son. Why dinna ye start from the beginning?"

Now that she saw them together, Kara was struck by how much Aiden resembled his father. They both had the same stern look, the same piercing gaze, the same tall, muscular shape. But there was something of Lucy in Aiden as well. His features weren't as sharp as Andrew's, his mouth softer, more used to smiling.

"An adventure?" he said. "I'm nay sure I'd call it that. More like a misadventure. As these things normally do in our family, it started with Irene MacAskill."

Aidan proceeded to tell his story, from his ride home with his men, meeting Irene on the beach and her cryptic message, to him stepping through the archway and into Kara's time. It was the first time Kara had heard his story in such detail and she found herself leaning forward to listen, spellbound by his words.

His family listened attentively, interrupting only to clarify certain points or to ask Aidan to repeat something so that all was clear. All the while Lucy and Andrew watched their son with a kind of wary intensity, as the details of his story played out.

When Aidan finally fell silent Lucy glanced at her husband and then back to her son. "And there was no sign of Irene when you and Kara returned to the beach?"

Aidan shook his head. "Nay sign at all. It's as though she's toying with me, playing some kind of trick. If protecting this Key is so important, why would she not be there to collect it? And why would she allow Kara to get caught up in this?" There was a hint of anger in his voice and his hand clenched into a fist where it rested on the table.

"I had thought we were done with her interfering in our lives," Andrew said, a menacing undertone to his voice. "It seems that Irene MacAskill is nay yet finished with my family."

"She might be a meddler," Lucy said. "But she's always been a friend of this family. Whatever her reasons, I don't doubt that she was acting from good intentions. As to why she wasn't there to meet Aidan? I don't know, but from my experience Irene doesn't do anything without a reason." She glanced at Kara. "Maybe we could figure out what that reason is if we hear your side of the story."

Kara swallowed. With a quick glance at Aidan she began her tale. "It all started with a man called Michael Devereux."

She told them everything, leaving nothing back. She described the man's shady dealings and the rumors of what his organization was caught up in. She described her encounter with Irene MacAskill and the cryptic message she'd given along with the clue that led her to her meeting with Aidan.

Lucy was especially interested in this and asked several times what Irene MacAskill's message had said. In the end Kara wrote it down and Lucy took it, studying the words carefully before tucking the message into her pocket. Kara's story ended with the fight by the railway bridge and their tumble back in time.

Finally, silence fell in the room, everyone taking their time to digest her words. Then Bhradain cleared his throat. Throughout Kara's tale he'd been listening intently, pausing every now and then to scribble something on a piece of parchment. "Ye are sure ye'd never met Irene MacAskill before she accosted ye?"

"Of course," Kara replied. "I think I'd remember, don't you? I've never seen her before or since. And I've no idea why she sent me to that place. Believe me, I've wracked my brain trying to think of a reason."

"But yer name," Bhradain persisted. "Buchanan. It's Scottish. A good Highland name."

Kara nodded. "Many generations removed. My great grandparents moved to America from Scotland."

Bhradain's eyes narrowed, his look calculating.

Kara shifted awkwardly. What had this got to do with anything? She didn't like the way Bhradain was looking at her. There was something in his gaze, like he knew something the others didn't.

"And this Key of Ages?" Bhradain asked. "Where is it?"

Aiden frowned at his foster-brother but then brought out a wrapped bundle and placed it on the table in front of him. "This is the thing Irene sent me to fetch." He unwrapped it and everyone leaned forward to get a good look.

Andrew picked it up and weighed it in his hand, inspecting it closely. The three curling gold prongs gleamed in the light. "I canna say what I expected from a Fae artifact," he said. "But this doesnae look anything special." He handed it to Lucy who also took a good look.

After a moment, she shrugged. "Who can say? If there's one thing I've learned about Irene, it's that appearances can be deceptive."

Bhradain reached out to take the Key but Aiden took it before Bhradain could lay hands on it and covered it with the bit of cloth. Annoyance flashed across Bhradain's face but he said nothing.

"I suggest we lock this up somewhere safe," Aiden said, looking at his father. "And tell nobody of its existence until Irene can be found to take charge of it."

"Lock it up?" Bhradain said, incredulous. "Why would ye want to do that?" His gaze flicked to Kara and back to Aiden. "If ye wish to send Lady Kara home, surely this is the method for doing so? We should use it, not lock it away!"

"Havenae ye been listening at all, Bhradain?" Aiden growled, rounding on his foster-brother. "It doesnae work. I suspect it will only work for Irene."

"There is only one course open to us," Andrew said. "And that is to find Irene MacAskill. I'll send out riders, have them take word to all settlements on Skye. Somebody must know where she is. We'll find her. Until then, this Key will remain locked securely in the treasury." He turned his stern gaze on Kara. "Dinna worry, lass. We'll find a way for ye to return to yer time. Until then Clan Harris would be honored if ye would treat Dun Arnwick as yer home."

"Ha! Finally!" Jamie leaned back in his chair and raised his goblet in a toast. "Now everything is sorted out, we can really get down to business! It isnae often we welcome back one of our own *and* a time-traveling visitor! I feel a feast coming on!"

Chapter 8

KARA FELT UNEASY AS she sat by the window in her chamber, pulling a brush through her hair. She knew the feast being planned for tonight was as much to welcome her to Dun Arnwick as it was to welcome Aiden home, but she couldn't help the nerves that coiled in her belly. She had never been good with big social events and in a few hours time she'd have to mingle with people she didn't know. She always felt out of place at such occasions and usually managed to make an idiot of herself in the process.

When she'd graduated from college and had gone up on stage to collect her scroll, she'd somehow managed to trip on her gown and sprawled flat on her face in front of hundreds of people, much to the uproarious laughter of her classmates. At her acceptance speech when she'd won her first award for journalism the microphone hadn't been working. Kara droned on through her speech for a good five minutes, whilst the audience couldn't hear a word she was saying and then she wondered at the stone-wall silence that greeted the end of the speech.

No, she wasn't good at these sorts of things. She was used to working alone, living alone. This sudden immersion into a tightly knit extended family was a little overwhelming and the fact that it was taking place in a time and culture completely alien to her made it worse.

Her worrying was interrupted by the door opening. Lucy poked her head around the door and, seeing Kara by the window, pushed her way inside, followed by Beth. She carried a tray set with cups and a teapot which she set on the small table.

"I thought we might have a cup of tea and a chat, if you're feeling up to it?" Lucy said.

Kara nodded. "I don't suppose there's coffee?"

Lucy laughed. "Afraid not. Beth, I forgot the cake. Would you be a dear and run along to the kitchens and get it?"

As Beth left, Lucy seated herself opposite Kara. Kara watched Aiden's mother. There was nothing to indicate she was anything but a Highland native—until she spoke, of course.

"I'll bet you have a hundred questions," Lucy said, pouring them both some tea.

Kara took the cup Lucy offered her and inhaled the minty scent. At home she was a coffee girl but tea would have to serve that role. Kara had no idea when coffee was first introduced to Scotland but she guessed it was many years distant yet. "More like a thousand questions," Kara muttered. She gestured at the room around them. "I don't even know where to begin."

Lucy smiled sympathetically. "If it's any comfort, I know exactly how you feel. I was so disorientated when I first came here that I refused to believe that I'd traveled in time. For a good while I insisted on thinking I'd been kidnapped and transported to Scotland without knowing." She smiled at the memory. "I came to my senses eventually."

"Do you miss it?" Kara asked. "Home, I mean?"

Lucy shrugged. "This is my home. To be honest, it's been so long that living in the twenty-first century feels like another lifetime. I adapted. I suppose being able to visit home helped with that."

"You mean you went back to our time?" Kara said, shocked.

Lucy nodded. "Irene left a portal open for Andrew and I so that we could visit my family in the twenty-first century. I was brought up by my Aunt Helen and Uncle Nathan and couldn't bear to leave them behind. In the first few years I was here they used to visit regularly and we used to go there. It was great for bringing medical supplies back too. If there's one thing that I do miss from my time, it's the medicine." She sighed wistfully. "But I've not been back in many years. Uncle Nathan and Aunt Helen are both gone now and after they died I never went back. It was too painful."

"I'm sorry," Kara said. Then the import of Lucy's words hit her. "Wait a minute! You said Irene left a portal open for you? That means there's an open portal here on Skye?"

Lucy shook her head and Kara's moment of hope was dashed. "I'm sorry, dear. The arch was destroyed many years ago. It formed part of a window in a church and the whole building came down during a particularly bad storm one winter. It's nothing but a pile of rubble now."

Kara tried to stifle the sudden feeling of despair that crashed in on her. What if she was stranded here? What if she never got home?

As if sensing her distress, Lucy put down her tea cup and squeezed Kara's hand. "Don't worry. We'll find Irene eventually. She wouldn't bring you here and leave you without any way to return. She may be annoying and meddlesome but she always has a plan. We just have to figure it out."

Kara smiled. "Thanks. I hope you're right." She squeezed Lucy's hand. "You've all been so kind since I got here. I want to repay you. Is there anything I can do to help around the castle? I'm not proud. Mucking out stables, doing laundry, cutting vegetables."

Lucy laughed lightly. "Anything you can do? You'll soon regret asking that question! There are always a hundred different jobs to be done around the castle so I'm sure we'll find plenty to keep you busy!"

The door opened and Beth came in carrying a large platter which she set down next to the teapot. She grinned at Kara and her mother. "Cook has put extra cream in the sponge cake and I promised I'd let you have an extra large slice, Kara. Cook takes her duty to her guests very seriously."

"Well don't just stand there!" Lucy said to her daughter. "Dish it out! Don't you know we have a cake emergency here? There's nothing better than tea and cake for curing homesickness. We'll have Kara as right as rain in no time! And then we have a party to get ready for!"

"THERE," BETH SAID AS she stood back and inspected Kara's hair. "Ye do look every bit the Highland lady."

Kara examined herself in the mirror. Beth had worked wonders. Kara's hair was pinned up at the sides, away from her face, leaving it to fall down the back in lazy waves. In addition, Lucy had lent her a pair of earrings with crystal droplets that dangled just above her jawline and sparkled in the lamplight.

"Wow," Kara murmured. "Who's that staring back at me? I'm sure I've never met her before."

Beth snorted. "Didnae anyone tell ye we have an important noble lady visiting us? Her name is Kara Buchanan."

"Oh, is that who this is?" Kara replied. "I didn't recognize her. It must be this gorgeous dress she's wearing."

"Must be," Lucy said, coming to stand behind Kara's chair. "I must say, you look better in that dress than I ever did. I was a jeans and T-shirt kind of girl back home and it took me quite a while to get used to wearing dresses every day – particularly dresses with so many hooks that I couldn't dress without help. If it wasn't for Annis, I doubt I would have ever learned to dress myself properly!"

Annis, the blonde-haired housekeeper, raised an eyebrow at her friend. "I had nay choice but to help. Otherwise ye would have gone around wearing jeans all the time. How would that have looked when ye went down to the village?"

Lucy waved her hand. "Oh they would have got used to it – it might have even caught on. Although I'm not sure starting a new trend and probably changing the whole history of fashion in the process would have pleased Irene MacAskill very much."

"We'd better be going," Beth said. "If we're late Uncle Jamie will have polished everything off before we arrive!"

Kara pushed the chair back and stood. Lucy gave her an encouraging smile and together the four women swept out of the chamber. Lucy and Annis walked in front whilst Kara and Beth followed behind, Beth linking her arm through Kara's good-naturedly.

"My mother is mighty glad to have ye here," Beth whispered, leaning close conspiratorially. "I think she's missed having someone to talk to about her homeland." She looked up suddenly and a wicked smile played across her face. "And I know somebody else who's equally glad ye are here."

Kara followed the line of Beth's gaze and saw Aidan leaning against the wall, waiting for them. For a moment her breath left her and it was all she could do not to stumble.

His eyes flicked over the group and settled on Kara. He hadn't shaved and there was a light dusting of stubble on his chin. Firelight from the braziers reflected in his stormy blue eyes and sent shadows dancing across the contours of his face.

He gave them a bow. "My ladies."

Lucy raised an eyebrow. "What are you doing here, son? I would have thought you and your father would have been well into your drinking by now."

"I came to escort ye all to the feast."

"Thank you, but I'm sure Beth, Annis and I are perfectly capable of escorting ourselves to the Great Hall. Lady Kara though, might be unsure of the way. Perhaps it would be best to ensure she gets there safely."

Then, before Kara could utter a word, Lucy, Beth and Annis walked off down the corridor. They turned a corner and Kara found herself alone with Aiden. His presence seemed to fill the narrow space.

"I...um...ye look nice," he said, finally.

"Thanks," Kara replied. "But I can't take any of the credit. Beth is the miracle worker. How she's managed to make me even halfway presentable I'll never know."

Aiden stared down at her for a long moment then he blinked and stepped back, offering her his arm. "If it would please ye, my lady, I would be honored to escort ye to the Great Hall."

Kara smiled and laid her hand on his arm. "It would please me a great deal."

They reached the Great Hall and from within Kara heard the drone of many voices in conversation. Kara balked, suddenly nervous, but Aiden gave her a reassuring smile then led the way inside.

"Lord Aiden Harris of Clan Harris, and Lady Kara Buchanan of Clan Buchanan!" shouted a servant as they entered.

The room fell silent and all eyes turned towards them. Kara swallowed, her stomach knotting. All those eyes. All staring at her

Oh God, she thought. *What am I doing here? What the hell am I doing here?*

Aiden began walking and Kara had no choice but to pace by his side. They made their way down the length of the Great Hall and Kara felt the eyes of the crowd on her the whole time. What would they make of her? She knew that Aiden's family had put out word that she was a visiting noble, some long-lost family friend or something, but she knew they'd be wondering exactly who she was and where she'd come from.

She stared straight ahead, feeling like a goldfish in a bowl, sure that any minute her shaky legs would betray her. But they reached the high table without mishap where Aiden bowed to his parents.

Andrew Harris scraped back his chair and stood. He raised a goblet. "Ye all know I'm not one for fancy speeches or fine words so I'll nay delay the feasting by blathering on. My son Aiden has spent years away from Dun Arnwick, serving King James. He's returned to his clan with honor. We also welcome Lady Kara Buchanan who is visiting with us from across the seas. I'm sure ye will show her a warm Dun Arnwick welcome. Now, let the celebrations commence!"

The crowd broke into a round of cheering and hollering and much banging of tankards on tables. She heard 'welcome home, Aiden!" shouted many times. Aiden led Kara to her seat and she slid gratefully onto a bench next to Beth, Aiden seating himself on her other side.

Beth leaned over. "See. That wasnae so bad, was it? Although I reckon ye'll be the talk of the whole of Skye come the morning. I reckon we ought to put it about that ye are some foreign princess – that would really set the cat among the pigeons."

"You wouldn't!"

Beth laughed and Aiden frowned at his sister, leaning close to Kara. "Nay, she wouldnae. Our Beth just doesnae know when to stop teasing. Dinna worry, lass, there will soon be some other point of gossip to take everyone's attention." He reached over to a pottery jug and poured out two drams of whisky, handing one to Kara. "I reckon we've earned a dram or two."

He didn't smile as he offered her the cup. Instead his eyes roved over the gathering and there was a look in his eyes Kara couldn't quite place. Wistfulness? Resignation?

"See?" Beth said, raising her cup and gesturing at the people filling the hall. "A few drams of whisky, some good music, and they've forgotten all about ye already."

Kara looked where Beth was pointing and saw that people were gathering in the center of the hall to dance. Benches and tables had been pulled back and a dozen or so people were forming lines facing each other. Some of the clansfolk had struck up a tune on a few instruments: a fiddle, a flute and some sort of stringed instrument that looked like a round-bellied guitar.

Lucy suddenly clapped her hands in glee, rose from her seat, and hurried to join them, taking down a fiddle that was hanging above the fireplace.

Beth rolled her eyes at Kara. "We've done it now. My mother likes nothing better than playing that fiddle until her fingers bleed and you've gone and given her the perfect excuse." She took a sip of whisky. "It's going to be a long night!"

AIDEN SAT IN STONY silence. Around him, the feast was in full swing. The Great Hall echoed to the sound of merry-making the like of which he hadn't seen since he was a boy. Everywhere he looked people were laughing and joking, gossiping about this or that, enjoying the food and drink or joining in the music and dancing, ably led by his mother, all to welcome him home.

But Aiden didn't join in. It was based on a lie. *His* lie.

He realized he was squeezing his cup tight and forced himself to relax. He was a small island of quiet in this sea of optimism. He responded when people spoke to him. He bantered and shared jests when necessary, but his heart wasn't in it. He churned inside. What would his people do if they knew the truth? Would they be celebrating like this if they knew he was going to turn his back on them?

His thoughts turned to the scroll sitting in a drawer in his room. He had intended to speak with his father about it the moment he got home, but his plans had changed since meeting Kara. His duty to keep her safe superseded any prior task and so he'd been given a stay of execution. He had exactly the amount of time it took to find Irene MacAskill and send Kara home to work out what he would say to his family, his clan. But what could he say?

My fate doesnae lie here. I've known it since I was a child. I'm sorry. I canna be the person ye need me to be.

He took a swig of whisky, and, surprised to find his cup empty, poured himself another. Things had been simpler on the road with Kara. Then all he had to worry about was finding them food and somewhere dry to sleep. He'd had none of the nagging doubts that plagued him whenever he returned to Dun Arnwick. On the road with Kara he'd been at peace, possibly for the first time in his life.

He glanced over at her. She was chatting to Beth, the two of them laughing like they'd known each other for years. His heart swelled at the sight. For a fleeting moment he wished with all his heart that this was an image of the future: Kara sat beside him for all time, part of his family. Part of him.

He pushed the thought away but he could feel Kara's presence by his side like a candle flame. She burned against his senses and he was hyper-aware of every movement she made, every word she spoke.

Annis called out to Beth, who pushed back her chair and made her way into the kitchen with the housekeeper. This was Aiden's chance to speak to Kara alone. But before he could say a word, Bhradain slid into Beth's vacant spot. He bent close to Kara, speaking softly, so softly that Aiden couldn't make out what he was saying.

Aiden sat stiffly, grinding his teeth. What was Bhradain saying to her? Why was she smiling like that? Didn't she realize that Bhradain Garrick was an oily snake with a reputation for chasing anything in a dress? Aiden gripped his cup as a strange mix of jealousy and protectiveness raged through him. Bhradain said something and Kara suddenly threw her head back and laughed.

Something in Aiden snapped. He pushed his chair back, thumped his cup down on the table, then strode from the room and out the main doors where he paused at the top of the steps. It was a cold, clear night and Aiden breathed in deeply, savoring the night air, allowing it to soothe his churning thoughts.

"Aiden?"

He spun, hand going reflexively to where his sword hilt would be. Kara stepped out, hugging herself to keep warm.

"What are you doing out here?"

Aiden stared at her. Moonlight reflected in her eyes as she watched him. "Go back inside," he said gruffly. "Ye are missing the feast."

"Damn the feast," Kara replied. "I saw you leave. Are you okay?"

Okay? he thought. *Not even close.*

"Go back inside," he repeated, his voice rougher than he intended. "Ye seemed to be enjoying yerself with Bhradain." He knew he sounded like a petulant child but he couldn't help it. The thought of Bhradain ingratiating himself with Kara made his blood boil.

Her expression hardened. "Bhradain was just being friendly. Which is more than I can say for you. You've barely spoken two words all night."

"I have naught to say."

"What's going on with you?" she asked. "I would have thought you'd be glad to be home."

Aiden blew out a breath. "I am. It's just that...ah, lass. It doesnae matter. Ye wouldnae understand."

Kara crossed her arms. "Why don't you try me?"

At that moment the door behind them opened and Bhradain stepped out into the night. He raised an eyebrow as he saw them together. "Ah! I hope I'm nay interrupting anything. Kara, that dance I told ye about is about to start—and I promised to show ye the steps if ye remember. Unless ye two have something more important to do?"

Aiden glared at Bhradain who watched him with a cocky little smile on his face. For a moment Aiden had the overwhelming urge to punch him. With a struggle he mastered himself.

"Nay, naught important," he growled.

Then, before either of them could say a word, he spun and descended the stairs two at a time, fleeing into the darkness of the bailey.

AIDEN SWUNG THE SWORD low in a one-handed grip, a blow designed to rip out his opponent's stomach. The dull-edged blade smacked into the practice dummy—two burlap sacks filled with straw lashed to a pole—with enough force to send a shiver of impact up his arm. Aiden ignored the pain. Without even pausing for breath, he spun on his heel and brought the sword around from the other side, his movements swift yet economical, using as little effort as possible for the maximum effect. This time the blade caught the practice dummy high on the left side, hard enough to take off an arm or even a head. If this had been a real fight, both of his opponents would be dead.

Still Aiden didn't stop. He dropped low to the ground, placing one palm flat on the icy ground and rolled, coming effortlessly to his feet on the other side of the dummy and slicing into it with an upper-cut designed to get through the defenses of an enemy coming at him from behind. Next he swung his sword in a series of arcs, taking one step with each swing, moving through exercises intended to keep his body lean and limber. He might not be on campaign at the moment but it was still important he kept himself in shape. Any warrior knew that it might mean the difference between living and dying on the battlefield.

Finally, after more than an hour, Aiden halted. Despite the cold wind blowing through the practice field, and the snow flurries falling from the white clouds above, a thin sheen of sweat covered Aiden's body, plastering his plaid to his skin and making his hair stick to his neck. Unable to sleep, Aiden had risen early, coming to the sparring grounds before dawn whilst the rest of the castle slept off last night's celebrations.

Around him, the rest of the garrison continued their sparring. They disliked training this early and more than a few were nursing sore heads. Over by the wall Jamie was taking a few of the new recruits through their paces with a pikestaff. The three youths were bleary-eyed and kept stamping their feet against the cold as Jamie demonstrated with a staff.

Aiden grabbed his cloak and wrapped it around his shoulders, watching the new recruits. Memories flooded him. How many times had he trained out here with Jamie and the others? How many times had he waited with ill-grace, just like those new recruits as Jamie explained something rather than letting them just get on with it?

The memories brought a flush of fondness but also a pang of regret. It things were different it would be Aiden himself putting those new recruits through their paces. As the eldest son and heir to the lairdship, his place was as commander of the castle's warriors but when Aiden had left to join the king's regiment, the duty had fallen to his uncle Jamie. So far, Aiden had managed to avoid taking the role back. He didn't want it. It was just another reminder of who he could never be.

Jamie set the new recruits to practicing their sparring and ambled over to Aiden.

"Lord above, lad," Jamie said. "What time did ye get out here? Ye will put us all to shame! Didnae ye realize last night was yer homecoming feast? Ye would be forgiven if ye didnae train the morning after."

Aiden shrugged. "Habit, uncle. I've been rising with the birds for four years. It isnae something ye can easily forget. Besides, I like to train."

Jamie rubbed his chin. "Aye, so I noticed. Just like I noticed ye disappeared early last night. What troubles ye, lad? Ye look as though ye have the weight of the world on yer shoulders."

Aiden looked at his uncle. There was more gray in his hair than Aiden remembered and the lines around his eyes were deeper. But for all that, he was still fit and hale. Still happy. Jamie was a warrior and yet he'd found contentment here, riding patrols, guarding caravans and keeping Harris lands safe. Couldn't Aiden find the same kind of contentment?

"I understand, lad," Jamie continued. "As does yer father. It canna be easy returning home after being away so long. It will take a little time but ye'll adjust, ye mark my words."

Aiden nodded. The comment was meant to cheer him up but it only made Aiden's morose mood worse. How could he tell Jamie that he would never adjust to this life? That his path lay elsewhere? His thoughts were like a tangled thorn bush. Whichever way he moved, they ripped at him like tiny thorns.

"Did...did everyone enjoy the feast?" he asked.

"Aye, lad, they did," Jamie replied. He eyed his adoptive nephew shrewdly. "But I dinna think ye are enquiring after me or yer folks. I think there's a certain wee lass ye are speaking of, am I right? Lady Kara retired to her chamber soon after ye left the feast. I'm nay great a judge of these things but I dinna think she was too happy with ye."

Idiot, Aiden cursed himself. *Why did ye storm off like that? Like a spoiled child because ye were jealous? Didnae ye promise to take care of her? Didnae ye give yer word?*

Shame washed through him, making his cheeks burn. He sighed. "I've made a mess of things since I returned havenae I, uncle?"

Jamie reached out and squeezed his shoulder. "Dinna fash, lad. Nobody begrudges ye a little time to get used to things again and there's naught that canna be fixed."

Aiden blew out a breath and then nodded. "Aye. Mayhap ye are right. Well, there is only one way to find out."

He turned and walked back towards the castle, running a hundred different apologies through his head.

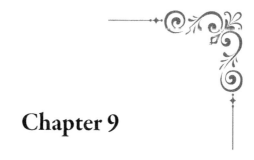

Chapter 9

IT WAS SNOWING WHEN Kara woke. She'd slept better than she had in a long, long time, and she woke feeling refreshed. Automatically she rolled over, expecting to find Aiden there, as he had been every morning for the last few days, but of course he wasn't. She was no longer out in the wilds with him but in Dun Arnwick castle.

And she was alone.

A pang went through her. They'd parted badly last night and she felt his absence keenly. It was like the anchor that held her in place had gone and she felt oddly adrift.

How had she gotten so reliant on his presence so quickly? It was dangerous. Hadn't she learned the hard way not to be reliant on anyone?

She threw back the covers, climbed out of bed, and crossed to the wardrobe. Biting her bottom lip, she considered the clothes in front of her. She picked a red dress that looked like it didn't have too many hooks on the back and struggled her way into it, pleased when she managed to do it up without help. Next she crossed to the fireplace and coaxed the fire back into life until a merry blaze sent heat stealing through the room. Then she sat in a chair by the window and brushed her hair.

There was a knock on the door. It opened and a fresh-faced maid stuck her head in. She took in the freshly made bed, the crackling fire, and an up-and-dressed Kara and her eyes widened slightly.

"Oh!" she said. "My apologies, my lady. If I had realized ye were up, I would have come sooner."

"It's fine," Kara said, smiling at her. "I'm an early riser and thought I'd make myself useful rather than lying in bed."

The girl smiled shyly back. "Is there aught else I can get ye?"

"No, I'm fine. Honestly."

The maid nodded although she seemed a little unsure about not being needed. "I'll let Lady Lucy know ye are up. Breakfast will be served in the Great Hall when ye are ready."

With that she turned and left and Kara busied herself brushing her hair once more. She was staring out the window, lost in thought, when there was another knock on the door.

"Honestly, I'm fine!" Kara called. Setting down the brush, she rose and opened the door. "I don't need anything else right now..."

Her words faltered as she saw Aiden leaning against the wall, arms crossed. He straightened and smiled tentatively.

"Good morning, lass," he muttered.

Kara's stomach did that annoying little flip at the sight of him. He was tousled and sweaty, as though he'd run here, but even so the sight of him sent heat flooding into her cheeks. It had only been one night but she realized she'd missed the sight of those stormy, brooding eyes. Of that self-deprecating smile. Of that messy, tangled black hair.

But she also remembered how he'd walked out on her last night.

She tilted her chin and said a little frostily. "Good morning."

Aiden shifted his feet. "Are ye...are ye well?"

"Fine. Thanks for asking."

She didn't invite him inside. If he thought she was going to make this easy on him he had another think coming.

"Good. That's good." He glanced at his feet then at the walls, the ceiling, and finally back to her. "Listen, lass. I came to apologize. I'm sorry for how I behaved last night at the feast. I wanted ye to enjoy yerself. I shouldnae have walked out like that."

His eyes met hers and Kara's irritation leaked away. "Why did you?" she asked.

He rubbed his chin. "I...I...it's complicated. But I wish to make it up to ye. How would ye like a tour of the castle?"

"With you?"

"Aye, with me."

Kara studied him. He held her gaze and her stomach did that little flip thing again. Yes, she'd very much like to spend some time with him.

"Apology accepted. Lead on."

Aiden held out his arm and Kara took it. Together they began walking through the corridors of the castle. A few servants greeted Aiden as they walked, and he responded politely, exchanging a few words of small talk and pleasantries. Everyone seemed to know him, from the young page boys, to the cooks in the kitchens, to the guardsmen standing guard on the door.

Kara tried to pay attention, to remember everything she saw and the people they encountered but her mind kept skipping back to the man at her side. He was the biggest enigma of them all, the one who held so many secrets.

Aiden led her through the castle and out into the bailey. The snow flurries had passed but the day was blustery and wind picked at Kara's hair, sending it streaming out behind her. True to his word, Aiden led her on a tour that took in most of the castle. First, they visited the stables and the kennels, then the kitchen and the herb garden. Lastly, they took a set of stone steps that led up onto the battlements.

The wind up here was stronger but it was worth it as the view was incredible. The cliff fell away, tumbling down to the beach and the ocean stretched away to the horizon, gray and roiling. If she turned to look the other way, Kara could see the undulating landscape of the island marching into the distance, purple, heather-clad hills mixed with pastures full of sheep, rising into the dark shadows of snow-capped mountains .

"It's...it's beautiful," Kara whispered. What would it be like to live in a place like this? This, wild, beautiful place surrounded by family and friends?

"Aye, it's beautiful," Aiden agreed, leaning his hands on the parapet and gazing out over the sea. His eyes scanned the horizon, his thoughts seeming far away.

Kara cocked her head and regarded him. "There's that look again."

"What look?"

"The same one you had last night. The one that says your body might be here but your mind is somewhere else entirely."

Aiden's hands clenched where they rested on the rough stone and he let out a long sigh. "Aye," he breathed, turning to look at her. "Mayhap I do. I had hoped things would become simpler when I returned, that my path would become clearer, but it hasnae." His eyes fixed on her and for a moment she thought he would tell her what was on his mind. But then his expression closed and he stared out to sea once more.

He didn't say anything for a long time and Kara kept silent, giving him space. Eventually he said, "I'm not the man ye and everyone else seems to think I am. I'm nothing but a cursed coward."

"Coward?" Kara said, taken aback. "Are you kidding me? You fought off Devereux's men, took the rap with the police and then agreed to go back through the arch with me, regardless of the fact that Devereux would likely be waiting for us. That's not the description of cowardice I know."

He fixed her with his deep blue stare. "Ye dinna understand, lass. This is all my fault. The fact that ye are trapped here is because of my cowardice."

She looked at him, puzzled. "I don't understand."

"Ye think I agreed to help Irene MacAskill out of honor? Nay, lass. The truth is, she gave me an excuse to run away. So I took it. I ran as far and as fast as I could from my responsibilities, from a decision I dinna want to make, and even centuries into the future wasnae far enough for me. And because of that, ye got embroiled in my mess. I'm sorry, lass."

Kara shook her head and jabbed a finger in his direction. "Oh no you don't. You don't get to take responsibility for my actions. *I* chose to go to Devereux's warehouse that night. *I* chose to follow you when you went to the arch. This is my mess just as much as yours. We're in this together."

He didn't say anything for a moment but watched her steadily. "In this together," he murmured at last. "I think I like the sound of that."

Before she could reply, a sudden rumble of thunder cracked overhead and a sheet of rain came hissing from the sky, turning the world gray. With a curse, Aiden unclasped his cloak and held it over their heads like a tent.

"What's with the weather?" Kara asked, huddling under the meager protection. "Did somebody turn on a tap?"

Aiden raised an eyebrow. "It's only a Highland shower."

"Shower? Then I'd hate to see what you call a deluge!"

He smiled. "Come then, we'd better get inside before we are soaked to our skin."

As they hurried across the bailey, the rain thickened into a downpour so strong the water bounced up when it hit the hard cobbles, making Kara doubly grateful for the stout pair of boots she wore.

They dived through a doorway and into the shelter of the castle. Aiden swung the door shut, cutting out the sound of the hissing rain. He shook out his cloak, making a puddle on the floor, before rolling it up and tucking it under his arm.

Kara squeezed out the hem of her dress, adding a few more drops to the puddle, then straightened, letting out a sigh. "So much for a tour of the castle. Seems like the weather has other ideas."

Aiden shook his head. "Nay, lass. If we Highlanders let the weather dictate our actions, we'd never do aught. There's still plenty more to show ye. I've just thought of a place ye will like."

Without waiting for an answer Aiden took her hand and led her down the corridor. It was such an unconscious gesture that Kara doubted Aiden was even aware that he'd done it, but his touch sent a thrill right through her body. She stiffened for a moment but then forced herself to relax. She curled her fingers around his and was rewarded when he gave her a surprised smile.

At the end of the corridor they reached a flight of steps that spiraled upwards. The steps had been worn smooth by the passage of many feet and had a beautiful gold and red runner down the middle. As they climbed they passed several landings and Kara soon realized they were climbing up the inside of one of Dun Arnwick's many towers. Through the narrow windows Kara could see the ground getting farther and farther away.

By the time they finally came to a halt Kara was puffing like a bellows. *Damn it*, she thought. *I never realized I was this unfit!*

"Don't say a word!" she warned Aiden when they reached the top and she bent over with her hands on her knees, breathing deeply. "I'll be fine in a minute, you'll see."

"Are ye sure, lass?" Aiden asked, who wasn't even breathing any quicker. "I could carry ye if ye would rather."

Kara gave him a flat look and didn't deign to answer. She followed Aiden over to a stout wooden door. It was closed but from the way the brass handle had been worn smooth, Kara guessed this room got a lot of use.

"It would be best if ye closed yer eyes, before I open the door, lass."

Kara eyed him suspiciously. "How do I know you're not going to lead me into a cupboard? Or a privy? Or a dungeon?"

"We dinna have any dungeons in Dun Arnwick," Aiden replied. "Although I do know a few good cupboards." He smiled mischievously. "Ye will just have to trust me, willnae ye?"

Kara held her frown for a long moment but then closed her eyes. A moment later she heard the door creak open. Aiden took her hands and slowly led her inside. Kara resisted the urge to peek.

"All right," Aiden said. "Ye can look now."

Kara opened her eyes and gasped. Four enormous windows illuminated a large, circular room stacked floor to ceiling with shelves. The shelves brimmed with books. Hundreds, if not thousands, of books.

"A library," Kara breathed. "It's a library."

She turned in a slow circle, taking it all in. The shelves were made from a dark wood and had been polished until they gleamed. Ladders on runners moved along the shelves to give easy access to the higher levels and many of the books' spines bore gold lettering that glittered in the sunlight.

Considering she was in sixteenth century Scotland rather than the downtown municipal library, the number of books here was staggering.

"This is amazing," she murmured.

"Ye like it?" Aiden asked.

"Like it? I love it! Where did all these books come from?"

"My mother's labor of love. She's collected works from all over Europe. There are books and scrolls here on everything from theology and philosophy, right down to folk tales gathered from the four corners of Scotland."

Kara walked over to one of the shelves and lovingly ran her fingers along the spines. So much knowledge. What hidden gems were contained within these pages? What secrets did they contain? A thrill of excitement passed through her. Lord, what might she learn given access to this place for a few hours? Historians the world over would be green with envy!

She gently pulled out a small, fat book with a faded leather cover. Carefully opening the cover she discovered it was written in Latin, each letter painstakingly drawn by hand in sweeping calligraphy. Brilliantly colored illumination marched up the pages and from her very rusty schoolgirl Latin, she was able to deduce it was a text on Christianity. She put the book back and took out another one. This was bigger and was written in Middle English that she could just about decipher. It had garish pictures of strange beasts and seemed to be a collection of folk tales.

She returned the book to the shelf and turned to gaze around the room. Under one of the windows sat a large desk on top of which a few books were lying open. A crumb-strewn plate and a goblet indicated that somebody had recently eaten their lunch here.

Just then the door swung open and Bhradain walked in. He was munching on an apple and had a big, leather-bound tome tucked under one arm. He froze when he spotted Aiden and Kara, apple raised for another bite. He raised an eyebrow and smiled.

"My apologies. I didnae expect to find anyone here. The library is usually deserted this time of day." He glanced at Aiden and the corners of his mouth quirked up. "Dinna tell me ye have become a student of literature whilst ye have been away? I thought drinking ale and shouting orders were more to yer tastes."

Aiden's mouth pressed into a line. "I was giving the Lady Kara a tour of the castle, not that it's any of yer business."

"Were ye now?" Bhradain turned to Kara. "And how does the Lady Kara find the library?"

"She finds it very impressive," Kara replied. "Just like the rest of Dun Arnwick."

"Ha!" Bhradain replied. "Dinna go around saying that too loudly. The compliments will make Aiden's head bigger than it already is!" Although he said it lightly, his dark eyes flicked to Aiden and there was no mirth in them.

Aiden's eyes flashed with irritation and Kara could see he was struggling to keep his temper. She didn't know what was going on between these two but there was clearly history here.

"What are ye reading, Bhradain?" Aiden asked through gritted teeth, nodding at the book tucked under Bhradain's arm.

Quick as lightning Aiden grabbed it and opened the cover. Kara caught a glimpse of diagrams and labels inside.

"Genealogies?" Aiden asked. "Why are ye looking at the bloodlines of the clans? Ye are nay a student of history."

Bhradain's eyes flicked briefly to Kara and a strange expression flashed across his face before his usual sardonic smile returned. "Well that's another thing ye didnae know about then, isnae it?" He held out his hand and Aiden placed the book in it.

Bhradain bowed. "Good day to ye both. I'll leave ye to yerselves." He took another bite of his apple, the crunching noise sounding strangely loud in the stillness, then with a wave to Aiden, he turned and left.

Aiden stared at the door for a long moment after he left. "What is he up to?" he muttered under his breath.

"He didn't seem very pleased to see you," Kara observed.

Aiden shook his head. "He never is. Bhradain is my father's ward. He's a Garrick, not a Harris, and never seems able to forget it even though he's treated the same as the rest of us. His father was Laird Callum Garrick and when his father died, Bhradain's mother sent him to foster with us." He shook himself and turned to Kara. "So, what do you think of my 'surprise'?"

"I think it's just about damned perfect," Kara said honestly. "There are so many books in here you'll have to prize me out of this place with a crowbar."

Aiden laughed suddenly, a deep, clear sound that echoed around the room. The sound of it sent a flash of joy right through Kara. "Well, it's a good job I have quite the collection of crow bars isnae it? Now, I dinna know about ye but I reckon I could eat a horse. How about we go get some breakfast?"

Kara rolled her eyes. "Finally! I thought you'd never ask!"

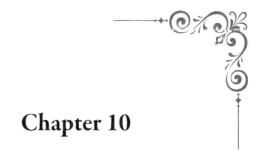

Chapter 10

THREE DAYS LATER AIDEN found himself striding through the corridors of Dun Arnwick with Jamie by his side. They'd been up since dawn training the garrison and sweat still clung to Aiden's skin from the workout. He'd not had time to go to his chamber and wash as a runner had brought a message that Aiden's father wanted to see them both in the Great Hall right away. Coupled with the snow flurries that were falling outside, the sweat made Aiden's hair and clothes stick to him uncomfortably. Still, there was nothing for it. His father wouldn't have sent for them if it wasn't important.

The heat from the fire in the Great Hall soon warmed Aiden's chilled skin and water began dripping off his clothes. Annis, who was busy serving breakfast at the high table, fixed him and Jamie with a withering stare for dripping all over a floor she'd obviously already cleaned. Aiden gave her an apologetic smile.

He and Jamie approached the high table where Andrew sat alone, perusing a set of documents, ignoring the breakfast of porridge and ale Annis had set out for him.

As Aiden took a seat, he found himself scanning the hall, looking for Kara, but there was no sign of her. He felt the bench shift and looked up to see Bhradain taking a seat next to his father. Bhradain inclined his head to Aiden and grinned. They'd not spoken since their altercation in the library three days ago but Aiden had often found Bhradain watching him when he thought he wasn't looking.

His father looked up from reading the parchment and, seeing they were all present, placed the parchment on the table between them. "A report has just come in of raiders attacking St. Margaret's Bay."

"Raiders?" Aiden asked, a shot of alarm going through him. "From where?"

"Details are sketchy but from the description of the boats, I'd guess they were Irish."

"Irish? At this time of year? Surely crossing the sea would be too dangerous?"

"Not if they're already hiding out somewhere on Skye," Andrew replied. "Ye know they've always seen us as easy pickings. They probably landed earlier in the season and have been biding their time, choosing their target. Nay doubt they're holed up somewhere, waiting out the weather before they return to Ireland."

Aiden swore under his breath. "Damn them," he growled. "Cowards, the lot of them. They willnae face us in honest battle and instead prey on those that canna defend themselves. We canna let this go unpunished, Father! I'll ride out. I'll take some of the garrison and we'll make these curs regret ever setting eyes on our island."

Andrew sighed, rubbing his eyes with the heel of his hand. He looked tired. "Aye, I dinna doubt ye would, son.

But they'll be long gone by now. They aren't stupid and will-nae hang around long enough for us to catch them."

"Then we should build defenses," Aiden said. "I've seen how effective coastal defenses can be. Build a watchtower near to St. Margaret's Bay, one that can give early warning of any approaching fleet. If we station a small garrison there and fresh horses for messengers, we can have a force there ready to repel anyone that tries to land."

Bhradain raised an eyebrow. "A plan fit for a king!" he said, his voice heavy with sarcasm. "But ye aren't lording it at the king's court now, Aiden. Ye are back in the Highlands and here we canna just snap our fingers and make coin appear out of our arses. How would we pay for such a thing?"

"We'd find the coin somehow," Aiden growled, glaring at Bhradain. "Or would ye abandon our people?"

"*Me,* abandon our people?" Bhradain snapped. "That's rich coming from ye! Ye rode off to seek fame and fortune without a second thought for yer people!"

Aiden rocked back in his seat, taken aback by the vehemence in Bhradain's tone. Then anger exploded through him. "Now listen here ye little—"

"Enough!" Andrew snapped, slamming his hand down on the table.

Aiden bit his lip to keep silent and Bhradain bowed his head. "My apologies, my laird. Worry for our people makes me speak out of turn."

Andrew waved the apology away. "For now, I want patrols doubled and scouts sent out, searching for any sign of these invaders. Aiden, Jamie, I want ye to drill the war band and have them ready to ride out the minute we get word of where the raiders might be holed up. Bhradain, examine our ledgers and see if we can squeeze out enough coin for Aiden's defenses. If not, I may have to petition the king."

"I'll see to it right away, my lord," Bhradain said. He hurried from the hall.

Aiden bid Andrew and Jamie farewell and quickly followed his foster-brother. He caught up with Bhradain in the corridor outside the Great Hall and grabbed him by the arm, spinning him around.

"What was that all about?" he demanded.

Bhradain quirked his eyebrow, a smirk curling the corners of his mouth. "What? Ye didnae like that I disagreed with ye? My apologies, my lord, I forgot that nobody is allowed to say aught ye might not like."

Aiden stepped back, looking Bhradain over. "What is wrong with ye, Bhradain? Ye have been hostile since the moment I returned."

Bhradain bared his teeth, his mask of cocky indifference slipping. "Ye really dinna ken? Then let me make it plain. Ye come swaggering back in here after all these years and everyone treats ye like a hero! The prodigal son returned, bringing honor to his clan. And I? I who have toiled by yer father's side these last years? I who have worked to make this clan stronger, to fill the gap ye left when ye went riding off to war? Not a word for me. Until ye returned yer father looked to me for advice, for words of counsel. Now all he does is listen to ye! Ye, who doesnae care about the future of this clan at all! Do ye think I dinna see it in yer eyes? Yer disdain? Yer yearning to be elsewhere? And yet, ye will be laird if ye so choose.

Where is the fairness in that? Until ye returned there was a chance yer father would adopt me, name me the next laird!"

"So that's what this is all about?" Aiden growled. "Jealousy? Power? Ye think just because ye have proven yerself an able administrator ye deserve to be named laird after my father?"

Bhradain stepped close, so close his face was almost touching Aiden's. "We both know I'd make a better laird than ye ever could. Ye have no stomach for it, Aiden Harris. Ye never did. Glory is all ye care about. So why stay? Why not return to the king's household where yer heart truly lies? Ye would be doing us both a favor."

Then, before Aiden could utter a word, he spun on his heel and strode away, leaving Aiden staring after.

KARA STIFLED A YAWN. It was barely past dawn. If she'd been at home, she'd have pressed the snooze button on her alarm clock and then gone back to sleep. As it was, she'd been up for over an hour and eaten a quick breakfast in the Great Hall with Beth and Lucy. It had been so early that nobody else had been in sight. No sign of Aiden and Kara had envied him the chance to sleep in. Now herself, Lucy and Beth were standing in a small room in a quiet part of the castle.

Lucy laughed. "You'll get used to it. Eventually."

Kara jumped, startled out of her thoughts. "Used to it?"

"The early mornings. When I first came here, it drove me crazy. Everyone seemed to get up at the crack of dawn and then go to bed just as the night was starting to get interesting. Our body clocks have shifted in the twenty-first century—we get up late and stay up late. Here it's the other way around. Don't worry, you'll soon adjust."

"I hope so," Kara admitted. "I feel like a zombie. I don't even have my caffeine kick to wake me up."

Lucy's face took on a wistful expression. "Ah, coffee. What I wouldn't give for an espresso! Or a mocha. Oh hell, even a cup of instant would do!"

Kara laughed. "So there *are* some things you miss from the future?"

"Of course! I don't think I'll ever get used to not having chocolate. Or hair straighteners." Lucy sighed dramatically. "The sacrifices we make for love."

Beth rolled her eyes at her mother. "Honestly, mother, anyone would think chocolate is the most amazing thing in the world the way ye go on about it."

Kara and Lucy shared a look then said at the same time. "It is!"

They all burst out laughing. Kara was amazed and delighted at how quickly Lucy, Beth and the rest of Aiden's family had accepted her. They were friendly and easy-going people who seemed content to accept people as they were, no matter their differences or where they might have come from. It was oddly refreshing. They weren't interested in where she'd gone to school, which newspapers she'd written for, which awards she'd won. They were more interested in her ability to tell a good tale in the Great Hall of an evening, or her ability to write letters for Andrew, small things that kept the clan running.

In return for their hospitality Kara was determined to help out as much as she could. Which is why she was standing in this small room with Lucy and Beth while the sun had barely risen above the horizon. It was a storeroom set in the northeast corner of the keep. It had no windows but was kept ventilated by grilles in the walls.

This was where the keep's medical supplies were kept. Bunches of dried herbs hung from the ceiling, giving the room a delicious aroma, and wooden shelves filled the space along the walls. Glass and pottery bottles sat on the shelves, each stoppered with a piece of cork.

Beth was busy picking up the bottles, checking the labels and putting what she needed into a leather satchel. Lucy and Kara were folding bandages and putting them in a second satchel.

When they'd got what they needed they left the storeroom, locked it behind them, and made their way down the winding staircase to the castle infirmary. It was a large rectangular room not much smaller than the Great Hall that had been divided into individual alcoves by wooden screens. A fire burned at one end, chasing away the chill, and bunches of dried lavender sat in vases, filling the room with its soothing, pungent scent. Three large windows let in sunlight, giving a sweeping view of the snow-covered landscape beyond.

There were only three patients in the infirmary today—a youth who'd been kicked by a horse, a middle-aged woman who'd come to have a dressing on a scalded wrist changed, and an elderly man with a bad cough.

Lucy led Kara over to the old man. He was sitting on his narrow cot, whittling at a piece of wood with a knife. He looked up as they approached and gave them a wide smile.

He appeared to be in his seventies with wild white hair and a short beard. Blue eyes peered out from a nest of wrinkles and they sparkled with intelligence.

"Ah, young Lucy! Is it that time again already?"

Before Lucy could reply, the man broke into a hacking cough. Lucy hurried to his side. She poured warm water into a mug, stirred in some honey and held it out to the man.

"Here, you old hound. Drink this."

The man took the cup gratefully and sipped it. "Thank ye, lass," he muttered, wiping his mouth. "I canna wait to be rid of this malady. Being cooped up in here will surely send me to an early grave!"

"Hush," Lucy admonished. "Don't say things like that. You'll be with us a good few years yet, old friend. You're as strong as an oak tree." She beckoned Kara over. "And I've brought someone to meet you. This is Kara Buchanan – the visitor you've heard so much about. Kara, I'd like you to meet Dougie Harris. He was Andrew's steward when I first came to Dun Arnwick. He's been retired a few years now, although you'd not realize it with the amount he likes to stick his nose in!"

Dougie frowned. "If I didnae stick my nose in ye'd all soon be in a mess!"

Kara held out her hand for Dougie to shake. "Pleased to meet you, Dougie."

Dougie smiled, making him appear much younger, then took Kara's hand and kissed the back of it as genteelly as any courtier. "Mighty pleased to make yer acquaintance, Kara Buchanan."

Lucy rolled her eyes. "You old charmer." She handed Kara a mug and some powdered herbs. "I'll go and check on Elaine. Make sure he takes his medicine, Kara, and don't let him wriggle out of it! He'll try and sweet-talk you given half a chance!"

Dougie gave her a wide-eyed innocent look. "As if I would!"

Lucy smiled and then left Kara alone with Dougie. He patted the chair next to his bed and Kara obediently sat. "I've been dying to meet ye since ye arrived but Tyrant Lucy reckoned I wasnae up to it. So, how are ye finding Dun Arnwick, lass?"

Kara thought about this for a moment. "Warm," she said at last. Dougie gave her a puzzled look and Kara laughed lightly. "It's the best word I can think of. I don't mean in a literal temperature type sense – it's downright freezing at the moment – I mean the people. Everyone has been so welcoming it's like being at home but not at home."

"I'm glad," Dougie said, smiling. "It must be very unsettling for ye being ripped away from yer home like that. Our Lucy was the same. I remember when she first came to us, all wide-eyed and unsure. But after a while it was like she'd always been here."

Kara's eyes came to rest on the piece of wood lying in Dougie's lap. "What are you carving?"

"I'm nay sure," Dougie replied. "It will find its own shape in the end – they always do."

He broke into another fit of coughing, chest heaving in great racking hacks. Kara patted him on the back then dropped the herbs Lucy had left into the water and stirred it. It gave out a sour, acrid smell. What she wouldn't give for a packet of lozenges right now. Or even better – some antibiotics!

"Easy," Kara mumbled, rubbing Dougie's back. "It'll pass in a moment."

The coughing fit eased and Kara handed him the medicine. Dougie took it gingerly, sniffed it, and pulled a face.

Kara gave him a flat look. "Drink it. All of it."

Dougie frowned. "My, ye are as bad as Lucy." But he drank the mixture, wincing at the acrid taste and handed her back the empty cup. "I hear there's been nay sign of Irene MacAskill. I'm nay surprised. That woman is mischief incarnate."

"Irene? You know her?" Kara asked eagerly. "Do you know where she lives?"

Dougie shook his head. "I've met the woman a few times is all. She came to attend Lucy when both Aiden and Beth were born. Didn't talk to her much. Scared me a little, truth be told." He scratched his head. "Ye have to be careful where the Fae are concerned and I'd rather say nothing at all then say something wrong and end up offending her. As for where she lives – nobody can answer that one. She turns up where she wills, when she wills it."

Kara sighed.

Dougie patted her hand. "But she'll be back when she's good and ready."

"I hope you're right," Kara said, forcing a smile.

The morning passed in easy companionship. Kara bustled around the infirmary, helping Lucy and Beth with the patients. She found herself singing softly as she worked.

She suddenly realized that the room had grown very still. The hum of Beth and Lucy's conversation had stilled. Kara looked up to find them both staring at her with an odd expression on their faces. She froze in the act of unrolling a bandage.

"What?" she asked. "Oh wait, I haven't got my dress on inside out have I? Or food smeared around my mouth?" She meant it as a joke but neither Beth nor Lucy smiled. Instead they shared a long look.

"What is it?" Kara asked again. "You're both looking at me like I've grown a second head!"

"What were you singing just now?" Lucy asked.

"I...um..." Kara stammered. "It wasn't that bad, was it? It's nothing. Just nonsense words."

"Not nonsense," Lucy said. "Gaelic. A very old dialect of Gaelic in fact."

Kara gave them a puzzled look. "But I don't know any Gaelic."

"And the song ye were singing was old too," Beth added. "A song every child knows. It tells the story of how the Fae founded Alba many millennia ago."

"Oh," Kara said. "Isn't that strange? I must have picked it up as a child." But for the life of her she couldn't remember ever having heard it before.

"Well, ye seem to have a knack for it," Dougie said from his bed in the corner. "Although yer pronunciation is a little odd." He rubbed his chin. "I could teach ye if ye'd like."

Kara thought of all those books in the library written in Gaelic. How much knowledge would she have access to if she could read them? "You'd do that?" she asked.

The old man waved a hand. "It's not like I've much else to occupy my time now is it? I'd be delighted."

"Then I'd be delighted to learn. Thanks!"

Kara finished her round in the infirmary and then made her way back into the castle proper. She was beginning to know her way around and managed to find her way down to the Great Hall without getting lost. She stuck her head in but saw that it was almost empty at this time of day, with just a few maids sweeping. She made her way outside and stood on the top steps, looking out over the bailey. Jamie approached her with a big bundle of sticks perched on his shoulder.

"Good day, lass!" he boomed. Jamie never seemed to do anything quietly. "How are ye this fine Highland afternoon?"

Kara smiled at him. Aiden's uncle was always ready with a smile or a joke. Kara had liked him immediately. "I'm very well. And if you call this a fine afternoon I'd hate to see an 'unfine' one." The sky was slate gray and the wind howled around the bailey like a banshee.

Jamie barked a laugh and moved past Kara and through the door. He paused on the threshold and looked back. "Oh, ye'll find him in the stables by the way." He winked at her and disappeared inside.

Kara didn't need to ask who he was referring to. Her cheeks warmed. Was she that obvious?

She hurried down the steps and across the bailey to the stables. She heard voices within and halted in the doorway where she got a good view of the dim interior. Aiden was standing on the far side, surrounded by a gaggle of Dun Arnwick children.

"And then what happened?" one of them asked. "My da says ye beat ten men with yer bare hands!"

Aiden laughed. "Yer da should know better than filling yer head with such stories. No man could face such odds." He crouched so he was at eye level with the children. "Aye, we won that battle but only because everyone worked together. A real warrior is really only as strong as the comrade guarding his back or the loyal steed carrying him." He reached out and ruffled the boy's hair. "Ye'll learn that when ye are old enough to begin yer training."

The boy, a small, sandy-haired youth of about eight, sighed dramatically. "But that's ages away! I want to start training now! I want to fight for the king just like ye did!"

Aiden shook his head. "There'll be plenty of time for that, lad. Dinna be so keen to grow up."

Kara smiled and her heart swelled at the sight of Aiden with the children. He was a big man, tall, muscular with an inborn strength. A warrior born and bred. And yet around the children he was gentle and patient. He would make an amazing father.

Aiden looked up suddenly and spotted her. "Now, why dinna ye go and pester the Lady Kara?"

The children looked her way and their eyes widened. They came rushing over and surrounded her, just as they had Aiden.

"Lady Kara!" said the same boy who'd been quizzing Aiden. "Can we have another story? I want to hear more stories from America!"

"Aye! America!" the others piped up.

Kara laughed. "Was the story of Tom Thumb not enough for you?" She'd soon discovered that sixteenth century highlanders were suckers for stories. They couldn't get enough of them. Kara had been dragged into telling one by the fire in the Great Hall every night since she'd arrived. It looked like she wasn't about to be let off the hook any time soon. "Okay!" she said, holding up her hands in surrender. "You win! How about I tell you the story of the Princess and the Pea tonight?"

The children cheered, nodding enthusiastically.

"Off with ye now," Aiden gently chided. "I'm sure yer mothers have chores ye should be doing and I have a horse to groom."

The children filed out, leaving Kara alone with Aiden.

"Ye've made quite the impression," he said. "Ye are a natural with them."

"As are you. Who would have thought it—Aiden Harris, baby-sitter extraordinaire?"

He laughed. "Who would have thought it—Kara Buchanan, clan storyteller extraordinaire?"

His gaze caught hers and held it. "Yes," she murmured. "Who would have thought it?"

For a moment they stared at each other in silence then Aiden cleared his throat and walked over to a stall at the back where his big black stallion was munching on a nose-bag. Aiden took a curry comb from the rack and approached the stable.

"What can I do for ye, lass?" he asked.

"I wanted to run an idea past you."

"Oh?"

"I want to do something to repay everyone's kindness. Dougie is going to teach me Gaelic so I can decipher the books in the library. A lot of them are histories and genealogies. I'd like to write a history of the clan. What do you think?"

Aiden thought for a moment. "A history of Clan Harris? I'm sure it will be a bloody tale. We weren't always as civilized as we are now. Still, it would be an interesting tale nay doubt."

"That's what I thought. There are scraps of stories and family trees in the library but they're all over the place. I thought it might be nice to collect them all in one place."

Aiden nodded. "And I'm sure Dougie and some of the older clansfolk can help ye out with oral histories as well. That tends to be the way stories are passed down. It's a shame Old Mona isn't with us anymore. She was the housekeeper when I was a lad. She was full of old stories."

"So you think it's a good idea?"

He smiled at her. "Aye, lass. Why not? Anything that keeps ye out of trouble is a good thing in my opinion."

"Trouble? I don't get myself into trouble!"

"Oh? Climbing fences, breaking into warehouses, stealing artifacts?"

"Oh, yeah. Apart from that."

They grinned at each other and Kara felt her breath catch in her throat. The shafts of light coming through the windows caught and illuminated Aiden's form, turning his skin to burnished bronze. Her stomach tightened.

She stepped back hastily and cleared her throat. "Right. Great. I'll leave you to her your...um...horsey things."

Aiden nodded. "Aye. I'll see ye tonight at supper?"

"You bet."

She turned and walked away thinking that the few hours between now and supper would seem like an eternity.

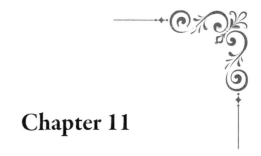

Chapter 11

"WOULD YE BOTH CARE for more mint tea?" Elsa asked.

Aiden shook his head but Kara held her mug out gratefully. The crofter made the most wonderful tea Kara had ever tasted. She smiled and nodded her thanks as Elsa refilled her mug from a big kettle hanging over the fireplace in this cozy one-roomed cottage.

Aiden handed his empty cup to Elsa and then leaned forward with his elbows resting on his knees. He looked at Machie, Elsa's husband, who was seated on a chair by the fire, enjoying a dram of whisky.

"So tell us what happened," he instructed the man, a balding farmer somewhere past his middle years. "Is it right ye saw Irene MacAskill?"

Kara found herself leaning forward eagerly. Word had come to Dun Arnwick this morning that Irene had been spotted near a croft to the east of the castle. It was the first news they'd received since Andrew had sent out riders over three weeks ago. She and Aiden had ridden out straight away, with three of Dun Arnwick's guardsmen for company.

Machie rubbed his bristly jowls. "I canna say whether it was this Irene woman ye speak of," he said in a deep voice.

"She didnae introduce herself but she fits the description that came down from the castle. I wouldnae have thought anything of it if we hadnae heard word ye were searching for such a woman." He threw back the rest of his whisky, put his cup down on the small, rickety table by the fire and leaned forward. "It was two days ago now. Late and already dark. I was doing my rounds of the fields, checking all was well before I turned in for the night. Normally I see not a soul, us being a long way from the road and all that. But this night I spied a light moving along the trail ahead of me. I thought it mighty strange as any traveler out here must be lost indeed so I caught up with the light. Turns out it was a tiny woman old enough to be me dearly departed mam. She was carrying a lantern and striding along as happy as they come."

He sat back in his chair and stretched out his legs, lacing his fingers over his ample paunch. "I asked her if she needed any assistance and she reached up and tousled my hair as though I was naught but a child and told me she was fine and to run along as Elsa would be waiting. And I did. I dinna know why but it was like I couldnae disobey her even if I wanted to. Well, I told Elsa about it when I got home but by the morning I'd all but forgotten her. It wasnae until yer father's messenger came this way with her description that I remembered."

"And this was two days ago ye say?" Aiden asked.

"Aye."

"Have ye seen any sign of her since?"

"Nay, lord. Naught. Not even any footprints in the mud the next day. She was heading east if that's any help."

Aiden nodded. "Ye have my thanks. It's the first news we've had of her and I'm grateful for ye bringing it to us."

Machie waved a hand. "Always a pleasure to be of service, my lord."

Kara smiled at Machie and Elsa. "You've been most hospitable. Thanks for your help." She frowned in concentration and then said, "Tapadh leat." *Thank you.*

Machie and Elsa smiled and replied. "S e do bheatha." *You're welcome.*

Kara nodded. She'd been at Dun Arnwick for over three weeks now and had taken every opportunity to practice the Gaelic Dougie was teaching her. In truth, she was enjoying learning it. There was something about the language that felt natural, like a language she'd once known and forgotten.

She and Aiden stood and, bidding farewell to the crofters, made their way outside where the three guardsmen were waiting with the horses. Kara balked at the sight of the big black mare she'd been given to ride. She'd been assured that she was the most placid horse in the Dun Arnwick stables but Kara was still less than confident as a rider.

"I'm sorry, lass," Aiden said. "I was hoping we'd get more. If the sighting was two days ago Irene could be anywhere by now."

Kara nodded. She'd been so excited this morning when word had come to the castle of a sighting of Irene. For the last three weeks worry had been gnawing at her. She wondered what Devereux would be up to, what damage he was doing. She had to get back to her time and stop him. And yet, as she thought about it, she wasn't quite as disappointed as she should be. She glanced up at Aiden then quickly away when she found him watching her.

"At least we know she's still nearby," she said. "And which direction she was heading."

"Aye," Aiden agreed. "I will send riders to the villages in that direction. Dinna worry, lass. We'll find her soon."

For some reason that thought didn't make her feel better. Instead, it made her sad. When they found Irene MacAskill, she would be going home and that meant leaving. Leaving Dun Arnwick and her new friends.

Leaving Aiden.

He was still staring at her. She couldn't read the look in his eyes but she didn't like the effect it had on her. More and more in the last few weeks she'd found herself drawn to him. She found herself looking for him when she walked into a room. She found herself thinking about him when he wasn't there. She found herself dreaming about him at night.

Idiot! she chided herself. *He's a sixteenth century warrior for pity's sake! You're a twenty-first century journalist! You come from different worlds and you'll soon be returning to yours. Get a grip!*

She sucked in a deep breath and marched over to her horse. "Looks like it might snow again. Let's get going shall we?"

AIDEN YANKED ON THE reins, keeping the spirited stallion under control. Smokey had been Aiden's horse for years and carried him into battle in the name of King James many times over. He was a loyal and dependable companion.

But he was also a trained warhorse who hadn't had enough exercise in the past few weeks. With the coastal trail stretching out in front of them, the stallion longed to stretch his legs.

"Easy boy," Aiden said, patting his neck. "Easy."

He glanced over at Kara who sat on the plodding mare by his side. Her riding was improving although she still sat straight-backed and rigid, as though she didn't trust the rolling gait of the horse not to pitch her from the saddle. Aiden had enjoyed teaching her. She was an attentive and quick student, always asking questions, always wanting to improve. Lord, he wished all his new recruits were as attentive as she. Right now though, she was staring straight ahead, a look on her face that suggested her thoughts were somewhere else entirely.

The biting sea breeze had put a pink tinge into her cheeks and tousled her hair, blowing it around her face in tangled locks. Aiden felt something shift inside him. Lord, she was beautiful. More beautiful than any woman he'd ever met. Being near her did strange things to Aiden. He found he couldn't concentrate when she was around. When she was close, his thoughts scattered like leaves in the wind and all he became aware of was her scent, her warmth, her nearness.

It was maddening and invigorating at the same time. What was happening to him? What was this twenty-first century woman, this woman from such an alien world, doing to him?

He wondered what she was thinking. About her home? Wishing she could go back there? Was she disappointed that

Irene hadn't been found? Was she desperate to return to her own time and leave Dun Arnwick—and him—behind?

He didn't like the feelings that thought evoked. Pushing his musings away, he forced himself to concentrate on the road. The castle still lay several miles distant but Aiden knew these lands like the back of his hand. He'd explored every inch of this coastline as a child, driving his mother to distraction by disappearing for hours with the other castle boys and coming home late in the evening, usually wet and dirty and thoroughly pleased with himself. Then later, as a youth, he'd ridden with his father on patrols and border inspections, and finally as an adult, led companies of his own on behalf of his father.

Spotting a path that branched off to the left he pulled his horse up suddenly. Around him the others halted their mounts as well.

Drake looked at him quizzically. "What is it? Is something wrong?"

Aiden suddenly grinned. "Nay, Drake," he replied. "There's naught wrong. Ye three head back to Dun Arnwick. We'll follow after. There's something I want to show Lady Kara."

Kara raised an eyebrow. "Out here? I can't see anything but moorland and sea."

"Ah, that's because ye dinna know where to look." He nodded to the three guards. "Go on ahead and tell my father what the crofters said. We'll return to Dun Arnwick anon."

Drake nodded then the three guardsmen nudged their mounts and carried on along the road. Kara watched Aiden.

"You're grinning like a Cheshire Cat," she said. "Am I missing something?"

"I havenae been this way in years," he replied. "But when I saw that trail I remembered something, a place I used to visit when I was just a lad. I reckon ye'll like it. Come on."

He swung his leg out of the saddle and dropped easily to the ground. Kara was a little more ungainly and slid out of the saddle like a sack, only keeping her footing by grabbing onto the cantle.

"Don't say a word!" she said, pointing a finger at Aiden. "I'll master this riding thing yet, you'll see."

Aiden held up his hands. "I wouldnae dare say a word! I value my head too much for that! This way."

Leaving the horses to crop grass, he led Kara over to the cliff-edge. A narrow trail wound its way to the beach below, winding through brush and around boulders. Below them the tide lapped at a narrow strip of beach.

"You want me to climb down there?" Kara asked.

"It isnae as steep as it looks from up here," Aiden replied. "And it will be worth it. I promise."

"Okay," Kara said, dubiously. "But if I fall and break my neck I'll come back and haunt you, Aiden Harris."

"Ye willnae fall, lass. I willnae let any harm come to ye."

She met his gaze and Aiden felt a surge of protectiveness swell within him. He wouldn't let anything hurt this woman. He would die first.

He cleared his throat and stepped forward. "This way."

True to his word, the path was easy to traverse and they made their way down to the beach without incident. Down here the wind was not quite as strong but the tang of salt-spray filled the air. The churning sea stretched to the horizon.

"What now?" Kara asked.

Aiden scanned the cliff, searching. Then he spotted what he was looking for and grinned at Kara.

"Come on."

She followed as he led the way along the base of the cliff for about a hundred meters or so. A large outcrop of rock stuck out of the cliff, covered in clinging, scraggly bushes and with a hardy coastal pine growing out of a crack in the rock. He halted in front of it.

Kara looked over the outcrop and then fixed him with a quizzical look. "What am I looking at? Seems like an ordinary cliff to me."

"So I thought, until I tried climbing that tree when I was ten years old. A branch snapped under me and the cliff revealed its secret. This way."

He strode in amongst the hanging branches of the tree. He held them aside so Kara could duck beneath their scratchy fingers. Once inside, a cleft in the rock was revealed, leading into the depths of the cliff.

"Careful," he warned Kara. "The rocks can be slippery."

She nodded and followed close behind as he carefully picked a way through the cleft. They soon entered a narrow tunnel. It was dark and dank, smelling of seaweed and from up ahead came the sound of the lapping sea. Aiden reached out and clasped Kara's hand to steady her. She looked at him gratefully and curled her fingers through his.

Together they made their careful way through the near-darkness, slimy rock walls close on either side. Then suddenly they rounded a bend and a huge sea-cave opened up before them, brightly lit by both a rounded entrance through which they could see the sea and a crack in the roof which let sunlight stream down from above.

Kara gasped. Her eyes widened as she took it all in. The cave was almost perfectly circular with clear calm water filling most of it, far more serene than the churning sea outside. Minerals sparkled in the walls and high overhead a cluster of stalactites hung from the ceiling, glittering like tiny diamonds.

Kara ran her hands over the wall. "It's beautiful," she murmured.

"Aye," Aiden agreed. *Like ye*, the thought came unbidden to his mind. "Like I said, I found it by accident when I was just a lad. After that, I used to come here when I needed to think." He smiled wryly. "Or to sulk after I'd had a hiding for some misdemeanor or other. Here, let me show ye something."

He led Kara over to the opening that led out to the sea. Here the rock wall had been weathered over time into a ledge that provided the perfect seat. He knelt down, running his hand over the wall. There, carved in crude, childish letters, was his name.

Kara grinned in delight, running her fingers over the letters. "So ten-year old Aiden used to come here," she said, taking a seat on the ledge and staring out over the sunlit cavern. "I bet you were a true little devil."

"I wasnae!" Aiden said in mock outrage, taking a seat by her side. "I'll have ye know I was adorable!"

Kara laughed. "I'll bet you were. And I'll bet you were the darling of everyone's eye—just like now!"

Her words sobered him abruptly. *Not if they knew the truth,* he thought. He looked away from her, staring out over the gently lapping pool. When he was younger this place had always soothed him. It was a place he'd come when he wanted to be alone, to think, to work out exactly what he wanted in life. He'd come here when he'd been deciding whether to leave and join the king's banners. He'd hoped it would soothe him now but found his thoughts churning worse than ever.

They'd failed to find Irene MacAskill. That should have disappointed him. After all, the sooner they found her, the sooner Kara could go home and Aiden could get on with his life. Wasn't that what he wanted? Hadn't that been the plan since the moment Kara had come back to Scotland with him?

But he found that was no longer the case. Far from being disappointed they hadn't found Irene, Aiden was glad. It meant Kara would be here a while longer. With him.

"What's wrong" Kara asked, laying a hand on his arm.

Her touch sent a thrill through him and Aiden sprang to his feet, staring out over the still pool. Kara stood and stepped up next to him. "Aiden?"

He turned to look at her. Her lips were parted slightly, her eyes large and round, deep enough to drown in. Desire swept through him, so hot and fierce that his thoughts shattered. Before he knew what he was doing, he stepped forward, gathered Kara into his arms and pressed his mouth against hers. Her lips were soft and warm, as sweet as he'd dreamed. Her scent filled his nostrils, intoxicating him, sending lust raging through his body. She melted into his arms, her arms going around his neck, her lips parting to let him inside.

He kissed her wildly, passionately, all the built-up desire he'd kept inside since the moment he'd met her exploding out in an uncontrollable tide. He yanked her hard against him, his hands in the small of her back, feeling her breasts crushed against his chest.

For her part Kara answered with equal passion, her tongue cavorting with his, her fingers tangling in his hair. Before he realized it, he'd pushed her up against the wall, his hands gripping her waist.

Some deep part of himself screamed a warning. If he went any further, he would be lost. He would lose himself in this woman, a woman who would soon leave him. This could be nothing more than a brief liaison and that would never be enough for him. He owed himself more than that. And, more importantly, he owed Kara more than that.

He broke the kiss but didn't let her go. Instead he stood looking down at her, his chest rising and falling rapidly, his raging desire making it difficult to think straight. She stared up at him, her lips swollen from his kisses, her hair tousled around her shoulders. Lord help him, but it was all he could do not to grab her, kiss her into submission, and take her, right here, right now.

It took all his battle-trained discipline to take a deep breath and say, "We shouldnae let this go any further, lass. It would be a bad idea."

He wanted her to disagree. He wanted her to give him an excuse, any excuse to taste her again. She breathed deeply through her nostrils and he could see her fighting with herself.

"You're right," she said eventually. "Bad idea. Maybe we should head back before we do something stupid?"

"Aye," Aiden breathed. For a moment he remained where he was, his body touching hers, his hands resting on her waist, savoring of the feel of her against him. It felt right. Natural. And when he stepped back he felt suddenly cold, as though he'd stepped away from the warmth of a winter's fire into a cold night.

"Come then," he said gruffly, not looking at Kara. "I hope the horses havenae wandered too far."

They left the cave in silence. They emerged onto the beach and made the climb back up to the top of the cliff. Aiden went first and helped Kara up the steeper bits, holding out his hand and supporting her as she climbed. She smiled her gratitude and Aiden felt his insides twist every time. If he'd thought he was hyper-aware of her before, now it was even worse. Every touch of her hand sent his skin tingling. Every look she gave him sent a thrill through his body.

He was glad to reach the horses and mount up. He set a brisk pace back to Dun Arnwick which precluded much talking. He almost breathed a sigh of relief when the castle came into view. They rode into the bailey and dismounted, two stable-lads running to take the horses.

"Aye, well, I'd best go report to my father. He'll want to know what the crofters said and I promised to lead a training session," Aiden said, shifting his feet awkwardly.

"Yeah, you'd better," Kara replied. "And I'd better go see Lucy. I said I'd help out in the infirmary again this afternoon."

"Then I'll bid ye good day," he bowed formally then turned on his tail and strode towards his father's study. He told himself he wasn't running away.

Chapter 12

"VERY GOOD!" DOUGIE said with a grin. "Now, one more time so I can check ye have the intonation right."

Kara concentrated and said the sentence again, pronouncing every word with care. "Conas atá tú inniu?"

Dougie nodded in satisfaction. "Perfect, lass. If I didnae know any better, I'd say ye were a native speaker."

He sat propped up in his bed in the infirmary with an array of books laid out on his lap. His chest infection had improved considerably and Lucy predicted he'd be able to leave the infirmary soon.

"You're just being kind," Kara replied. "Beth says I sound like a bear with a sore tooth."

Dougie barked a laugh. "Ha! Our Beth likes to tease. Ye are a natural, lass, take it from me!"

Kara smiled and reached out for another book. She'd been spending a lot of time in the library learning everything she could about Dun Arnwick, sixteenth century Scotland, and anything that might lead her to Irene MacAskill.

"How's yer reading coming on?" Dougie asked.

Kara made a face. "Not well. Reading Gaelic is much harder than speaking it."

Dougie frowned, his bushy eyebrows pulling together. "Nonsense! 'Tis practice, that's all, just like everything else."

Kara sighed dramatically. In truth, she was enjoying learning Gaelic from Dougie but they both enjoyed acting the part of impatient teacher and recalcitrant student as well. Kara picked up one of the books she'd brought from the library. The tome had caught her eye immediately. The script inside was ornate and looked very old, the pages brittle with age and carefully decorated with beautiful illuminations. In her time, such a book would be priceless and historians and curators the world over would be falling over themselves to get hold of it.

She propped the book on her knee and opened the cover.

Dougie pointed at the book and his tone took on that of a teacher addressing his student. "Ye can start by reading the first few pages. It's a child's book—perfect for a beginner!"

Kara rolled her eyes at him. He'd taken to his role as teacher with alacrity but Kara kind of enjoyed it. Dougie was fun to be around and was like the kindly grandfather she'd never had. Lucy said that Dougie had been improving more quickly since he'd taken on teaching Kara and she was more than happy to do anything that might aid his recovery. So she pulled her chair closer to Dougie's bed and angled it so he could see the book in her lap. Then she began to read.

Like she'd said, her reading of Gaelic was very rudimentary and she found herself having to stop and be corrected by Dougie three or four times every sentence. But she persevered and as she continued, she found it becoming easier.

The book appeared to be a collection of fairy stories. The first one talked about a stone circle high on a lonely hillside. According to the story it was a portal between worlds and each full moon the Fae would come forth and kidnap any mortals stupid enough to wander into the circle.

Kara paused suddenly. Something tickled the back of her mind. A memory, faint and slippery like a dream. She frowned, trying to remember. Something...

Suddenly she remembered cold air on her skin, branches clawing at her as she climbed. Tall, dark stones rising up around her like jagged teeth. And voices. Voices calling, *Ye are ours. Ye have come home.*

"Are ye well, lass?"

Kara jumped as Dougie laid a hand on her arm. She hadn't realized she'd been staring into space, or that the book had slipped from her knee, forgotten. She blinked, forced herself to focus on Dougie. "I...I'm fine."

"Ye dinna look fine," the old man said, concern creasing his weathered face. "Ye look like ye've seen a ghost."

A cold overcame her, a cold so bone chilling it seemed to sink right into her soul. Shadows danced on the edge of her vision...*Ye are ours. Come to us.*

Kara shivered. A fire roared in the hearth but cold seeped through Kara's veins and with it came a sense of dread. Of foreboding. As though something terrible was about to happen. She looked around quickly. Sunlight poured through the windows and on the other side of the infirmary Beth was changing sheets, humming as she worked.

Kara breathed out slowly. All was as it should be. There was nothing to worry about.

You're being ridiculous, she told herself. *Get a grip.*

The door opened and a maid burst in. Beth and Lucy looked up from where they were working.

"What is it?" Lucy asked.

"My lady," the maid said. "Laird Andrew requests yer presence in the Great Hall immediately. There's been another attack."

AIDEN BENT HIS KNEES, careful to keep his back straight, and got his arms around the big block of stone. He straightened his legs, grunting at the effort, and slowly lifted the block before carefully carrying it over to the wall foundation and laying it on top. He crouched, checking it was in the right place whilst Ceardach measured it and gave a grunt of affirmation.

"Aye, that'll just about do it," Ceardach said.

"Hear that, lads?" Aiden said to the men gathered around him. "We've got it lined up. Now put yer backs into it and we'll have this wall built by noon!"

The eight other men groaned but set to work. They were out in the northern paddock, repairing a wall that had come down during a recent storm. It ran close to the cliff-edge and if they didn't repair it before the winter snows set in in earnest, the rest of the wall would likely collapse and go crashing into the sea.

The men fell into easy companionship, each man knowing what they needed to do, and exchanging good-natured banter as they worked.

Aiden was soon puffing and sweating but found himself enjoying the work. There was something simple about working with his men to achieve a goal. No politics. No worrying about the future. They knew what they had to do and got on with it.

"Easy, lad," said Ceardach, standing with his hands on hips. "Ye've moved three of the damned things already. What are ye trying to do? Shame the rest of us into working harder?"

Drake came up and gave a wink. "Nah, he's hoping a certain young lady might be watching. What better way to impress her than by showing how big and strong he is?"

The rest of the men burst into laughter and Aiden scowled. "I dinna think ye are one to talk, Drake Harris," he said. "What did I see ye doing the other day? Following Myra around the market whilst she looked at dresses!"

The men laughed again—at Drake's expense this time. Aiden returned to his work. Lord, was he that obvious that even the men had noticed? He thought he'd hidden his feelings for Kara but that obviously wasn't the case. In the last fortnight since they'd returned from the sea cave he'd just about being going out of his mind with thoughts of her. He found himself dreaming about her at night and finding excuses to bump into her during the day. In the evenings, when they all gathered in the Great Hall, he sat with her and they talked, told stories, played chess and tafl.

But he'd been careful not to be alone with her. If he did, he wasn't sure he'd be able to control himself. The way he'd lost control at the sea cave scared him a little. He was a warrior, trained and disciplined. He could keep calm in the chaos of battle. He could remain detached, able to make rational decisions whilst chaos raged around him. So why was he unable to think straight whenever Kara was around? Why did her presence turn his thoughts to mush and his legs to water?

It made no sense. No sense at all.

He lifted another stone into place under Ceardach's careful instruction. Skilled in engineering, Ceardach was Dun Arnwick's master builder. He eyed the newly laid stones with a quizzical eye, checking they were straight and placed correctly to bear the wall's weight. Only when he was satisfied, did they continue.

They worked like this for several hours and gradually the wall repairs took shape. Aiden lost himself in the work. The physical labor and the banter of the men around him meant he was able to push away his worries and live just in the moment. They'd almost finished the repairs when a figure came hurrying out of the gates of Dun Arnwick towards them.

The figure seemed to be in a hurry and all but ran the distance to the edge of the paddock. Aiden straightened. It was Bhradain. He was out of breath and waved his arms to get their attention.

"Come quickly," he said, gasping. "Great Hall...now. Raiders....another attack."

Aiden's heart thudded. In an instant his light mood evaporated to be replaced by a churning anger. Without a word he broke into a run for the gates, Bhradain by his side. He took the steps up to the Great Hall two at a time and hurried inside. His parents were already seated at the high table, with a group of villagers standing in front of them. His father waved for Aiden and Bhradain to join them and they took seats at the high table. Aiden sat by his father's side, palms resting flat on the smooth oak surface. In front of the table a sorry band of survivors were telling their tale. There were only five of them, all that was left of a small community over by St. Margaret's Bay. Everyone else had either been killed or carried off by Irish raiders who had hit the settlement that morning.

"We hid, my lord," an old man said, wringing his hands in his grief. "I didnae know what else to do. We hid in the cellar and by, the grace of God, they didnae find us. When we came out, they'd set the village alight and scattered whatever animals they couldnae take aboard their ships. I should have helped my people. I'm a coward, lord."

Andrew rose from his seat and approached the man. Laying one of his meaty hands on the man's shoulders, he looked him in the eye. "Ye did the right thing. If ye'd have fought, ye and yer family would also likely have been killed or taken. Ye were wise to hide, there's nay shame in that."

Aiden met his father's eyes. His gaze smoldered with anger. Aiden could see the desire to ride out himself battling with the knowledge he had to stay to lead the clan.

"Ye know what to do, son," Andrew growled. "Find them and bring them to justice."

Aiden punched his hand to his heart in salute. "Aye, sir. Jamie, Drake, to me. Have the war band muster and be ready to ride within the hour. Gather in the courtyard and make sure everyone is kitted for battle."

Jamie and Drake ran off to do his bidding and Aiden hurried through the castle to his own chamber. Once there he pulled off his sweat-covered clothes and donned a fresh shirt and plaid. Over this went a leather hauberk, greaves and boots. He strapped a brace of daggers around his waist and deposited two into the tops of his boots. His claymore and shield lay propped against one wall. He would grab them before he left.

As he donned his battle-gear Aiden felt his mind settle into that calm detachment he found only before battle. His thoughts retreated, his worries became something for another day. There was only this moment. This time. The next heartbeat. The next indrawn breath. The next moment that might be your last. Deep inside him a roiling anger burned. Fury that these bastards would harm his people. But his anger was distant, something he was aware of, but it did not control him. He was cold, clear-headed, ready to fight.

There was a knock on the door. Aiden yanked it open, expecting to find one of his warriors on the other side. He went stock-still when he saw that it was Kara. She had her arms wrapped around herself as if cold and her face was pale.

"Can I come in?"

Aiden pulled the door wide. "Of course."

She strode past him and stood by the fireplace, staring down into the cold ashes. Aiden closed the door and turned to face her.

"Is somewhat wrong, lass?"

She whirled to face him and Aiden was shocked by the expression on her face. She looked desolate, her skin like alabaster.

"Don't go," she choked out. "Please don't go."

His calm detachment shattered like glass. In its place a fierce protectiveness welled up. Kara looked more vulnerable than he'd ever seen her. The brave facade was gone and instead she looked terrified. He longed to step forward and enfold her in his arms, to hold her like he never wanted to let her go. But he didn't.

"I must, lass," he said gently. "It is my duty. Who else would go in my place?"

"None of you should go!" she cried. "This is wrong. Wrong!"

"What do ye mean? We must bring these men to justice. If we dinna—"

"But not like this," she interrupted. "This isn't how it's supposed to happen. I can feel it." She looked at him and for a second he thought he saw shadows shifting in her eyes. He remembered a ring of standing stones high on a hillside and a shiver of unease ran down his spine.

"Dinna worry, lass," he said. He stepped close and put a finger under her chin, tilting her head back to look at him. "We've faced brigands such as these many times and each time we've defeated them. This will be nay different. Ye have to trust me. Ye trust me dinna ye?"

She gazed up at him for a long moment and some of the anguish receded. "I...I...." she looked around, trying to find the words. "I just have this terrible feeling." She squeezed her eyes shut and took a deep breath before opening them again. "Promise, me," she demanded. "Promise me you'll be careful. Promise me you'll come back."

Oh, how he longed to hold her in his arms. How he longed to bend down and kiss those lips. But he knew where that would lead and it was too dangerous. He needed to be cold, detached, focused for what was to come. So instead he raised her hand to his lips and kissed her fingers.

"My lady," he said formally. "I give ye my word as a Harris that I will return."

She straightened and nodded. "Good. I'll hold you to that."

He nodded in turn then bade her farewell, grabbed his sword and shield and walked out of the door. As he neared the end of the corridor he looked back. Through the open door of his chamber he saw Kara standing there, watching him leave.

His heart twisted. *I'll always come back to ye*, he thought to himself. *Always*.

Chapter 13

KARA DIDN'T WATCH THEM leave. The terrible sense of foreboding hadn't left her but she did her best to push it to one side. Aiden was a trained soldier and had fought in many battles, just like he'd said. He had the garrison of Dun Arnwick around him to face a ragtag bunch of raiders. He would be fine. He would. She was being irrational.

So she tried to forget what she'd sensed and busied herself around the castle. She went down to the kitchens and enquired if there was anything she could do to be helpful and was promptly sent to collect firewood from the stack by the outer pasture.

She wrapped her cloak about herself against the cold wind and made her way out to the log pile.

There was a wheelbarrow here for transporting the wood and Kara began filling it with logs. It was hard, heavy work, and Kara was glad of the exertion. It soon pushed her worries to the back of her mind. By the time she'd filled the barrow, she was sweating, despite the cold wind. She grabbed the handles of the barrow and was just about to start pushing it back to the kitchen when a sudden wave of dizziness washed over her. She crashed to her knees, pressing her hands to her temples.

Her vision blurred and when it cleared she didn't see the barrow, the log pile or Dun Arnwick anymore. Instead, she saw a rocky path through a wooded valley at the base of a sharp escarpment. A group of mounted men came riding down the road and Kara's heart leapt as she recognized Aiden in the lead. Then shouts suddenly echoed around them and men came pouring out of a cleft in the escarpment, shouting in a language Kara didn't recognize. They ran towards Aiden's group, weapons flashing in the sunlight.

Then her vision shifted and she saw a ring of standing stones outlined against the sky. Voices whispered in her head. *Embrace who ye are. Come to us. Ye are ours.*

A terrible, roaring pain rampaged through her skull and she clamped her fingers over her temples, trying to drown out the voices, the images. "No! Leave me alone! Thu cha toir mi!"

Then someone was kneeling next to her and hands were gently taking her shoulders. "Kara, what is it? Kara?"

She opened her eyes to see Lucy and Beth crouched on either side of her, their eyes wide with concern.

"I have to see Andrew," Kara gasped, pushing them aside and climbing to her feet. "It's a trap. They're riding into a trap." She took a few steps but staggered as the dizziness returned. Lucy and Beth shared a look and then took her by the elbows.

"All right," Lucy said. "This way."

They guided her to the Great Hall where Andrew was sitting with Bhradain, going over some papers. The laird looked up in alarm when he saw his wife and daughter enter, supporting Kara between them.

"What is it?" Andrew asked. "Kara, lass, are ye well?"

She pushed away from Lucy and Beth's support and faced Andrew. "Go after them," she rasped. "Aiden and the others. You have to stop them. It's a trap."

Andrew frowned. "Trap? What do ye mean, lass? However could ye know that?"

Kara shook her head. She didn't have time for this. She had to make them believe her. She knew, with a cold, hard certainty that the vision she'd seen was true. "I can't tell you how I know because I don't know myself. But I do." She met the laird's stern gaze, imploring him to believe her. "Please," she said. "If you don't go after them, Aiden is going to die."

Lucy gasped and Andrew stared at her in shock. "Listen, lass. I can see ye are upset by Aiden riding into danger but ye must get a hold of yerself. Ye canna go around making such claims without evidence. I suggest ye retire to yer room. Ye will feel better once ye've rested."

Kara slammed her fist down on the table, upsetting a jar of ink that spilled a black puddle across the oaken surface. "You're not listening to me! I'm right on this—I know I am! You have to go after them! If I'm wrong, you can throw me in a cell or whatever you like, just as long as you go after them!"

Lucy stepped up beside Kara. "Husband, I think you should listen to her. I think there's more to this than we realize. When we found her she was shouting in Gaelic and the words she was using." She glanced at Kara and her eyes were wide and wary. "The only person I've ever heard speak those words before is Irene MacAskill."

Andrew glanced from his wife to Kara and back again. He rubbed his chin and then finally threw up his hands.

"Very well. Bhradain, summon the rest of the garrison. Leave only a skeleton command to protect Dun Arnwick. We ride out immediately."

Bhradain's expression turned incredulous. "What? Ye canna be serious, my lord! Surely ye dinna give credence to such superstitious nonsense? I'm sure Lady Kara believes what she's saying but tis nay more than silly womanish worrying!"

Andrew turned to his foster-son. "Bhradain, if there is one thing I've learned, it's not to be complacent where Irene MacAskill is concerned. Now do as I bid."

He began striding from the hall and Kara fell into step beside him.

"Where do ye think ye are going?" Andrew demanded, turning to her and putting his hands on his hips.

"With you," she replied. He opened his mouth to reply but Kara held up a hand to stop him. "You'll have to tie me up to make me stay behind."

"Let her go," Lucy said. Her voice was filled with worry. "Andrew, bring our son safe home."

Andrew nodded. "I will." Then to Kara he said, "Ye will stay in the middle of the group and do exactly as I say."

Kara nodded. She would agree to anything as long as she got help for Aiden and the others.

Andrew nodded tightly and together he and Kara strode from the hall.

AIDEN HELD UP HIS HAND for silence. Around him, the men pulled their horses to a halt and silently slid their weapons from their scabbards, eyes scanning the terrain. Aiden went perfectly still, listening. There was only silence. No call of birds, no whisper of the wind. But there was something...

He slid from the saddle and landed lightly on the ground. Placing his hand flat against the damp earth, he closed his eyes for a moment, letting the sounds and smells wash over him. Ahead, something moved in the underbrush. Signaling for the men to wait, he drew his sword and held it in a two-handed grip. He padded silently forward, eyes trained on the patch of shadow in the undergrowth.

Something exploded out of the bushes. He managed to fling himself to the side just as a wild boar and her family of piglets hurtled by, squealing loud enough to wake the dead. They thundered past him and disappeared into the woods to Aiden's left. He blew out a long breath and ran his fingers through his hair, thankful there hadn't been a male with that family otherwise it would likely have attacked rather than running.

He returned to his horse and remounted, signaling the column on its way. The men obeyed without a word, his uncle Jamie passing him a water skin from which Aiden took a long drink. Lord above, but he wished it was whisky in there rather than water.

He'd felt uneasy since the moment he'd ridden from Dun Arnwick. They'd thundered away from the castle, pushing the mounts to a gallop but as they'd neared their destination Aiden had slowed them to a walk. It was likely that the enemy had scouts and pickets around their camp watching out for visitors and Aiden wanted to avoid giving their quarry any advance warning. So for the last half an hour they'd picked their way with care along a trail that wound across the steep side of a river valley. Below them the valley fell away to a dark, tangled mass of vegetation that surrounded the river and to their right rose a sheer limestone escarpment. It was along this escarpment that they made their careful way.

He pulled up his horse and scanned the terrain ahead.

"What is it, lad?" Jamie asked. "What do ye see?"

"Look how the valley narrows ahead, with those two rocks sticking out on either side. If ye were a brigand where would ye position scouts?"

Jamie studied the view. "Aye," he said at last. "If they'd positioned scouts, then it's likely they'll be atop those spurs."

"But they're not," Aiden replied. "I've been watching those positions from the moment we arrived and there's been nay movement up there at all. Why would they ignore the best scouting spot around here?"

Jamie shrugged. "Perhaps they're nay very good brigands?"

"Maybe," Aiden muttered. "But I dinna like it."

They carried on moving and after ten minutes or so the trail wound around a bend in the escarpment and Aiden found himself face to face with a rockslide. Some of the escarpment had fallen away and the trail ahead was blocked by a gigantic pile of rocks and debris. A second, smaller trail branched off from the one they were following and descended into the valley bottom, towards the river.

Jamie stood in his stirrups and examined the rock face. "Looks recent. Maybe the recent snows dislodged it." He glanced at the second trail. "Seems we've only got one path to take."

He nudged his horse down the second trail but Aiden held up his hand.

"Wait."

The men looked at him expectantly.

"There's something wrong here. This doesnae feel right."

"We dinna have much choice, lad," Jaimie replied. "There's nay other way to go. It's either take this path or turn around and retrace our steps around the valley. That will take all day."

"We havenae ridden all this way for naught," Angus added from behind. "If we leave now, these bastards will attack again. We have to finish it."

There were rumbles of agreement but still Aiden hesitated. His instincts, honed from years of fighting for his life against impossible odds, were screaming at him that something was wrong.

He pulled a breath, trying to calm his doubts. *It's just what Kara said*, he told himself. *Ye are on edge because of her warning, that's all. And Angus is right. We need to finish this.*

He nodded tightly. "Stay alert. Eyes wide and weapons drawn. Angus, Jamie, take point. Roald, Sean, Grant, form a rearguard. The rest of ye follow me, those with horse bows, have them ready."

With that they moved off down the trail, Aiden in the lead, Jamie and Angus off in the trees to either side, the rest of his men spread out behind. To begin with the ground was relatively open, free from underbrush and they were able to move in formation but the trees soon closed in, thick bushes appearing to either side and they were forced together, their lines of sight reduced to only a few meters.

A shiver walked down Aiden's spine, a sudden sense of danger. He held up his hand and everyone went still. They stood in a small clearing, surrounded on all sides by trees and thick vegetation. Ahead of them the trail disappeared into the shadow between two holly bushes. A thick carpet of moss blanketed the ground and the trunks of the trees, deadening all sound. And then Aiden realized what had been bothering him. It was silent. Too silent.

"Ambush!" he yelled, wheeling his mount just as ten, twenty, thirty figures, materialized from the underbrush, each bearing wicked-looking weapons. Aiden pulled his mount around in a circle but it was no good.

They were surrounded.

FIRE BURNED DEEP WITHIN Kara's belly. It felt as though liquid flames surged through her veins, making it almost impossible to think straight. She had to get to Aiden. She had to.

Around her, the men of Dun Arnwick rode in grim silence, expressions stern, hands never far from their weapons. Laird Andrew rode at Kara's side, his eyes set on the road ahead. Bhradain rode on her other side, his expression thunderous. He'd not approved of them coming on this mission but once the laird had made up his mind he'd insisted on coming along. He kept glancing at Kara and she didn't like the look in his eyes. It looked like he was appraising her, as if trying to work out exactly what he was looking at.

Kara pushed all such concerns from her mind. Nothing mattered but reaching Aiden. Nothing. Not once did she stop to consider whether her hunch was correct, nor where her certainty came from. She knew. That was all.

They were cantering along a broad, well-trodden road that wound through the interior of the island. Andrew's intelligence had suggested the brigands had left the coast and had used one of the rivers to make their way inland, hoping to throw off the trail of Andrew's patrols that rode the coastal roads and had made camp in a narrow valley. Although they were moving as fast as the muddy terrain would allow, this wasn't fast enough for Kara. Every moment they delayed put Aiden in greater danger.

They reached a cross roads and Andrew called a halt. He looked around, studying each road in turn. Kara didn't hesitate. She pulled her mare on the eastern path and continued riding. Behind her, she heard Andrew curse and then spur his horse to catch up with her.

"What are ye doing?" he demanded. "We need to check the map. I canna be sure this is the road they've taken."

"I'm sure," Kara replied without slowing. "This is the right way. Follow me."

The fire in her belly tugged her, pulling her ever onward. Andrew swore loudly then barked orders to his men. In moments they'd fanned out on either side of her, keeping pace but letting her lead. They soon found themselves riding into a river valley. The road they followed hugged the upper slopes of the valley but they soon found their way blocked by a landslide. Kara pulled her horse onto a path that snaked further down the hill towards the valley bottom. The fire in her belly was increasing. She was near her goal now. So near her goal. Fear for Aiden made her reckless and she pushed the horse to ever greater speed, even though the trail was steep and muddy.

Then she heard it.

The unmistakable sound of fighting came from ahead: the clash of steel, the hoarse shouts of men. Around her Andrew and his warriors drew weapons but Kara set her heels to her horse and sent it springing away.

She rounded a bend in the path and found a scene of carnage. A battle raged on the road ahead. She saw scores of strangely-dressed men engaged in fierce fighting with the men of Dun Arnwick who appeared to have been surrounded in a clearing. Aiden himself had been unhorsed and was on his feet fighting three men. They wielded axes and clubs as well as swords and hacked at Aiden with savage ferocity. He parried the blows with blinding speed, blocking one stroke and answering with a riposte that took one man across the throat, before spinning and lopping the head off another. One man got through his guard and raked a blade across Aiden's arm. He grunted with pain, one arm going limp, before head-butting his attacker and then running him through.

But the tide was endless. More men replaced those Aiden had dispatched.

"Aiden!" Kara screamed.

Andrew barked orders to his men and they rode to the aid of their kinsmen but Aiden was on the far side of the clearing, a wall of brigands between them.

Kara threw herself from her horse and waded into the press of battle. Down here at ground level the fighting was terrifying. Everywhere she looked there were struggling bodies and flashing blades. The stench of sweat and blood filled the air.

Some rational part of her mind was screaming that this was crazy, that she would surely be killed, but that rational part of her was drowned out by the need to reach Aiden. The fire welled up in her, burning through her veins, burning away fear and doubt, bringing with it a strange clarity. She knew what she had to do.

Around her, time seemed to slow. A brigand moved to intercept her. He was dirty and unshaven and a leering grin split his face as he saw her—an easy target. He reached out, grimy hands grabbing, but to Kara he seemed to move in slow-motion. She ducked easily under his reach, and moved on, stepping away as another man swung a sword at snail-pace in her direction. She heard a 'twang' and turned to see an arrow moving towards her. It shifted so slowly through the air that she stepped out of its path and it stuck into a tree instead. Time moved like treacle dripping from a spoon. She was only yards from Aiden now. He had his back to a large boulder and was battling with a large man more richly dressed than the others.

A she stepped into his vicinity, time caught up and the clash of fighting rolled over her once more. Aiden and the big man fought viciously, their blades clashing in a series of blows so fast she could hardly track them. They were evenly matched and the brigand was clearly a skilled swordsman. Aiden dropped to the ground, swept the other man's legs out from under him and sent him crashing to the ground. But the man rolled, coming to his feet, swinging his blade at Aiden's neck. Aiden caught the blade on his own and the two men strained against each other, neither able to gain the advantage.

Then Kara heard another 'twang' and turned to see an arrow speeding at Aiden. He had no chance. The arrow would take him right in the back.

With a strangled cry Kara threw herself between Aiden and the arrow, raising her hand, words streaming out of her mouth. They were Gaelic but she had no idea what they were. The arrow slowed then stopped, hanging in mid-air just inches from Kara's outstretched palm. Then it fell to the ground with a thud.

Aiden disengaged from the man he was fighting, spun around and ran at the boulder. He vaulted atop it then used its height advantage to leap on the brigand. The big man brought his blade up to defend himself but Aiden's momentum carried his down-swing straight through the man's defenses and into his neck. The man collapsed to his knees, clutching at the wound. Aiden swung his sword, taking the man's head from his body.

He spun towards Kara. "Get behind me! This isnae over yet."

He grabbed her arm and pushed her towards the boulder, just as another wave of men charged Aiden. The brigands fought ferociously. Aiden seemed to be their target. Three more came at him and Aiden stepped forward to meet them, short-sword held in one hand, a knife in the other.

"Stay back!" he bellowed at the men. "Ye willnae get near her!"

If Kara had thought he'd fought fiercely before, she was mistaken. Aiden moved so fast she barely registered his movements. He stabbed and kicked and parried and punched, his movements so smooth and economical it was almost a dance. In no time at all the three men lay dead at his feet.

Aiden looked around for more opponents but the battle was over. Andrew and his men were finishing off the last of them and rounding up those that surrendered. Aiden dropped his weapons and spun to Kara.

The look in his eyes almost stopped her heart. His expression was full of raw, wild fury and something else. Fear. He grabbed her arms. "What, by all that's holy, are ye doing here? Have ye lost yer mind?"

"Isn't that obvious?" she said, facing down his anger with her chin raised. "I came for you."

"Ye could have been killed!" he bellowed. He shook her. "Do ye hear me? Ye could have been killed! And then what would I have done?"

"Aiden, you're hurting me," Kara gasped.

He released her and stepped back but his eyes lost none of their intensity. He opened his mouth to speak but Andrew strode up.

"They're captured or scattered," he said to his son. "What happened here?"

Aiden forced his attention to his father. "My thanks for riding out, Father. It was an ambush. They knew the road we were taking and lay in wait. I suspected they caused the rock fall in order to force us onto this narrower path, better suited to taking us unawares." He looked at the Harris men gathered around him. There were plenty of wounded but seemed to be no fatalities. "As grateful as I am for miracles—what are ye doing here, Father? How did ye know about the ambush?"

"I didnae," Andrew replied. "It was Lady Kara that warned us. Wouldnae rest until she'd convinced me to ride out after ye and if I'd have refused I reckon she would have ridden out on her own anyway."

Aiden turned to look at Kara. There was a question in his eyes, one that she couldn't answer. Her memories of the battle were becoming hazy, like dream images, but she remembered dodging through the combatants and stopping an arrow meant for Aiden. She shivered. What the hell was happening to her?

"I would like some answers," Andrew said. "How did they know where ye and yer men would be? How did they learn of our plans? Was it lucky happenstance or do we have a traitor among us? Bring him!"

Two of Andrew's men approached, dragging a struggling figure between them. He was a large boned man with wide shoulders, a shaven head and a bushy beard. A swirling tattoo covered one half of his face. As he was forced to kneel on the ground he glared up at Andrew and then spat at the laird's feet.

"Who are ye?" Andrew demanded. "Why have ye come to our lands?"

The man answered in a thick accent that made him difficult to understand. "Isnae that obvious? Yer lands are fat and rich. Easy plunder."

Andrew stiffened. "How did ye know where my son would be? Who told ye where to wait for them? Answer me or by God, I'll make ye wish ye'd never been born!"

The man smiled, showing bloody teeth. He looked around the group and his eyes narrowed when they rested on Bhradain. "Well, that is quite a story."

Suddenly Bhradain jumped forward brandishing a knife. With a cry he plunged it into the man's neck. The man's eyes flew wide and he scrabbled uselessly at the blood welling from the wound. With a horrifying gurgle, the man toppled forward and lay still.

For a heartbeat there was shocked silence in the glade then Aiden grabbed Bhradain by the tunic and pulled his face close. "Have ye lost yer mind? He was our way of gathering information! We are Harris Clan! We dinna murder prisoners!"

"He was going to attack the laird!" Bhradain spat back. "See for yerself!"

Andrew stepped forward and rolled the man's body over. Sure enough, he had a small dagger, no longer than his little finger, nestled in the palm of one hand. Andrew blew out a breath, and leaned with his elbows resting on his knees. "It seems we'll find nothing here. We shall have to look elsewhere for the answers we seek."

Aiden let Bhradain go but continued to glare at his foster-brother. Bhradain ignored him and instead stepped up to Andrew. "What I would like to know, my laird, is how Lady Kara knew there would be an ambush and where to come to intercept it."

Andrew rose to his feet. "What are ye suggesting?"

Bhradain's eyes fixed on Kara and she almost quailed under his cold, calculating look. "Nothing," he said aloud. Then under his breath, so low that only Kara could hear, he added, "but I suspect much."

Kara wrapped her arms around herself and looked away. She suddenly felt exhausted, like a wrung-out dishcloth.

"Burn the bodies, see to yer wounds, then mount up," Andrew instructed. "We return to Dun Arnwick."

Kara took a step towards her horse and stumbled as exhaustion turned her legs to water. Aiden caught her before she could hit the ground and carried her over to his own horse who'd been retrieved by one of the other men. Without a word he lifted her into the saddle.

In short order they'd dealt with the bodies of the brigands, had addressed the most urgent wounds of their own men, and were mounted and ready to leave. Aiden nudged his horse into a walk and Kara felt herself slumping back against him, his chest a welcome solidity in this crazy, shifting day. He didn't speak and Kara was reluctant to break the silence. Fury still rolled off him in waves and Kara struggled to understand it. Wasn't he pleased she'd led Andrew to them? Would he rather have faced those brigands alone?

She couldn't figure out what she'd done wrong and she was too exhausted to think straight. The rolling gait of the horse lulled her and she found herself dozing in the saddle. When the horse stopped suddenly she came awake with a start to see the inner bailey of Dun Arnwick around her. Beth and Lucy were hurrying down the steps, an army of healers and servants behind them.

Aiden dropped from the saddle and Lucy enveloped her son in a fierce hug. "You're okay?" she demanded. "You're not hurt?"

Aiden glanced up at Kara who still sat in the saddle. "Nay, mother. I'm nay hurt."

"Thank God," Lucy breathed before moving off to greet her husband.

Aiden held up a hand and helped Kara out of the saddle. The clamor of voices surrounded her, asking questions, relaying everything that had happened. To Kara it sounded like the clanging of a hundred discordant church bells. She wanted nothing more than to get away from that noise and find some quiet.

"I have to get out of here," she muttered. She pushed away from Aiden and took two steps before Aiden caught her arm, spinning her around.

"Where are ye going, lass? My father will want a full report."

She shook her head. "It'll have to wait. I need some space."

Aiden looked at her intently and then nodded. "Aye, mayhap ye do." He turned to his father and they had a quick, quiet discussion, before Aiden returned to Kara's side. He took her arm and helped her to stagger up the steps and into the keep.

On their way through the castle Kara could feel Aiden like a glowering presence at her side but he said not a word. They reached Kara's door without speaking. He pushed open the door to her chamber and helped her inside. She slumped gratefully onto a chair by the window.

It was blessedly quiet here and for the first time since the battle she could finally think straight.

"I must return to my father," Aiden said tightly. He didn't look at her but spun on his heel and headed for the door.

"Is that it?" Kara asked.

Aiden stopped in his tracks then turned to face her. "Is that what?"

"Is that all you're going to say?"

A vein in his temple throbbed. "What would ye like me to say?"

Anger shot through her. "Oh, I don't know, Aiden! Maybe *I'm glad you turned up when you did, Kara.* Maybe *how are you doing, Kara?* Maybe *I'm sorry I scared you witless today, Kara, but I'm okay so you can stop worrying now!*"

Aiden said nothing. He stared at her and she could see the shifting emotions behind his eyes. Finally he said, "Ye shouldnae have been there today."

"What is wrong with you?" she shouted. "You've barely spoken two words on the way home. Why are you annoyed with me? Because I saved your life?" She quailed suddenly as memories flooded her. Of arrows stopping in mid-air. Of time seeming to slow. Had Aiden seen that? "Or is it because of what I did in the glade? Do you think I'm a witch?"

AIDEN STARED AT KARA. He could hardly believe his ears. Did she really not understand? Did she really think he gave two figs about the abilities she'd demonstrated? The incident at the standing stones had told Aiden there was something different about Kara and her actions had only confirmed it. But that's not what was bothering him. He was grateful to her for riding out to rescue him but that didn't override the dominant emotion coursing through his veins. Anger. Or was it fear? He could no longer tell.

"Ye think I care about such things?" he snapped. "Ye think I'm annoyed because I think ye are a witch? Give me more credit than that!"

"Then what?" she demanded, jumping to her feet and glaring at him. "Because from where I'm standing all I did was save your life and get a whole load of agro for my troubles!" Her eyes flashed and her chin tilted defiantly.

His restraint snapped and he grabbed her forearms. "Dinna ye understand? I'm angry because ye could have died today! Any of those men could have killed ye! A stray arrow, a sword-point in the back, Lord, even a fall from a horse would have done it. Ye could have died, Kara! And then where would I be? Dinna ye understand that it's my duty to protect ye?"

"I don't hold you to your vow—"

"I'm not talking about that! Vow be damned! It's my duty to protect ye because I love ye! Havenae ye figured it out by now?"

She went very still. Her eyes were big and round as she stared up at him. There. He'd said it now. The words had been gnawing away inside him for weeks, trying to find a way out but it was only when he'd seen her in danger this afternoon that they'd grabbed him, made him face up to what had been inside him all this time. He loved her. Lord help him, he loved her more than life itself.

"Aiden," she breathed and there was a world of promises in that single word. "Oh my God. Aiden." She reached up and cupped his face in her hands. Her touch sent a thrill right through his body. He stared at her, unblinking, hardly daring to breathe. She studied his face, her eyes roving over his features as though drinking them in. And then she said it. Those words he'd dreamed of hearing.

"I love you too."

FOR ONE LONG, TIMELESS moment, Aiden said nothing. He stood frozen, his hands still gripping her forearms, his expression unreadable. Then his lips found hers and she answered hungrily, allowing all the pent up emotion of the day to sweep her up on a tide of need and desire. He loved her. Oh God, he loved her. In all her life she would never get tired of hearing those words.

Then all of a sudden he had her up against the wall, her back pressing painfully into the hard stone. Kara barely noticed it. Her senses were deluged by Aiden. By his mouth on hers, by his hot breath on her face, by his hard chest crushing her breasts between them, by his hands that roved up and down her sides, sending tingles of sheer pleasure across her skin. Kara wrapped her arms around his head and pulled him close. She wanted no distance between them. She wanted every part of him to touch every part of her.

Aiden's kisses moved down the line of her jaw to her neck and Kara threw her head back, letting out a low moan. Her fingers gripped his shoulders and then his back, feeling how his muscles had gone taut and as hard as rock. Where his body pressed against hers she felt the solid swell of his desire pressing against her stomach and the sensation sent her almost senseless with desire.

Aiden spun her around and whilst one hand hiked up her dress to caress her thighs and buttocks, the other quickly undid the myriad of clasps and buttons on the back. When he turned her back to face him, Kara had never been so glad to be rid of a garment. The dress fell to the floor between them, pooling by her feet, leaving her in only a thin chemise. Aiden's eyes raked over her, gone dark with lust.

"Beautiful," he whispered. "Every inch of ye."

Kara grabbed him, pulled him to her, wanting to feel his hands on her body. Aiden obliged, finding her mouth with his whilst his hands gripped her tightly, one on her waist, the other sweeping down her back. Kara plucked at the knot that held Aiden's plaid in place. It came undone easily and it slid between them to pool beside Kara's dress. This left Aiden in only his linen shirt but this was still too much for Kara. She wanted nothing between them. Nothing. She grabbed the linen and tugged it. Aiden raised his arms over his head, tore off the shirt, and tossed it away before kicking off his boots as well.

Kara drank in the sight of him. Naked from head to toe, he was more than she'd ever dreamed in a man. His body was tight and toned, the light playing over the contours of his muscles. But it was his eyes that caught and held her, sent her thoughts spinning in a mad dance. They were so filled with desire and need that it took her breath away.

With a low grunt Aiden grabbed her shift in his fist and pulled. The thin fabric tore easily and Aiden tossed it nonchalantly away. The cool air played across Kara's naked skin, sending goosebumps riding up her arms.

Aiden growled deep in his throat and yanked her hard against him. There was nothing between them now. Just skin and heat and desire. Kara wrapped her arms around him and Aiden lifted her, pressing her back against the wall, supporting her with his hands beneath her buttocks. She wrapped her legs around his hips and felt the tip of his manhood touch the spot between her legs that ached for him.

He looked into her eyes and in them she saw a future stretching out. A future for them.

"I love you," she whispered.

Aiden's eyes slid closed and he leaned forward, pressing his forehead to hers. Then he shifted his hips and entered her, his shaft piercing that hot, dark spot, finding her burning core of warmth and burying himself deeply. She tilted her hips, taking all of him, needing all of him, until she could feel him filling her.

Kara gasped, almost losing herself with the sensation of it. It felt right. She felt complete.

Aiden began to move inside her. His forehead dropped to her shoulder, his breath coming hot and ragged by her ear. Kara gripped him tightly, her hands on his shoulders, her legs around his hips as his thrusts became deeper, more urgent. Tiny gasps of pleasure began to escape Kara's lips and Aiden's breath came in a low, animal growl.

He was pounding her now, spearing her hard and deep, passion overwhelming both of them as they lost themselves to their desperate, hungry need for each other. The world around Kara disappeared until nothing mattered but this moment with Aiden, their bodies joined, as they should be.

The fire raging in Kara's core ignited her blood. Pure, blinding ecstasy engulfed her as she reached her climax and screamed Aiden's name. A moment later he groaned and shuddered, hips bucking as he emptied himself into her core.

For a long, timeless moment they stood there, each coming back to an awareness of the other, until finally Aiden raised his head and looked at her. His hair was tousled, his cheeks flushed and a thin sheen of sweat marked his brow. To Kara he was the most beautiful thing she'd ever seen. She leaned forward and gently wiped away the sweat and then kissed the end of his nose.

Aiden grinned, his face transformed into a look of pure delight then, still with her legs wrapped around his waist, he carried her over to the bed and laid them both down on the soft covers.

He crouched over her, his hair falling forward to tickle her face. "My wee lass," he breathed. "My Kara."

He leaned down and kissed her, gently this time, his lips moving slowly, tenderly across hers. Emotion swelled up in Kara and she felt the hot burn of tears in her eyes. How could she have found something like this in so unexpected a place? She'd never felt the way she did now. Complete. Like she'd come home. For the first time in her life, she was where she was meant to be and could finally stop running.

So she kissed him back. Kissed him so thoroughly she hoped he could read how she felt about him, pouring all her emotion into the act. Aiden kissed her cheeks, her nose, her forehead before rolling onto his back and pulling her into the crook of his arm. She snuggled against him, fitting her body against his and his arms came around to hold her close, circling her protectively.

"Ye have unmanned me, Kara," he mumbled into her hair. "I'm good for nothing now."

She looked up at him. "I hope there's one thing you're still good for because I haven't done with you yet." She raised herself up on her elbows and looked down at him. He watched her, eyes dark with lust once more. Slowly, she made circles across his skin with the tips of her fingers and was rewarded when goosebumps rippled across his torso.

He groaned and, glancing down, she saw the swell of his desire begin to grow once more. An answering ache lit deep within her. She leaned down to kiss him, passionately this time, and he suddenly grabbed her, lifted her atop him.

"I'll be good for that for as long as ye want me," he breathed.

Kara's thoughts exploded into fragments.

Chapter 14

IT WAS A LONG TIME since Aiden had slept so well or so deeply. Whilst on campaign he'd learned to sleep lightly because you never knew when the sudden order might come for you to wake or when a surprise attack would come in the night. So he slept lightly, weapons always within arms-reach. But not tonight. Tonight he fell into a deep slumber, every inch of him sated. His limbs were heavy with contentment, his mind settled and free of worry for what felt the first time in years.

And yet he remained aware. All through the night, he felt her against him, curled up against his chest and with her presence beside him, came a peace he'd rarely known. The ache inside of him was gone. He was at peace.

The first rays of sunlight falling through the window woke him the next morning. Beside him, Kara slept, her hair spilling across the pillow, her naked breasts rising and falling with her breath. Desire took Aiden and he wanted nothing more than to wake her, make love to her again. He couldn't remember how many times he'd taken her last night but he'd soon discovered that Kara's passion matched his own and it had gone on late into the night. But he could never get enough of this woman. Never.

He reached out and brushed a stray strand of hair from her face. She mumbled something but didn't wake. He tried to calm his arousal. No, he wouldn't wake her. Better to let her sleep. And besides, there was plenty of time for that now that she was his.

Mine, he thought, hardly able to believe it. *She's mine. She loves me.*

Just the very thought of it left him stunned.

Careful not to wake her, he climbed out of bed and stretched to work out the last vestiges of sleep. Then he dressed and planted a soft kiss on her head.

"Where are you going?" she mumbled, reaching out to twine her fingers through his.

"I'm sorry, lass," he replied. "I didnae mean to wake ye. I must be about my duties. I have training this morning. Ye sleep. I'll see ye later."

"You'd better," she muttered.

He kissed her again, untangled his fingers, and left the room. He seemed to float through the castle. He couldn't seem to stop grinning. The few servants he passed gave him quizzical looks but he didn't care. He wanted to shout to the world that Kara Buchanan was his. His!

When he reached his own chamber, he took a quick wash and changed his clothes. He was just strapping on his sword belt, ready for training, when there was a knock on his door. A page stood outside.

"Begging yer pardon, but yer father requests yer presence immediately, Aiden," the boy said.

"At this hour? What's this about, Rab?"

"I dinna ken, lord. I only know he's waiting for ye in his study."

"Very well, I'll attend immediately. My thanks."

The lad nodded and hurried off. Aiden finished buckling on his sword belt and then left his chamber. As he hurried through the corridors of the waking castle, a sense of unease descended on him. What could his father want to speak to him about at this hour? Surely a report on yesterday's events could wait until later? Had he learned of what had happened between him and Kara? Gossip in Dun Arnwick was rife and no doubt someone would have noticed that he'd spent the night in her chambers. He didn't care. He didn't care if the whole world knew he loved Kara Buchanan.

He reached his father's study, knocked on the door and entered. He found his mother and father waiting for him inside, both standing by the fire. His father was holding a parchment. The look on their faces made him pause.

"What is it?" he demanded. "I dinna know what ye may have heard of myself and Lady Kara but my intentions are completely honorable—"

"This isn't about Kara," Andrew interrupted him. "We wanted to talk to ye about this." He nodded at the scroll he was holding.

Aiden waited, saying nothing.

Andrew blew out a breath. "I think I've prepared ye well for the lairdship, son. Ye've learned the arts of governance and of leadership. Yer skill in battle was never in question." His eyes snapped up to meet Aiden's. "But yer conviction is."

Aiden frowned. "What are ye talking about?" He glanced at his mother to see that she was pale and her eyes filled with sadness. "Mother? What is going on here?"

She just shook her head mutely.

Andrew unrolled the scroll and began to read. "I, James, fifth of that name, King of Scotland, do hear by grant to Aiden Harris the title of Earl of Marischal and the estate of Dunnottar."

"Where did ye get that?" Aiden exploded. "How dare ye look through my private things?"

"Why didn't you tell us?" Lucy asked, her voice stricken. "Why didn't you tell us you were leaving? You've let us think you were back to stay, you've let us make plans for yer future, get used to having you around again. How could you deceive us like that?"

Aiden opened his mouth for an angry retort but the pain in his mother's eyes made him pause. "It wasnae like that," he began. "I meant to tell ye as soon as I returned but then the complications with Kara and Irene happened and it never seemed like the right time."

"That's yer explanation?" Andrew snapped. "That it wasnae the right time? Lord above, I would hope for a little honesty from my only son. Havenae I taught ye better than that?"

His words stung. "Aye, lord," Aiden said. "Ye taught me well. Ye taught me to consider my decisions before making them. Ye taught me to always put my duty to others first. That's why I didnae tell ye. Firstly, I havenae yet given my decision to the king. The Earl of Marischal is a border baron, a military post designed to protect his borders in the East. The king gave me time to deliberate before I answer him. Secondly, I had a duty to Kara. To see her safely home." He fixed his father with a challenging stare. "That is why I didnae tell ye."

Andrew stared at him for a long moment. Then he blinked and looked away. For the first time he realized that his father looked weary. He was getting older and now Aiden was the bigger and stronger of the two. The realization filled him with sadness.

"How did ye get that scroll?" Aiden asked. "I dinna like being put on the spot. I would have told ye when it was the right time. Lord, I would even have brought it to the two of ye to ask yer advice. Why did ye go through my things?"

"Bhradain brought the parchment to us," his mother replied. "He said it arrived by courier at dawn and he opened it by accident, thinking it was addressed to him."

"That's a lie," Aiden growled. "I brought the scroll back with me and kept it amongst the papers in my room. He must have gone in there and looked through them. I'll kill the sneaking bastard!"

What, by all that's holy, was Bhradain up to? Why was he trying to sow discord between Aiden and his parents? Then he remembered their altercation outside the Great Hall all those weeks ago. *If ye hadn't returned, there was a chance yer father would have adopted me and named me laird after him!* He knew Bhradain was bitter about Aiden's return but he'd never thought he'd act on it. Stupid. Bhradain's discontent obviously ran deeper than anyone realized. Then Aiden remembered something else. The leader of the brigands kneeling, hands bound. Bhradain suddenly darting forward and running him through—right before he was about to be questioned.

Aiden's blood ran cold. "Who knew the route we were taking to intercept the brigands?"

Andrew looked startled at the sudden change of topic. "Nay many. Why?"

"Who? Give me names."

"Yerself, me, Jamie and Bhradain."

Bhradain.

Everything suddenly fell into place and a ball of ice formed in his stomach. Bhradain had planned the ambush. But his plans had been thwarted by...

"Kara!" he shouted.

He turned and bolted from the room.

"YE ARE DOING IT AGAIN," Beth grumbled.

Kara looked up, startled out of her thoughts. "Doing what?"

"Staring into space like some loon. I'm trying to capture ye whilst ye are writing, remember?"

"Oh yeah. Sorry."

She picked up the quill and once more set to her task. Her history of the Harris clan lay open on the desk before her. It was almost finished and she hoped the family would like it. Beth sat in a chair by the window, sketch pad on one knee, feverishly sketching whilst Kara wrote. They were the only ones in the library this early in the morning, for which Kara was grateful.

She'd woken more rested than she could ever remember—despite not getting much sleep. Her cheeks flushed as she remembered the night she'd spent with Aiden. The first night of the rest of their lives if Kara got her way.

So this is what it's like, she thought. *To be in love. To feel so alive, like every minute of every day holds something new and exciting to look forward to.*

The realization that she loved him hadn't come as a shock. Since the moment she'd first met Aiden Harris, he'd done strange things to her, made her feel things she never had, made her think things she never had. She'd felt it creeping up on her, this thing that had been growing between them, until yesterday it had risen up and swallowed them both.

There was no going back now, nor did Kara want to. She could never, ever get enough of Aiden Harris. He was part of her, as integral to her as breathing.

But what about when you go home, a traitorous little voice whispered in her head. *What then?*

She pushed the voice away, refusing to let it ruin her mood, but it hovered at the back of her mind like a storm cloud.

Beth threw up her arms in exasperation. "There ye go again!"

Kara fixed her friend with a sheepish smile. She'd been daydreaming again, her arms dangling at her side, quill and ink forgotten on the table. "I can't seem to concentrate this morning."

Beth raised an eyebrow. "Mayhap ye need to get a little more sleep."

Kara's cheeks flushed. Did Beth know about her and Aiden? Holy crap, was it round the whole castle already? But more to the point, did she care? *No,* she realized. *I don't care who knows. In fact, I want to shout it from the rooftops.*

She longed to tell Beth but didn't. Sure, Beth was her friend but she was also Aiden's sister. How would she react to knowing what was going on between Kara and her brother?

She was spared making a decision by the door opening suddenly. Bhradain came striding in. He halted, looking them over for a second.

"Ah, Beth, I'm glad I've found ye. Aiden wants to see ye right away. Something about a loom ye asked him to fix?"

Beth rolled her eyes. "Finally! I've only been badgering him about that since he returned!"

She climbed to her feet and hurried to the door. "I'll see ye later," she called to Kara before exiting the room.

Kara expected Bhradain to leave, but he didn't. Instead, he walked slowly over to her table and stood looking down at the book on her desk.

"It's a history of your clan," she explained. "I've been gathering together all the record fragments I could find and copying them into one document."

He looked at her sharply. "Nay my clan," he said. "I'm nay a Harris. I'm a Garrick."

The vehemence in his voice shocked her. "From what I understand, a ward is practically the same thing as family."

He glanced at her but didn't answer. His fingers lightly traced the open page. "Ye would do well to write yer own history, Kara Buchanan. It's far more interesting."

Kara snorted. "Hardly. There's nothing interesting about a down and out city girl like me."

"Really?" he said, raising an eyebrow. "Is that what ye really think? How could ye be so ignorant, Kara Buchanan? Or should I say, Kara MacAskill?"

She frowned at him, puzzled. "What are you talking about? Why would you call me that?"

He stepped closer, placed his palms flat on the table and leaned down so that his face was only inches from her own. In a soft whisper he said, "I saw what ye did at the battle. I saw the way ye slowed time and saved Aiden's life. Ye canna lie to me, Kara. I know what ye are."

A sudden jolt of alarm went through her. Her heart was suddenly racing. "I...don't know what you're talking about."

"Oh yes ye do. Dinna worry. I willnae tell anyone. Ye canna imagine how irritated I was when ye thwarted my plan. It took quite some effort to set up that ambush. If it had gone according to plan I would have finally been rid of Aiden Harris, and I would have been named the heir to the lairdship. Then all I would have had to do was arrange for Andrew to have a little 'accident' and I would have gotten what I deserve."

Kara's eyes widened. She scrambled up from her chair and backed away. "You!" she breathed. "You set Aiden up!"

A sardonic smile curled his lips. "Aye, I did. And I was mighty aggrieved when ye thwarted it. I considered killing ye. But then I saw what ye did at the battle and everything fell into place. I finally put the pieces together and realized what ye truly are. It's took me quite some time and lots of digging, but I finally have the truth."

Kara thought back to all those times she'd encountered Bhradain in the library, poring over old manuscripts, family histories and genealogies. What had he been looking for? She glanced at the door and considered making a run for it but Bhradain had placed himself between her and escape. She could scream and hope somebody heard but the library was high up in one of the towers and it was unlikely anyone would hear.

She squared her shoulders and lifted her chin defiantly. "What do you want, Bhradain?"

He held up a finger. "Ah! Now we get to it." He stalked towards her and Kara backed away until she was up against the wall. She looked around for a weapon, a poker, a candlestick, anything, but there was nothing within reach.

"Stay away from me!" she warned.

He halted a few paces away and took a cloth-wrapped bundle from his pocket. He unwrapped it, revealing the Key of Ages that she and Aiden had stolen from Devereux all those weeks ago. It glinted in the sunlight.

Cold settled into her bones. "What are you doing with that?"

"Ye will see. We had better be going, Kara. We have a long way to go."

"Go where? What the hell are you talking about?"

"Haven't ye guessed it yet? This trinket may be called the Key of Ages but that is an error. The Key of Ages is something else entirely." His eyes fixed on hers. "The Key of Ages is ye."

There was a sudden blur of movement. Something struck the side of her head and she knew no more.

AIDEN BURST INTO KARA'S chamber without knock-ing. "Kara!" he yelled. "Are ye here, lass?"

Her bed was neatly made, her fire had been banked and her room tidied, but there was no sign of her. Aiden cursed. He strode out of the chamber and nearly collided with Beth coming the other way.

"Careful!" his sister cried. "Ye just about trampled me! I'm glad I found ye. What did ye want to see me about? Have ye managed to fix my loom?"

Aiden frowned at her in puzzlement. "Yer loom? What are ye talking about?"

Beth frowned in turn. "Ye mean ye havenae fixed it? So what did ye want to see me about?"

Aiden shook his head. He didn't have time for this. "I've nay idea what ye are talking about. I didnae ask to see ye."

"Oh. But Bhradain said ye had asked for me."

Aiden's head came up at that. "Bhradain said so?"

"Aye. A little while ago. He came into the library where Kara and I were working and said ye wanted to see me."

Aiden's neck prickled. "Where is Kara now?"

"Still in the library most probably. I left her with Bhradain and came to find ye."

Aiden whirled and sprinted down the corridor to the staircase of the east tower.

"Aiden! What's going on?"

He didn't answer. He had to find Kara. He took the steps two at a time and after a moment he heard Beth's footsteps coming up behind him. They hurried up the spiraling staircase and together he and Beth burst into the library. It was empty. A big book lay open on the desk, a quill and inkpot standing next to it. Beth's sketchpad and charcoal lay on a seat by the window.

Heart pounding, Aiden forced himself to keep calm and scan the room for any sign of what might have happened. He narrowed his eyes as he spotted something over by the far wall. Hurrying over to it, he went down on one knee and examined it.

A small puddle of blood marked the flagstones with a man's boot print clearly outlined within it.

Beth's hands flew to her mouth. "Lord! What's happened?"

Aiden stood. "Bhradain is a traitor. He's kidnapped Kara. Go warn Father. I'm going after them."

Without waiting for an answer, Aiden hurried through the door and down the stairs, taking them so fast he risked tripping and breaking his neck. He didn't care. That fire was in his belly again. That urgency. But this time it was from fear. For Kara.

Kara, he thought as he jogged through the castle corridors. *I'm coming, lass. I'll find ye. I promise.*

He exited the main doors and hurried to the stables, throwing open the doors with a bang and spooking the horses inside. A figure was lying prone in the straw between the stalls: Drew, the stable master.

Aiden knelt by the man's side. A bruise the size of a duck's egg was forming on his temple but other than that he appeared unharmed. Aiden shook his shoulder. "Drew?"

The stable master groaned and his eyes fluttered open. They alighted on Aiden and widened in alarm. "Bhradain!" he cried. He lurched upright and then groaned again, putting a hand to his head.

"Easy, man," Aiden said, placing a hand on his shoulder. "Tell me what happened."

"Bhradain came in demanding I saddle his horse. He seemed in a right temper," the stable master said. "I didnae question him—he often goes out riding alone. He was carrying a large bundle over his shoulder and I didnae question that either. Until that bundle groaned. When I asked about it, he got very angry. Hit me with something. Next thing I know I'm waking up here." He found Aiden's eyes with his own. "I fear he's up to something evil, Aiden. It was a lass he had wrapped in that bundle, I swear it."

Aiden nodded. "Aye. This is very important, Drew. Do ye have any idea where he might be heading?"

Angus shook his head. "I dinna. But he had something else with him as well. I saw it sticking out of his pocket. Some sort of jewelry I reckon. Gold, with three interlocking swirls. I've nay seen the like before."

The Key of Ages, Aiden thought. *That bastard is trying to get to Kara's time.*

And there was only one place he would be able to do that.

"My thanks," Aiden said, straightening. "When my father arrives, tell him all ye know." He hurried to his horse.

"But where are ye going?"

Aiden swung up onto Smokey's back without a saddle. "I'm going to stop Bhradain."

Clutching Smokey's mane he guided him from the stable and then kicked him into a gallop out of the gates of Dun Arnwick and down the road at breakneck pace. He knew where they were heading.

The arch through time.

KARA RAN AS FAST AS she could with her hands bound behind her back. Thick clumps of heather tried to trip her but she kept going, fear and desperation giving her speed. Then something struck her from behind and she went tumbling to the ground, whacking her chest hard enough to knock the breath from her lungs. Something flipped her over and she saw Bhradain glaring down at her.

"If ye try that again," he growled. "I will beat ye unconscious. I dinna need ye awake for this."

Kara glared at him. The ride from Dun Arnwick had passed in a blurry haze. Bhradain had hit her hard and it had taken most of the ride for her to come to her senses. Finally they'd stopped at the edge of a cliff and Bhradain had dismounted and then pulled her off the horse. Kara had seized her opportunity and ran.

"You're never going to get away with this," she hissed at him. "Aiden is coming."

"Ye reckon I fear yer lover?" Bhradain said, amusement shining in his eyes.

"You should. He's going to kill you."

"Really? I dinna think so. Not even the great Aiden Harris can follow us where we're going. Get up and behave yerself or ye'll regret it."

He hauled her to her feet and over to the cliff-edge where a zig-zag path snaked its way down onto the beach below. Bhradain pushed her ahead of him as they descended, the tip of a short-sword pressing into her back to make sure she did as she was told. As they reached the bottom, Kara suddenly realized where they were. Ahead of her was the eroded piece of cliff face that formed a natural archway through which she could see the churning gray sea.

It was the arch through time.

Her eyes widened as realization dawned on her.

"Aye," Bhradain breathed. "We are going to yer time."

"You're crazy," she replied. She spun and tried to run again but Bhradain grabbed her arm in a pincer grip and dug the tip of the short-sword against her neck.

"Final warning," he growled.

He yanked her towards the arch until they both stood underneath it and then took out the Key of Ages.

"It doesn't work," she spat at him. "You were there when we told all of this to Andrew and Lucy. Aiden and I already tried it. It can't take us anywhere. Only Irene MacAskill can do that."

Bhradain raised an eyebrow at her. "Do ye think I dinna know that? Ye underestimate me, Kara MacAskill, just like everyone else. All those books in the library? I'll bet ye were told Lucy collected them. In fact, a good portion of them were ones I managed to find—especially the family histories and the genealogies. I've been very interested in Irene MacAskill and her family since the time I learned of her involvement with my adopted family. Those fools dinna ken the half of what she really is or how old she is. I do. I pieced it together. I collected all the scraps and folk tales, half-whispered legends, any old documents I could lay my hands on." His eyes were alight now, warming to his subject. "Do ye know what I found? That Irene MacAskill has been walking this Earth for hundreds of years. That she had children and that she went to great lengths to hide her descendants. For that reason they took her maiden name." His eyes narrowed and his gaze turned predatory. "That name was Buchanan."

Kara stared at him for a moment, letting his words sink in. "You think I'm one of Irene MacAskill's descendants?" she said incredulously. "Just because I have the same name? Do you have any idea how many people there must be in my time with the name Buchanan?"

"But she didnae choose to send any of those back in time did she?" Bhradain countered. "I first started to suspect what ye were when ye started speaking Gaelic without ever having learned it. Dougie told me that ye picked it up more quickly than anyone he'd ever taught—as though it was a language ye already knew. Then what ye did at the battle confirmed it." He stepped forward, so close he could have touched her and gave her a grin full of malice. "Like I said, it isnae some trinket that is the Key of Ages. It's ye, Kara MacAskill."

She shivered and wrapped her arms around herself. She tried to denied his words but memories suddenly surfaced. A dark night. Standing stones rising up into the sky and sibilant voices whispering.

"Why are you doing this?" she asked. "The Harris clan took you in. They've been nothing but kind to you and this is how you repay them?"

"Kind?" Bhradain spat. "They took me in out of pity and that's all I've been shown since! I've made myself invaluable to Laird Andrew. There's nobody a better administrator than I. I tally his land grants, I collect his rents, I manage Dun Arnwick's stocks. But what reward do I get for my efforts? None at all! Everyone with half a brain knows I would make a fine laird. I should be his heir but the second Aiden cursed Harris comes simpering back into our lives it's as though I dinna even exist! Everyone bows and scrapes like he's some kind of conquering hero. They forget that he rode out and left us!"

"So that's it?" Kara said. "Jealousy? You're jealous of Aiden and this is somehow your revenge?"

"Jealousy? Ye think I'd be driven by so mean an emotion? Nay, woman, this is about far more than that. It's about getting what's mine. It's about fulfilling my destiny. Aiden is in my way. And ye know what the most ridiculous thing is? He doesnae even want the lairdship! He's going to be Earl Marischal and go live on the other side of the country! They fawn over him and they dinna even know the level of contempt he holds for them!"

Kara gasped. Aiden was going away? Why hadn't he told her?

Bhradain's eyes narrowed. "I can see ye didnae know. But why would he tell ye? Ye are only the latest of a long line of his doxies. Aiden Harris is not the man everyone thinks he is. Come, time grows short."

He grabbed her arm and before she could react, he scored the tip of his short sword along her forearm. Stinging pain ignited and a line of blood welled up. Bhradain caught the blood on the tip of his blade and then used it to transfer a drop to the rough stone of the arch through time. Gripping her arm so she couldn't escape he began to speak. Kara didn't recognize the language but the sound of it set her hair on end. It sounded as though it had been dredged up from the bowels of the Earth, an ancient language not meant for mortal tongues.

Suddenly the air beneath the archway began to shimmer like heat-haze.

Bhradain glanced at her, a grin curling his mouth. "Ready to go home, lass?"

Then he dragged her through. There was a moment's disorientation where Kara felt like she was falling. She cried out and threw out her arms to steady herself but her questing grip met nothing but empty air. Then her feet hit something hard and she fell to her knees. Fighting back a sudden wave of nausea, she lifted her head and took in her surroundings. The beach, the sea, the arch were gone. Instead she was kneeling on damp mud below a railway bridge.

Bhradain was already on his feet and Kara forced herself to stand, preparing to run. But a gun-barrel suddenly poked her in the chest.

Four men detached themselves from the shadows beneath the bridge and surrounded them.

"Boss!" yelled one of them. "You'd better get in here!"

Another man appeared from somewhere beyond the bridge. He walked quickly and with a grace that reminded Kara of a predator. He approached her and Bhradain then stopped, looking them both over with snake's eyes. Suddenly the man smiled.

"Well, well, the prodigal daughter returns. Welcome home Kara Buchanan," said Michael Devereux.

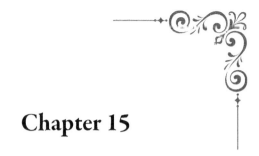

Chapter 15

AIDEN RODE LIKE HE had the very devil on his tail. It was dangerous to ride the cliff-top trail at breakneck speed but he dare not slow, even for an instant. Dun Arnwick was far behind him and he'd been riding all day, stopping at a local croft to change horses when his became lathered. He paused from time to time only long enough to check the trail. Sure enough, each time he dismounted, he found the tracks of Bhradain's horse in the mud, moving quickly but not as fast as he with its burden of two riders. He was gaining on them. Just a little further...

He yanked his horse to a halt as he reached the place where the trail split, a branch leading off down the cliff to the beach where he and Kara had originally come through the archway. He hurried to the trail and careened down it, slipping and sliding and sending showers of rocks sliding over the edge. At the bottom he found the arch exactly as he remembered only this time two sets of tracks showed clearly in the sand. They led right up to the archway—and then disappeared.

There was no sign of Kara or Bhradain.

Aiden's heart leapt into his mouth. Fear raced through his veins. He pelted up the beach, following the tracks until they disappeared under the archway. They didn't emerge on the other side. Letting out a string of curses, Aiden turned in a circle, eyes scanning the terrain.

"Kara!" he bellowed. "Kara! Are ye here, lass?"

His shouts died into silence. Gritting his teeth, Aiden drew his sword, took a deep breath and stepped through the arch.

Nothing happened. He exited the archway on the other side, his footprints clearly showing in the wet sand. He passed back through and tried again. Nothing. Whatever magic the arch employed, it wouldn't work for him. Not without Irene MacAskill.

He threw back his head and screamed his fury to the sky. How was he to find Kara now? Irene was nowhere to be found and only the Fae could work the portals.

He paused as a sudden thought struck him. *Only the Fae.*

Suddenly he was off and running, sheathing his sword and sprinting back up the switch-back trail to where his horse was idly cropping grass. The beast snorted in alarm when Aiden vaulted onto his back but Aiden grabbed his mane and dragged him around, digging his heels into his flanks and sending him galloping inland, using the same path he and Kara had taken all those weeks ago.

Only the Fae could open the portals. Only the Fae.

The words kept going round and round in his head. A plan had come to him. A desperate one that might very well end up costing his life but it was the only plan he had.

He drove the horse to as fast a pace as possible and eventually he reached the valley where he and Kara had camped in the cave that night. The stones of Cullmaggin reared up on the valley's rim, seeming to stare malevolently down at him as he rode alongside the river at the valley's bottom. When he reached the ford, he pulled the horse to a halt, dismounted, and quickly forded through the shallow water.

The narrow trail that climbed the valley's side on the other side of the river was even slippier than the last time he'd come this way. Twice he lost his footing and was driven to his knees, but he dragged himself up and drove himself on.

He finally reached the top and came out onto windswept moorland. A few paces away Cullmaggin reared up out of the ground, looking like a giant, clawed hand had broken the surface of the land.

The last time he'd been here it had been dark and the place had been one of shadows and moonlight. It had been terrifying. Now, in daylight, it was little better. The stones seemed to capture and devour the light and Aiden could feel their gleeful, malicious stares. Steeling his courage, he marched into the stone circle.

All light vanished. What had been bright daylight became deepest night. Above him the cloudy sky was replaced by stars, cold and distant, giving off little light. There was no moon and it was so dark Aiden could barely see his hand in front of his face.

He sensed movement nearby and he spun, trying to discover its source, but all that met his gaze were twisting shadows. He resisted the urge to draw his sword: he knew such defenses would be ineffective here.

"I've come to make a bargain!" he called.

Soft laughter. Then a voice whispered, "What bargain do ye offer us, mortal man?"

"I need yer help. I need ye to send me into the future. I know the Fae have power over time. Please. Send me to the twenty-first century."

The laughter came again, seeming to echo from all sides. There was no mirth in it. Only malice. Aiden's heart hammered in fear but he forced himself to raise his chin, put his shoulders back.

"Will ye help me?"

"Ye ask much, mortal. There can be no bargain without a price paid first. Are ye willing to pay it, Aiden Harris?"

Something inside him screamed a warning but he pushed it aside. If this was what he had to do to reach Kara, he'd do it. He'd pay the price, whatever that may be.

He opened his mouth. "I—"

"Stop!" a voice cried suddenly. "I willnae allow this!"

The voices suddenly hissed, bubbling with anger. "Ye have nay place here! He is ours! Ours!"

"He is mortal and so belongs to me!" the voice said. "Be gone!"

The voices hissed again and suddenly the night vanished. Aiden was once more standing in the light of day. He spun and was astonished to see Irene MacAskill striding towards him. She came to stand in front of him, hands clasped and head cocked to one side, glaring up at him with annoyance in her eyes.

"Just what exactly did ye think ye were doing, lad?"

Aiden opened his mouth and closed it again. "Me?" he exploded. "What do ye think I was doing? Trying to find a way to save Kara is what! And since ye brought us both here and abandoned us, I could think of nay other way!"

She shook her head, eyes glinting. "I canna allow this, no matter the need. Not all my kind can be trusted, Aiden Harris. Those who dwell here are such. Do ye know what they would have asked in return for their help?"

He stepped back, suddenly wary. "What?"

"Yer soul."

Aiden gazed around at the dark stones. On the edges of his hearing he heard laughter. He scrubbed a hand through his hair in frustration. "And I would have paid it! Dinna ye understand, woman? Bhradain has taken Kara! They've gone to the future and lord alone knows what danger she's in! I must save her!"

"Why?" Irene asked.

Aiden startled. "What do ye mean 'why'?"

"Why must ye save her?"

"Because it's my duty! I swore to protect her and I failed!"

"Is that all?"

"Is that nay enough?"

"Nay, it isnae. Now I ask again: why must ye save her?"

Aiden stared at Irene MacAskill who stared right back, her black eyes like pits reaching back into eternity.

"Because I love her," Aiden breathed. "Because she's the better half of me and if aught happens to her, then I truly will have lost my soul."

Irene suddenly smiled. "Aye, lad. Ye will have. When I first met ye, I gave ye a task. Do ye remember what it was?"

"Ye told me to protect the Key of Ages."

"Aye, and that is why ye now feel the burning desire to do just that. Because ye have failed to protect her. Ye have failed in yer duty." Her eyes found his. "Kara is the Key of Ages, Aiden Harris. She is my granddaughter many generations removed and the first to show the gift for centuries. She has a destiny, lad, one she must fulfill if she is to ever find peace. Just as ye do. Yer destinies are intertwined, neither of ye able to fulfill yers without the other."

"Why didnae ye tell us any of this? Why did ye disappear without so much as a word?"

"Choice, lad. There must always be a choice. Would ye and Kara still have fallen in love if I had told ye from the very start who ye both were? Who can say? But ye have to be free to make yer own decision. Without them, everything will come to ruin."

She took his hand and led him from the stone circle. The sun had come out from behind the clouds, illuminating a huge oak tree growing out of the steep valley side. One of its branches had bowed under its own weight and curved down to the ground, forming a natural archway. The space beneath it shimmered like the air over a campfire.

Irene smiled up at him. "Now, lad, are ye ready to go rescue yer destiny?"

Chapter 16

THE TWO GUARDS LEANED together, murmuring in low voices. Kara took advantage of their momentary distraction to pull fiercely at the bonds that bound her wrists. It did no good. The two henchmen clearly knew how to tie a knot and all Kara was doing was chafing her skin red raw attempting to loosen them. With a growl of frustration, she looked over at the desk where Bhradain and Devereux were talking.

They'd been taken back to Devereux's warehouse, to the very room where she and Aiden had stolen the Key of Ages what seemed a lifetime ago. The room hadn't changed, and nor it seemed, had Devereux's plans. Since her and Aiden's disappearance he'd been guarding the railway bridge until either he found a way to use the arch or someone came through from the other side. The man was nothing if not patient.

Bhradain was tied to a chair in front of Devereux's desk although this didn't seem to particularly bother Bhradain. He was supremely confident in his plan, despite being suddenly pulled out of his time and confronted by men who would shoot him as soon as look at him. Idiot. Did he really think he would pull this off?

"Who are you?" Devereux demanded of Bhradain. "You're not that muscle-bound meathead she ran off with."

"Nay, I am not," Bhradain answered. "My name is Bhradain Garrick, ward of Andrew Harris, laird of Clan Harris of the Isle of Skye."

Devereux's eyes lit up suddenly and he leaned forward. "A Scotsman. Tell me Bhradain Garrick, what year are you from?"

"We left my homeland in the year of Our Lord 1541."

Devereux went very still. For a long moment he said nothing and Kara could almost see the plans boiling behind his eyes. "So it works then," he muttered, almost to himself. "The arch really works."

"Aye," Bhradain replied. "If ye know how to use it."

"Why have you returned?" Devereux demanded. "From the way she glares at you its plain Kara Buchanan is no friend of yours but even so she must have warned you we'd be waiting on the other side."

"Oh, I was counting on it. I've come to offer ye a deal, one that will benefit us both. To ye I will grant the power of the arch. In return..."

"In return what?"

"Ye will give me the men and weapons I need to conquer Skye. I will rule the islands."

The two men looked at each other, neither blinking, and Kara was struck by how alike they looked. They both had that cold, predatory gaze.

"Tell me," Devereux said after a moment. "Why do I need you? Why shouldn't I just kill you and the girl and take the Key of Ages? That way the power of the arches is mine anyway, with no need for your paltry deal."

"That would be unwise," Bhradain said. "The Key of Ages willnae work, as ye've already seen."

This was true. The second Devereux had found the Key of Ages in Bhradain's pocket he'd tried to use it to activate the arch. Nothing had happened.

"At least, not by itself," Bhradain continued. "There are other ingredients needed and words that must be said at the right time. For those ye need both myself and the girl. Everything ye need is stored in here," he tapped his head. "So ye see, killing me would be very stupid indeed."

Devereux looked between Bhradain and Kara and then he suddenly laughed. "Ha! You are a man after my own heart I see, Bhradain Garrick. Very well, you shall have your men and your weapons. And I? I will hold the power of time in my hands. Release him."

One of Devereux's heavies cut Bhradain's bonds and he stood. Devereux held out his hand and the two men shook.

A cold shiver walked its way down Kara's back. If these two were able to carry out their plan, then she dreaded to imagine the devastation they would wreak on Skye, on the Highlands. Hell, on all of history. Devereux able to travel to any time he chose and do God-knows-what? The thought was too terrible to contemplate.

No, she told herself, gritting her teeth and steeling her courage. *It's not going to happen. I will not let it happen. Because I'm going to escape.*

And I'm going to stop them.

AIDEN EMERGED FROM the archway carefully. He gripped a knife in his fist but hadn't drawn his sword in case the blade glinted in the light and gave him away. From his first experience he knew that the area under the railway bridge was dark. If luck was with him, he could slip into the shadows on the other side, unseen.

Sure enough, he found himself stepping through into shadow. His boots made no sound as they came down on the hard tarmac of the twenty-first century. In front of him he saw four men guarding the archway but they had their backs to him and hadn't heard him emerge. Silently, Aiden hugged the wall of the tunnel, relying on the shadows to conceal him. Then he looked around, assessing his enemy, just as he did when scouting before a battle.

The four men all carried guns and all looked to be alert. They were spaced out, one behind the other, watching the entrance to the tunnel. Clearly they were watching for someone trying to enter the arch, not exit. Their first mistake. Their second was to space themselves in such a way that Aiden could sneak up on one without the others knowing. Rudimentary errors. No Highland captain worth his salt would arrange his warriors that way.

Aiden stepped noiselessly up behind the first guard, wrapped his arm around the man's throat, and tightened. The man's eyes went wide and he struggled for a heartbeat before he slumped unconscious to the ground. Without pause Aiden moved to the second man and did the same. The third man turned at the last minute, perhaps alerted by a sound behind him, but Aiden smacked the hilt of his knife against the man's temple with enough force to snap the man's head to the side. His eyes rolled in his head and he began to topple backwards. Aiden caught him before he fell and lowered him gently to the ground.

A click sounded behind Aiden and something hard and cold was pressed against the back of his head.

"Hands where I can see them," growled a voice.

Aiden spread his arms wide. "All right. I dinna want any trouble."

But even as he spoke the last word he was moving. He spun, grabbed the barrel of the gun and used it to yank the man towards him, then buried his knife in the man's stomach up to the hilt. The man's eyes widened and he opened his mouth to shout a warning but all that came out was a long, low hiss as his life left him.

Aiden stepped over the man, crouched close to the tunnel wall, and peered out. It was night and in the distance Aiden could see the lights of the city sparkling like hundreds of fireflies. Devereux's warehouse rose into the night several meters away across a stretch of wasteland. Lights burned in the windows. He made out other guards stationed at various points around the warehouse, two by the doors, one on the roof, another standing at the top of some metal steps by a fire exit.

Aiden assessed his options. He needed to get inside that building, and without alerting Devereux he was here. Kara was inside and there was no telling what Devereux would do to her if he discovered Aiden had come after her. He burst from his hiding place and sprinted across the waste ground, keeping low and using the scraggly brush and burned-out cars as cover. He made it round to the side of the warehouse without the alarm being raised and pressed himself against the wall. The guards on the main doors were just around the corner and he heard them talking in low voices. He couldn't take them both on at once. He had to separate them. He picked up a handful of pebbles and tossed them at the ground a few paces away. They made a rattling sound as they scattered.

The two guards went silent. One of them said, "What was that? You go check it out."

Aiden pressed himself back against the wall, clutching his knife and waiting. A heartbeat later one of the guards came round the corner. Aiden grabbed him before he even saw he was there, landing an uppercut into his chin that laid him out flat. He caught him as he fell and dragged him into the shadows. One down, one to go.

"Simon? What you doing? Did you see anything?"

Aiden leaned against the wall and sure enough the other guard appeared around the corner. He was more cautious than the first, holding his gun in front of him and treading softly but he wasn't careful enough to stop Aiden. He dropped into a crouch, below the man's line of sight then kicked out viciously, taking the man's legs out from under him and kicking the gun out of his hand. A blow to the temple and the man was out cold.

Aiden hurried to the doors and slipped inside. He found himself in a small entranceway that led to a bigger room beyond. A door on the other side lay ajar and Aiden crept over to it and peered through. Devereux was sitting at a desk talking on one of those devices that his mother called a 'cell phone'. Two more guards stood nearby. Aiden's eyes scanned the room and alighted on Kara bound to a chair close to the desk.

His heart thudded, sending a jolt right through him. It was all he could do not to burst in there and rush to her side. He dug his nails into his palm to steady himself. He would only get one chance at this. He had to do it right. Taking a deep breath, he forced himself to listen.

"That's what I said!" Devereux growled down the phone. "All of them. At least a hundred. Tell them to be here by first light and to bring weapons. I suspect the garrison at Dun Arnwick will be easy to subdue, what good will swords and arrows do against guns? But be ready anyway. They might give us some trouble." He paused whilst the other person said something. Then he smiled. "You should never have doubted me. I told you I'd find the Key of Ages and I have. This time tomorrow Dun Arnwick will be mine. After that the whole of the Highlands. After that the Fae and power of time itself. Now get your boys over here. We invade at first light." He snapped the phone shut.

Cold horror drenched Aiden. Michael Devereux was planning to use the arch to take men back to Dun Arnwick and conquer it. Conquer his home.

Devereux stood and made his way around to crouch in front of Kara. She glared at him, seeming not the least bit afraid. Aiden tensed, ready to spring to her defense, but Devereux didn't touch her. Instead, he smiled.

"You know, things would have been so much easier if you'd taken my advice. I told you not to poke your nose into my business, didn't I? Gave you fair warning. Now you'll pay the consequences of not listening to me."

"Go to hell," Kara growled.

Devereux laughed and straightened. "Come on," he barked at his heavies. "The rest of our boys are on their way. I want to make sure we have enough weapons for everyone. Let's go check the armory."

Devereux and his men left by a door that led further into the warehouse. Aiden let out a long, slow breath and forced himself to look around and check there were no more guards in the room. There weren't. Devereux obviously felt those he'd stationed around the perimeter were enough to keep this place secure. Fool.

Aiden padded from his hiding place and over to Kara. He went on his knees in front of her.

Her eyes widened. "Aiden!" she whispered. "What are you doing here?"

"Isnae that obvious," he replied, lifting her chin to look at her face. She appeared unhurt, thank the Lord. "Did ye really think I'd leave ye in his hands?"

"No," she answered. "I knew you'd be coming. But Aiden, you have to listen to me. Devereux is planning—"

"I know what he's planning, lass," Aiden cut in as he began sawing at the bonds around Kara's wrists. He cursed. They were thick and didn't give easily.

He heard the step behind him too late. He whirled just as something smashed into the side of his head. Pain exploded through his skull and he was driven to his knees. A face swam into view, a face with dark eyes and a cruel smile.

"Well, well," said Bhradain. "The faithful hound has followed us. I should have guessed. Ye are a right royal pain in
the arse. Do ye know that, Aiden?"

"I'll kill ye for this," Aiden growled.

A second blow cannoned into his temple. The last thing
he heard as everything faded around him was Kara screaming his name.

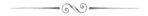

"TAKE YOUR HANDS OFF him!" Kara yelled. She struggled against her bonds but the rope didn't give an inch.

Bhradain merely grinned at her. He pulled a chair over
beside Kara's and then dragged Aiden over to it. Blood was
dripping from Aiden's head and the wrench that Bhradain
had hit him with lay on the floor in a small pool of blood.

Oh God, oh God, oh God, Kara thought as she stared at
Aiden, searching for signs of life. There. His chest was rising
and falling. He was only unconscious.

The relief that washed through her was strong enough to
make her giddy. She'd never been so elated as when Aiden
had appeared in front of her and she'd never been as mortally
afraid as when Bhradain had suddenly appeared from behind them, had hit him with that wrench and he'd collapsed
bonelessly to the floor. If Aiden died, it was over. She would
die with him, whether she carried on breathing or not.

Bhradain manhandled Aiden into the chair and tied him
in the same way she was: arms behind her back, ankles lashed
to the chair-legs. When he'd done this he dumped a mug of
water over Aiden's head.

"Wakey, wakey!"

Aiden spluttered awake. He raised his head, eyes bleary, and for a second didn't seem to realize where he was. Then his gaze fixed on Bhradain.

"Ye," he growled, "are a dead man." Aiden flexed his arms, straining against his bonds but even Aiden's great strength wasn't enough to break them. He turned his gaze on Kara. "Are ye well, lass? He hasnae hurt ye?"

"No," Kara replied. "Oh my God, Aiden. I'm so glad you're okay."

"Ah, isnae that nice?" Bhradain said, his voice dripping with sarcasm. He leaned close to Aiden and whispered loudly. "Just between ye and me, I think she likes ye. Bit stupid of her to show that, dinna ye think? Now we have a way to make her do what we want. If she doesnae, I'll carve bits off ye."

"Do what ye will with me," Aiden replied. "But leave her be."

"Oh, I dinna think so. Dinna ye realize yet what she is? She's the key to giving me Dun Arnwick."

"Dun Arnwick will never be yers."

"Now that's where ye are wrong, my friend." Bhradain gestured around them. "In case ye hadnae noticed, we're in the twenty first century, with twenty first century weapons. Dun Arnwick will fall in minutes when faced with guns."

Aiden glared at him. "Ye think that's all there is to it? Ye conquer the castle and Skye will fall? Ye are an idiot, Bhradain. Ye will never win the clan's loyalty. They will never accept ye as laird."

"They will if it means their sons and daughters get to live," Bhradain hissed. "They will if it means their crops dinna get burned to the ground around them. That they keep the hovels they call homes. Skye will be mine within the week and after that? The whole of the Highlands. When I'm finished, even the king will bend his knee to me."

"I will stop ye," Aiden growled.

Bhradain barked a laugh. "Really? Because ye've done such a grand job so far ye mean?"

Devereux and his men suddenly burst into the room, weapons drawn.

"My men have been taken out!" Devereux grated. "We've got a breach!"

Bhradain stepped aside so Devereux could see Aiden tied to the chair. He raised an eyebrow. "I've already taken care of it. See? I told ye ye needed me. If I hadnae been keeping an eye on Kara, she and Aiden would be halfway back to Dun Arnwick by now. Ye really should pay better attention to yer prisoners."

Devereux scowled at him then stalked over to Aiden and stood looking down at him, eyes narrowed. "How did he get through the arch?" he asked Bhradain. "I thought ye said the girl was the only one who could operate it?"

"Actually, I said the *Fae* were the only ones who could operate it. My guess is Irene MacAskill sent him through—she's the old woman I told ye about. It seems she's intent on stopping us from taking Dun Arnwick."

"Is she now?" Devereux said softly. "It's a little late for that." He waved his hand at one of his men. "Kill the newcomer."

Kara opened her mouth to scream but Bhradain got in there first. "Nay! Aiden is mine!"

Devereux paused then waved his men away. "Very well. Do with him as you wish."

A cruel smiled played across Bhradain's features. "Ye hear that, Aiden? Ye are mine. I won't kill ye, oh no. Ye are gonna come back with me to Dun Arnwick. Ye will watch as I take everything ye hold dear and make it mine."

"Enough of this," Devereux said. "Settle your petty squabbles on your own time. The rest of my boys will be here soon. Before they arrive I want to be sure you can deliver what you promised."

Bhradain looked at Devereux. "Do ye still doubt me?"

"I always doubt," Devereux replied. "You say you can work that arch? Show me."

Bhradain shrugged. "Fine."

Devereux nodded to his men and they quickly cut the bonds tying Kara and Aiden to the chair and then hauled them to their feet. Aiden fought in his captor's grip and managed to take a few steps in Kara's direction.

"Hold on, lass," he whispered. "I'll think of something. Be ready to move."

She nodded before her captor grabbed her roughly by the shoulder and pushed her through the doors and out into the night. They were marched unceremoniously across the waste ground to the railway arch. Here they encountered several of Devereux's men nursing injuries and one that didn't move at all. Devereux scowled murder at Aiden who stared back, unflinching.

Devereux nodded to the arch and then said to Bhradain. "Do it. Activate this thing."

Bhradain grabbed Kara and dragged her to stand under the archway. He made a big show of taking the Key of Ages out of his pocket and holding it up. Kara knew it was just a worthless piece of metal but Bhradain had kept up the pretense with Devereux, the better to pull the wool over the crime-boss's eyes and make him believe he needed Bhradain. Kara flinched as Bhradain drew a knife. She met Aiden's gaze and gave a slight nod. He inclined his head slightly in response, showing he'd understood her unspoken message.

"Ye need three things to work the arch," Bhradain said. "Firstly, the Key. Secondly, the knowledge in here,"—he tapped his forehead, "And lastly, the blood of the Fae."

Aiden and Kara exploded into motion at exactly the same time. Aiden threw his head back, ramming his head into the face of the man gripping him, whose nose exploded in a shower of blood. He spun, kicking the man savagely in the head. With a roar, he flexed his arms and the bonds tying his wrists snapped. He grabbed the fallen man's gun and, even though the weapon was alien to him, expertly shot Devereux's remaining two guards.

Kara jabbed her elbow into Bhradain's stomach and was rewarded when he grunted in pain. She tore out of his grip and aimed a savage kick between his legs. Then she turned and opened her mouth to shout for Aiden but a hand suddenly clamped over her mouth and something hard and cold pressed against the back of her head.

"This is starting to get very tiresome," Devereux growled by her ear.

Aiden raised the gun, but froze when he saw Kara in Devereux's grasp, his eyes going wide with fear.

"Put the gun down," Devereux said. "And I just might refrain from spattering your girlfriend's brains all over the archway."

"Dinna hurt her," Aiden said, dropping the gun and kicking it away. "I'll do what ye ask. Just please dinna hurt her."

"You're in no position to ask favors," Devereux grated. "You've injured a lot of my men tonight. I'm not inclined to kill you quickly."

"Let me do it," Bhradain growled, straightening with a grunt. "I'll take him a piece at a time."

He drew a sword and held another, hilt-first towards Aiden. "What do ye say, *brother*? Should we settle this the Highland way? Nay guns for us. Only cold steel."

Aiden took the offered sword but said nothing. He let the tip of the sword drop, resting it against the ground and watched Bhradain as though he was a viper.

Kara swallowed thickly. Her heart was hammering in her chest so hard she feared her ribs would crack. Devereux still held the gun against her head and so she was forced to watch, helpless, as Bhradain circled Aiden, a cruel smile curling his lips.

Aiden merely turned to follow him, sword still held in a loose grip.

Then suddenly Bhradain attacked. He moved like lightning, his blade singing out to rake across Aiden's throat. Only Aiden wasn't there anymore. He ducked under the blade, pivoted behind Bhradain's back, and raked him across the shoulder. Bhradain grunted in pain and a red line welled through the arm of his tunic.

Bhradain cocked his head. "First blood to ye. Well done. But this is to the death."

He sprang at Aiden, his face contorted in a mask of rage and hatred. His attack was so furious that Aiden was suddenly battling for his life. He parried Bhradain's blows, but only barely. The air was filled with the clang of metal on metal, the thump of boots in the dirt and the grunt of exertion. Kara bit her lip, hardly able to breathe as she watched it unfolding. She felt more helpless than she ever had in her life.

Aiden was driven back several paces. Bhradain followed, swinging his sword in deadly arcs, the silver blade glittering in the night. Aiden brought his own sword up, catching Bhradain's blade and for a moment the two men were locked, straining against each other, faces close.

"Bitterness has twisted ye, Bhradain," Aiden growled. "But it ends right here, right now."

"At last something we can agree on," Bhradain growled back.

He aimed a kick at Aiden's knee, forcing him to shift his stance to defend against it. Taking advantage of the distraction, Bhradain punched Aiden in the face hard enough to snap his head to the side and then, with a look of savage glee, brought his blade swinging for Aiden's neck. But Aiden dropped to one knee, picked up a handful of dirt and flung it in Bhradain's face. As his foster-brother staggered back, wiping his eyes, Aiden caught Bhradain's sword with his own and flicked it, sending it flying from Bhradain's hand to land in the dirt with a clang. Aiden pressed the tip of his blade against Bhradain's chest.

"It's over," Aiden growled. "Give it up."

Bhradain glanced down at the blade and that familiar sardonic smile curled his mouth. He raised an eyebrow. "It will never be over until ye are dead," he said.

He danced backwards and drew two small, wide-bladed knives from inside his cloak, holding them loosely in each hand.

"An assassin's weapon?" Aiden said. "Have ye no honor left at all?"

"Honor be damned," Bhradain growled. "Yer death is all that matters."

He pulled back his arm and threw. The two knives spun through the air like little silver stars. Aiden brought his sword around and knocked one from the air but the other buried itself in his shoulder with enough force to send him staggering backward. Aiden grunted and his sword fell from suddenly nerveless fingers.

"Aiden!" Kara screamed.

She fought against Devereux's grip but he held her fast.

Bhradain sauntered up to Aiden, smirking. "Well, it seems the great Aiden Harris isnae so great after all." He stooped to pick up his fallen sword and gripped it in both hands. "I'm going to enjoy this." He raised his arms high to swing the blade but in that moment Aiden yanked the throwing knife out of his shoulder in a shower of blood and rammed it with all his might into Bhradain's chest.

Bhradain's eyes went wide, his arms falling to his sides and the sword dropping from his grasp. He crashed onto his knees. He plucked at the knife-hilt weakly but hadn't the strength to pull it out. His gaze sought Aiden's.

"Nay," he whispered. "It's nay supposed to be this way. I win. I always win."

Aiden, chest heaving with exhaustion, stepped up to his foster-brother. There was no elation in his face, no thrill of victory. Only sadness.

Bhradain opened his mouth as if to speak but only a long sigh escaped him. Then he toppled onto his side, sightless eyes staring at the stars above.

For a moment nobody moved. The moment was frozen in time. Then Aiden spun towards Kara and Devereux. Blood was pouring from the wound in his shoulder but he barely seemed to notice.

"Yer pet is dead," Aiden growled. "He willnae be taking ye anywhere. It's over, Devereux. Let her go."

Devereux raised an eyebrow. "Enough of this bullshit."

He raised his gun and shot Aiden. The bullet cannoned into the meat of his upper arm, spinning him around, and bringing a grunt of pain. Even as Aiden staggered to his knees, Devereux fired again.

Kara screamed as the bullet sped straight at Aiden's heart.

"No!"

And suddenly power blasted out of her like a sound wave.

It was so strong it seemed to shake the very foundations of the ground beneath her feet. Suddenly she was standing in darkness. Around her a circle of standing stones reared up out of the ground, leering at her like jagged teeth. Shadows danced on the edges of her vision, melting away when she turned to look at them.

Laughter. Harsh and cruel.

Dead! Voices cried around her. *He'll be dead in a moment. He has only seconds. What will ye do, daughter of the Fae?*

"Who are you?" she cried. "What do you want from me? Take me back right now! Take me back to him!"

Ye know who we are, the voices whispered. *And ye know what we want. We want ye to embrace who ye are. Join us. Embrace yer power and ye can still save him.*

Kara went very still. Save Aiden? Was it possible?

"How?" she cried. "What do I do?"

Accept us into yer heart and we will give ye the power ye need. All ye have to do is agree to our price.

"What's that?"

Only yer soul. Such a small price to pay for the man ye love.

They were right. Such a small price to pay if it meant Aiden would live. She'd pay any price for that, a hundred times over.

She opened her mouth to accept their offer but the wind suddenly stirred, howling around the circle in a gale and snatched the words out of her mouth. Within the wind she heard another voice, a gentle, kind voice.

Nay, lass. It doesnae have to be this way. Ye have the power already within ye. Ye dinna need any bargain from them to do what ye must. Only look inside yerself and see what's already there.

"Irene?" Kara whispered.

Look inside, Kara Buchanan. Ye will find what ye need.

Kara closed her eyes and remembered a cloudy day and a clearing full of fighting. She remembered an arrow speeding for Aiden. She remembered it halting in mid-air. She hadn't needed any dark bargain then. She didn't need one now.

"No," she said, opening her eyes to the dark circle. "I don't accept. I am of the Fae but I'm not one of you. But I accept my heritage. My power."

The voices broke into hissing fury and the stone circle vanished. She was once again in front of the railway arch, Aiden crouched a few paces away, Devereux standing with his arm outstretched, the gun clutched in his hand.

And a bullet speeding across the space between them.

Kara stepped forward and held up her hand. "No."

Time stopped. The bullet froze in its path. Kara stepped forward and calmly plucked it from the air then tossed it away. Then she raised her hand again and time reasserted itself.

Devereux's eyes went wide as he realized the bullet hadn't found its target. A quick look of understanding swept across Aiden's face as he glanced at Kara. Devereux tossed the gun away with a snarl and spun towards Kara, pulling a knife.

"Bitch! I'll take your blood a drop at a time if I have to."

Quick as a snake he darted forward, swinging the knife at Kara's chest. She saw the blade coming but didn't have time to react, or even scream, as it came slicing through the air at her.

But then Aiden was there.

He'd grabbed his fallen sword and threw himself between Kara and Devereux, catching Devereux's knife on his own blade.

"Ye will not touch her," he growled.

Then, with a flick of his wrist, he sent the knife skittering from Devereux's grasp and then plunged his sword into the man's stomach. Michael Devereux looked down at the sword impaling him and his face twisted into a mask of rage. He reached out, clawing for Aiden's face before his strength evaporated and he slumped, sliding off Aiden's blade to lie lifeless in the dirt beneath the arch.

For a frozen heartbeat, Aiden stared down at him, chest heaving. Then he dropped his sword and spun to Kara.

With a cry, Kara flew to him. He wrapped his good arm around her, the other hanging limp and dripping blood from both the bullet wound and where Bhradain had stabbed him. But he held her close against him and Kara clung to him, tears leaking from the corners of her eyes. Tears of horror at what had just happened. Tears of joy and relief that Aiden was safe.

He held her for a long time, neither speaking, just savoring the feel of being alive, being together. Then Aiden pushed her to arm's length and looked her up and down.

"Are ye all right? He didnae hurt ye?"

She shook her head. "I'm fine."

He squeezed his eyes tight shut and took two shuddering breaths. She could feel him trembling. "Thank the Lord," he whispered. "Thank Irene MacAskill, the Fae, anyone who's listening. I thought I'd lost ye, lass." He stared hard into her eyes. "I dinna ever want to feel like that again. I dinna ever want to be without ye again."

He brushed a stray strand of hair from her face. "This isnae the most romantic of spots but I canna wait. I have to know, lass. I want ye beside me every day for the rest of my life. Will ye be my wife?"

Kara reached up, cupped his face in her hands. "Of course I will. You're my life, Aiden Harris. I don't want to ever be apart from you again."

He breathed out, one long shuddering breath as though letting go of tension. "And ye willnae be," he said. "I will always be by yer side. I will always be there to keep ye safe, nay matter what might come." He kissed her tenderly and then took her hand. "Come. Let's get out of here. I suspect yer law makers will come at the sound of gunfire. We can be back at yer apartment before they arrive." He took a pace but halted when Kara didn't move. He looked back. "What is it, lass?"

"Not here," she breathed. "This isn't my home any more. I know who I am now. *What* I am. And my home is Dun Arnwick."

His eyes widened slightly. "Are ye sure, lass? I thought ye wanted to come back to the twenty-first century. I'll stay here with ye, if that is what ye wish."

She shook her head. "It's not. It wasn't till I returned here that I realized how empty my life in this time is. Always chasing a story. Always moving on and never putting down roots. In Dun Arnwick it was different. I had a place, a purpose, and now I have the greatest story of them all about to unfold before me." She met his gaze. "My life with you."

He stepped up to her, caught her hands in his. "Aye, lass. It will be a grand adventure."

Kara cocked her head. "As long as you aren't planning on leaving, that is. I know about the king's offer of giving you an earldom. Bhradain told me. Why didn't you?"

He winced. "Because I'd already decided to tell my king no. Because I'd already decided that I would go wherever ye did. Ye are my home, Kara. Wherever ye are."

Joy rushed through her and she felt a stupid, idiotic grin spreading over her face. She tightened her fingers around his. "That's settled then. Let's go home. And when we get there, you're going straight to the infirmary."

With a wave of her hand she activated the arch and they both stepped through.

Chapter 17

KARA LOOKED AT HERSELF in the mirror. She barely recognized the woman who looked back. There was no longer any sign of the twenty-first century journalist with her sharp business suits and her unquenchable drive. Instead, a Highland bride stared back at her, one whose eyes were filled with a peace that Kara had never expected to see there. She sighed.

"I don't know how you did it, but you've gone and made me look at least half presentable," she said to Lucy, Beth and Annis. "You all deserve a medal."

"Half presentable?" Lucy replied. "My God, Kara, you look more than that. You look...oh, you know. I'm so happy. Who would have thought it? My Aiden settling down and with a lass from my own time no less?" Was Kara imagining it or did Lucy look a bit misty-eyed?

Lucy, Beth and Annis had been working on Kara's wedding dress for the past week, only letting her catch sporadic glimpses. But now, on the day of her wedding, it was revealed in all its splendor. It was a rich purple, like the heather that clad the hills of Skye, with the Harris plaid worked into the bodice. It was stunning. Lucy, Beth and Annis wore a matching outfit, if not as grand, as they'd all agreed to be her bridesmaids.

There was a knock on the door and Old Dougie walked in. He halted when he saw Kara.

"Oh my," he breathed. "Ye are a sight to behold, my dear. Everyone's assembled downstairs. Are ye ready?"

Kara's heart skipped. Butterflies flew in her stomach. "Yes, I'm ready."

Dougie nodded and then broke into a fit of coughing.

Lucy rushed over and patted him on the back. "Are you sure you're ready for this?" Dougie had only been allowed out of the infirmary yesterday.

He frowned at Lucy. "Of course I'm ready! Ye dinna think I would let a little cough stop me from giving away our Kara did ye?" He held out his hand for Kara who took it. "I'm sorry yer own father canna be here to give ye away, my dear. I know he and yer mother would have been very proud of ye."

Kara swallowed against a sudden lump in her throat and forced a smile. "Thanks, Dougie."

"We'd better be going. If we keep young Aiden waiting much longer I fear he'll barge his way in here and carry ye down to the altar himself."

Kara laughed. "We can't have that can we?"

Together they left the room and made their way through the castle to the Great Hall, Kara on Dougie's arm, Lucy, Beth and Annis walking behind. They paused at the doors to the Great Hall and Kara saw that it was crammed full of people. It seemed that everyone in the village and a good number from all over the island had come for the wedding. The warriors from Aiden's old command had turned up which Kara knew Aiden was exceptionally pleased about. Hell, even a representative from the king himself had ridden up yesterday, bringing the king's personal good wishes and accepting his rejection of the Earldom of Marischal.

The room grew quiet and all eyes turned towards Kara as Dougie escorted her up the aisle towards the high table which had been converted into a makeshift altar. There, Andrew waited to marry them as was his right as laird. And there also waited Aiden, Jamie at his side.

Kara's eyes met his as he watched her, unblinking, his gaze like a lodestone pulling her in. He seemed to fill her vision, everything else receding to unimportance. Sure, the hall was full, but to Kara it felt as though she and Aiden were the only people in the whole world. God, he was gorgeous. There was a faint blush to his sculpted cheeks and his eyes were wide, full of love and longing. He wore the traditional Harris plaid, his wide-shouldered physique only heightened by the way it pulled taught over his frame.

And then he smiled and Kara's heart seemed to explode in her chest.

That smile was like seeing the sun after days of rain. She would never get enough of it. Of this man. Her man. Her Aiden.

And then she was standing by his side and he was gazing down at her, his eyes speaking a thousand promises. They held hands and stared at each other as Andrew said the ritual words that would bind them together forever. And then Aiden was bending down and kissing her soundly enough to make her toes curl and to bring an answering cheer from the people in the hall before picking her up and whirling her around, a huge laugh of pure joy escaping him.

He set her on her feet and leaned down, his forehead touching hers. "Mine," he whispered in her ear. "Ye are mine. Wife."

"Yours," she agreed. "For now and forever. Husband."

BOY, COULD HIGHLANDERS party. They shared a joy that was infectious and everyone in the Great Hall, and in the great pavilion erected in the bailey outside for those who couldn't fit into the hall, joined in the fun, from the smallest child right up to gray-haired grandmothers. There was feasting and drinking and singing and dancing, the like of which Kara feared would take the roof off Dun Arnwick.

Lucy led much of the music, playing the fiddle with several of the villagers accompanying her along with Dougie playing the spoons. Kara danced with practically everyone in the room and by the time she managed to take a breather, settling onto her seat at the high table, she was sure her feet would be killing her in the morning. Aiden, dancing with Beth, excused himself from his sister and came up to meet her. Settling onto a seat by his wife's side he gave her a lopsided grin.

"Surely nay tired already? The night's only just begun."

"Only just begun?" Kara replied incredulously. "It must be well past midnight and it looks as if there's no chance of anyone going to bed anytime soon."

"I did warn ye that we Highlanders like a good knees-up."

"You did," she said, leaning over to kiss him, "And I wouldn't want it any other way."

He returned her kiss and after a moment it deepened before they both remembered where they were. Aiden watched her, eyes dark with lust.

"Although there's naught to say the bride and groom have to stay until the end. In fact, it's expected that we'll slip out at some point to be...alone."

"Is it now?" Kara said, raising an eyebrow. "Well I'd hate to break with tradition. What say we slip out now before anyone notices?"

"I'd say that was a grand idea."

He took her hand and together they scraped their seats back and made a quick dash for the door behind the high table. It didn't go unnoticed though. A round of cheers followed them. Kara blushed but Aiden only grinned at them. He paused at the door and gave the audience a flourishing bow before turning and leading his wife up the stairs.

Passion overtook them before they even made it to their chamber. Aiden pulled Kara into an alcove where a large window looked out over the grounds and kissed her fiercely. Kara's back pressed against the cold wall but she hardly registered it. Aiden's mouth and questing hands robbed her of all thought. She kissed him hungrily, her body coming alive with desire as she wrapped her arms around his waist and pulled him hard against her.

For one wild moment, Kara wanted him right then and there and be damned with the consequences but common sense reasserted itself. Aiden broke their kiss.

"Come, wife," he said hoarsely. "I canna wait any longer. I have to have ye."

Without waiting for a response he picked her up and carried her down the corridor. Kara laughed, wrapped her arms around his neck and rested her head against his chest, thinking how never in a million years would she have believed that she'd be experiencing this moment: being carried to their marriage bed by her new husband. She had to keep reminding herself that it was real.

Aiden pushed open the door to his chamber— their chamber—and then kicked it closed behind him. A maid had been in before them. A fire was burning in the hearth and scented candles had been lit all around the room, filling the place with flickering candlelight and the smell of summer flowers. Pristine white sheets had been laid on the bed.

"Oh!" Kara said as Aiden put her down and she took in the room. "It's beautiful."

"Aye," Aiden breathed. "Just like my wife."

His eyes roved over her, seeming to undress her with his gaze. They were huge and dark, full of desire. He curled his fingers through hers then raised her hand to his mouth and kissed it.

"Ye are all of me, lass. Do ye realize that? My heart and soul."

Kara gripped his hand tight, feeling tears prick the back of her eyes. "Just as you're mine, Aiden Harris. Everything. Always."

He stepped closer, closing the distance between them until she could feel the heat coming off his body. Tenderly he placed a finger under her chin, tilted her face up to his and kissed her gently, his lips brushing over hers with the gentle touch of a feather.

Kara's eyes slid closed and she breathed in the scent of him. He smelled of open skies and pine needles.

"Well that's done it," she breathed. "You're going to have to help me out of this dress. I warned Annis that if she put so many buttons on the back they'd probably end up getting ripped off."

Aiden laughed softly. "We canna have that can we?"

He turned her away from him and then stepped up behind her. His lips found the back of her neck, even as his fingers worked free the clasps on her dress. Kara's eyes slid closed, a low moan escaping her. Aiden worked with deft fingers and a moment later pushed the dress off her shoulders so it fell to the floor. He pulled her against his chest, his lips caressing her neck, her shoulders, her earlobe, and Kara felt his desire for her pressing against her buttocks.

It was too much. She couldn't wait any longer. She spun, catching his lips with her own, even as she reached down and stroked his bulge through the material of his plaid. Aiden's eyes slid closed and something close to a growl escaped him.

Then his hands were on her, sweeping over the contours of her belly, her hips, her breasts. He grabbed a fistful of the thin shift she wore under the dress and yanked. With a tearing sound the material came away, leaving her standing before him naked. He yanked off his own plaid just as quickly, along with the linen shirt underneath. The candle light played light and shadow over his muscled body and Kara couldn't help but eye him hungrily. She ran her hands over the hard muscles of his chest, his arms, feeling the puckered scar where Devereux's bullet had been removed, before trailing her fingertips down the tight V of his hips and then his manhood which stood tall and proud, aching for her.

With a hiss of in taken breath, Aiden scooped her up and carried her over to the bed, laying her on her back. For a moment he knelt over her, looking down as if trying to fix the memory of her in his mind but then all his restraint snapped and he was atop her, kissing her with feverish passion.

Desire exploded along Kara's nerves. She'd never wanted anything as much as she wanted this man, right here, right now. The feel of his strong body atop her, pinning her to the bed, the sensation of his hot skin against hers, the taste of his tongue and the smell of his scent all combined to devour her.

He nudged her knees apart with his own and positioned himself atop her. The tip of his manhood bumped the space between her legs and Kara groaned, tilting herself to meet him. Aiden shifted, pushing his hips forward and drove himself inside her with a sharp, powerful motion that made them both gasp in pleasure. A core of warmth flared to life as Kara felt him slide into her right up to the hilt.

Kara tilted her hips up to meet him as he began to move. Slowly at first but then with gathering force, he drove into her and their bodies met in an explosion of delicious passion. The core of warmth burning in Kara exploded through her nerves, sending sizzling bliss radiating through her blood. Nobody had ever made her feel this way. Being with Aiden felt right. It made her feel complete.

"I will always want you," she gasped into his ear. "Always want this."

In answer his tempo increased until he was driving into her with enough force to send the bedhead smashing into the wall. Kara screwed her eyes tight shut as her climax overcame her, a white-hot, blinding tide of ecstasy that swept her away and broke her into a million pieces. Aiden jerked as he reached his own climax, emptying himself inside her and then lying still for a long moment, head resting on Kara's shoulder.

Kara breathed deeply, coming back to herself slowly, loving the way her body melded with Aiden's, loving the feeling of him atop and within her.

After a moment Aiden raised his head and looked at her. He smiled, kissed her forehead and then rolled away from her, pulling her into the crook of his arm.

A heavy, contented feeling was spreading through Kara's limbs. It had been a long day. A perfect day. Now, it had a perfect ending. Her husband's arms tightened around her and she snuggled against him, the heat from his skin keeping them both warm.

"Thank ye, Kara," he said suddenly.

"For what?" she asked.

He turned to look at her and his eyes were so full of emotion that it made Kara's heart swell with love for him. "For turning up at the warehouse that day. For getting chased by that dog. If ye hadn't, we might not be here now."

Kara barked a laugh. "I'd forgotten about that dog. Wow, he really was a match-maker wasn't he? He deserves a bone or two."

Aiden laughed, a clean, pure sound, like the tinkling of rain. Kara laid her head on his shoulder thinking of all the steps that had led her to this point, to this man and her destiny. One thing was for sure, she could spend the rest of her life listening to that laugh. It was like the wind through trees. She would never get tired of it.

He rolled to face her, leaned forward and kissed her again. His fingers trailed across her hips, her belly, then down to the sweet spot between her legs.

After that, all thinking stopped.

KARA DROPPED ONTO THE sofa in her little apartment and flattened the newspaper onto her knee. The headline read: *Local businessman revealed as crime-boss*. A big picture of Michael Devereux sat beneath the headline and the by line for the story, printed at the bottom, read *story by Kara Buchanan*.

She read the words meticulously, ensuring her editor hadn't cut out anything important. He hadn't. All the essential information was there. Kara had obviously kept out any details of herself, Aiden, and time-travel, and instead brought to light the many shady deals and protection rackets that Devereux had been involved in. His corruption turned out to be deeper than even she'd suspected. Since she'd penned the story, more and more people had come forward to give evidence of what they'd suffered at Devereux's hands and Kara had included their evidence in what she'd delivered to the police. Devereux himself might be gone, but his criminal network remained, and it was Kara's fervent hope that her story, along with all the evidence she'd been able to obtain, would help dismantle that network.

The McQueen estate had been promised to the National Museum of Scotland in Edinburgh and the Key of Ages, its principal treasure, along with it. Kara felt particularly pleased about that. Finally, those artifacts would be where they belonged where everyone could enjoy them.

Kara sighed as she finished reading. At last, she had her story. It was done. She folded the newspaper, put it down on the coffee table, and looked around. She'd come full circle, back to where she started. Her tiny apartment, where all of this had begun, hadn't changed. The clippings from her father's murder where still pinned above the mantelpiece and her apartment was still cold and impersonal. She doubted her landlord would have any problems letting it out once she was gone. With a sigh, she rose and crossed to the mantelpiece, looking up at the faded clippings.

"Well, I did it, Dad," she whispered. "I got my story. Turns out that it was bigger than I could ever have imagined."

Oh, how she wished her parents were here now. What would they make of how her life had turned out? What would they make of her new husband?

"They'd be mighty proud of ye, lass."

Alarmed, Kara spun. Irene MacAskill stood behind her, smiling gently.

Kara took a step back, heart suddenly thumping. Here was the woman who'd started all this, the one who'd set Kara on this course. "What are you doing here, Irene?"

"I thought it about time we had a little chat."

"Now? Here? After all this time?"

"What better place and time? This is where yer two worlds cross."

Kara schooled herself to calm. "What do you want?"

"Only what I always want. To see ye on yer rightful path at last. Aiden has chosen his. Will ye choose yers?"

"You've spoken to Aiden?"

Irene shook her head. "Nay, lass. I didnae need to. He chose without my help. His path is to love ye and protect ye with his life, and in so doing, protect the very Highlands themselves. It was an easy choice for him."

"That doesn't make sense," Kara said. *Like almost everything you say.* "How does Aiden protecting me help the Highlands?"

Irene's eyes were like pools of ink as she regarded Kara. "Because it will allow ye to fulfil yer own destiny. The fact that ye are here suggests ye have figured it out already, even if ye havenae admitted it to yerself. Ye managed to use the arch by yerself to come here—without telling anyone ye were coming. What does that say do ye reckon?"

Kara felt a twinge of guilt. Irene was right. She'd not told anyone, not even Aiden, that she was planning on returning to her time. Aiden would only have insisted on coming with her and this was something she'd needed to do alone. She needed closure, so she'd gone to the arch and passed through it to the railway bridge by Devereux's warehouse. Using the arch had become instinctual to her, as easy as breathing. She was sure she could return to Dun Arnwick at the exact same time she'd left. Nobody would miss her.

Kara squeezed her eyes shut and drew in a deep breath. "I'm like you, aren't I?"

Irene laid a hand on her arm. Her skin felt warm and as dry as paper. "Aye, lass. Ye are my granddaughter many generations removed and carry the same legacy in yer blood as I. We are of the Fae—at least partly—and we have a job to do." Her grip on Kara's arm tightened and her eyes became intense. "We are guardians of the Highlands. It is yer destiny, lass, and ye canna escape it any more than I could escape mine all those years ago. Do ye accept?"

Deep down Kara had always known there was something different about her, but she'd never realized what that was until she'd been offered a bargain in a dark circle of stones high on a lonely hillside. Strangely, she didn't feel frightened by Irene's words. She felt...content. Since she'd met Aiden it seemed like her life was realigning, finally falling into the pattern it was meant to. Now that pattern was almost complete.

"What happens if I say yes?"

Irene shrugged. "Ye will carry on with yer life. Ye and Aiden will live a long life together, ye'll raise a family and do all the small things that make a life worth living. But ye will also have another role to fill. Ye will become a guardian of the Highlands and a keeper of the arches through time."

Kara watched Irene. She said it so lightly, but the responsibility must be enormous. How had she carried it alone for so long? "So I'd be able to travel back here whenever I want?"

Irene shook her head. "Nay, lass. Only when the need is great. Only when the currents of time have shifted out of their course and need correcting. There are rules we must obey."

"Rules?"

"Aye. Starting with choice. We canna influence anyone's free will. Aught that is given must be given freely. Nor can we interfere with the normal flow of fate. We canna save some-one who must die, nor end a life if fate has decreed that they live. We are guardians, my dear. We keep the balance of life. That is all." She smiled warmly. "I will guide ye and show ye all ye need to know. Do ye accept?"

Kara placed her hand over Irene's where it rested on her arm. "I accept."

A wide smile curled Irene's mouth and just for a second Kara got a glimpse of the beautiful young woman Irene must once have been.

"That makes me mighty glad, my dear. Have ye done here? Are ye ready to go home?"

Kara huffed out a breath and looked around her little apartment. "One moment." She crossed to the mantelpiece, carefully took down the clippings about her father, and put them in her pocket. "Oh and one other thing." She hurried into the kitchen and collected a few things from the cup-board which she stuffed into a bag.

Irene raised an eyebrow and Kara smiled sheepishly.

"Coffee and chocolate. You can't expect a girl to give those up, can you?"

Irene barked a laugh, merriment dancing in her eyes. "I suppose I canna. And there has to be some benefit to being a guardian doesnae there?"

Kara grinned. "Exactly. Right. I'm ready now."

Irene took her hand, tugged her to stand under the arch-way of the door, and spoke a few words. Kara's apartment melted away, and she found herself standing in the library of Dun Arnwick, below the high window which formed a pointed archway above them. It was dark outside, the small hours of the night.

She crossed to the desk on which sat the history of the Harris Clan she'd been writing. She ran a hand down the cover. It was finished. Tomorrow she'd present it to Andrew and Lucy, her gift to them.

"A fine work, lass, although unfinished," Irene said behind her.

Kara glanced at the book and then back to Irene. "Unfinished?"

Irene turned to the book and flipped through to the back page. "See? There's naught in here about ye or Aiden or yer children. Yer story comes next and what a story it will be! Now, off with ye. Ye will have a busy day tomorrow. That's when it all begins."

"What begins?"

Irene rolled her eyes. "Why, the rest of yer life of course!"

Kara nodded. She walked towards the door but paused on the threshold and looked back. "Thank you, Irene—"

But the old woman was gone.

Kara closed the door behind her and made her way down to the chamber she shared with her husband. She slipped into bed beside him, curling up against his warmth. He shifted, his arm coming around to hold her close against him. Peace flooded through her. Peace born of the knowledge she was where she was meant to be. She was safe and protected and loved. She knew this man would be by her side no matter what the years brought them, no matter the demands her Fae nature might put on them.

She kissed his forehead. "Tomorrow, my love," she whispered. "It all begins tomorrow."

THE END

Want some more Highland adventure? Then why not try the other books in the series? www.katybakerbooks.com[1]

Would you like to know more of Irene MacAskill's story? *Guardian of a Highlander*, a free short story is available as a free gift to all my newsletter subscribers. Sign up below to grab your copy and receive a fortnightly email containing news, chat and more. www.katybakerbooks.com[2]

WHAT DO YOU DO WHEN destiny comes knocking?

---

1.   http://www.katybakerbooks.com

2.   http://www.katybakerbooks.com

Irene Buchanan is running from hers. Gifted with fae blood, she is fated to become the Guardian of the Highlands.

But Irene wants none of it. Soon to be married to her childhood sweetheart, she has everything she ever dreamed of. Why would she risk that for a bargain with the fae?

But Irene can't run forever. When a terrifying act of violence rips all she loves from her, she realizes she must confront her destiny. If she doesn't, she risks the destruction of all she holds dear.

The fate of the Highlands lies in her hands.

Printed in Great Britain
by Amazon

19618824R00171